MOLLIE WALTON

The Suffragette of Ironbridge

MLP

First published in 2026 by Mountain Leopard Press
An imprint of Headline Publishing Group Limited

This paperback edition published in 2026

1

Cataloguing in Publication Data is available from the British Library

Paperback ISBN 978 1 0354 2493 1

Offset in 10.32/13.76pt Sabon LT Std by
Six Red Marbles UK, Thetford, Norfolk

Printed and bound in Great Britain by Clays Ltd, Elcograf S.p.A.

FSC
www.fsc.org
MIX
Paper | Supporting
responsible forestry
FSC® C104740

Headline's policy is to use papers that are natural, renewable and recyclable
products and made from wood grown in well-managed forests and other
controlled sources. The logging and manufacturing processes are expected
to conform to the environmental regulations of the country of origin.

Headline Publishing Group Limited
An Hachette UK Company
Carmelite House
50 Victoria Embankment
London EC4Y 0DZ

The authorised representative in the EEA is Hachette Ireland,
8 Castlecourt Centre, Dublin 15, D15 XTP3, Ireland (email: info@hbgi.ie)

www.headline.co.uk
www.hachette.co.uk

Praise for the Ironbridge Saga

'Saga fiction at its very best. Mollie Walton writes with superb empathy for her believable characters so that the reader really cares what happens to them'
Margaret Dickinson

'I really enjoy Mollie Walton's books and this one brings into focus the sacrifices that an entire generation made. I loved the way Jo unfurls like one of Alfie's plants to forge the way for women everywhere. An excellent read but one that will make you think. Thoroughly recommend'
Shirley Mann

'In her own inimitable and challenging way, Mollie Walton brings to her readers a tense and moving story of a lonely child who craves to be loved; in adulthood she finds love which is snatched away from her and yet, in the midst of a violent war finds friendship when she least expects it. A tense, vivid and absorbing read'
Val Wood

'A historical masterpiece highlighting the grit and determination of working-class women in the first two decades of the twentieth century'
Jean Fullerton

'A story of strength and belonging in times of great turbulence, and the importance of family and friends. Jo's journey of self-discovery and agency had me turning the pages until the early hours . . . A vivid and poignant rendering of life in times of peace and war'
Tracy Baines

'A compelling blend of real history, rich period detail, and a gritty, authentic story brimming with love, loss, intrigue, hope and bitter revenge'
Lancashire Evening Post

'A gritty, emotional saga that broke my heart yet was ultimately hopeful'
Vicki Beeby

'Feisty female characters, an atmospheric setting and a spell-binding storyline make this a phenomenal read'
Cathy Bramley

Also by Mollie Walton

The Raven Hall Saga

A Mother's War

A Daughter's Gift

A Sister's Hope

The Ironbridge Saga

The Daughters of Ironbridge

The Secrets of Ironbridge

The Orphan of Ironbridge

The Shopgirl of Ironbridge

This dedication is in three parts, as all were equally resident in my mind as I wrote this novel.

The memory of my grandfather – Arthur Leslie Chadwick – who fought in the Great War as a young man and lived. I wouldn't be here writing stories for you now if he hadn't survived and I'm exceedingly grateful for his bravery.

Yet many others did not survive and paid the ultimate price for their sacrifice. This book is dedicated to all of them – the soldiers, the civilians, the refugees, the home front, the children – all who found themselves caught up in a war none of them asked for or wanted, just as today, so many of our fellow human beings are trapped by wars not of their own making. Let us always extend the hand of friendship to all who suffer under the movements of history against their choice.

The brave women who gave up their time, their freedom and even their lives to fight for women's suffrage. Without them, I dread to think where we'd be now, in a system today that is still rife with misogyny, the women and men who fought for women's suffrage so long ago were courageous warriors against a brutal system, which threw them in jail and subjected them to torture. Yet the will of the suffragettes was never broken and they pushed onwards until women were given the same voting rights as men in the UK in 1928. I thank them for everything they suffered to give me the freedoms I enjoy today.

The Ironbridge Saga

- Woodvine
  - Matthew Woodvine b.1770
    - Ebenezer Woodvine b.1790
      - Josiah Woodvine b.1810
        - Reuben Woodvine b.1830 d.1885 — Rebekah Weston b.1833 d.1889
          - **Charlie Woodvine b.1865** —
            - **Alfie Woodvine b.1893** — **Jo Darlington b.1893**
              - **Henry (Harry) Woodvine b. 1913** — **Rosina Lazenby b.1895**
  - James Woodvine b.1771
    - **John Woodvine b.1793** — **Rachel Woodvine b.1799**
      - **Anny Woodvine b.1823**

The Raven Hall Saga

Chapter 1

Jo

June 1900 to April 1902

When she was six years old, Jo Darlington secretly watched from the darkened hallway outside her parents' room as her mother held a pillow over the face of Jo's father and ended his short brutal life. He'd been lying on their bed in a drunken stupor after he'd beaten his wife in the kitchen. Mrs Darlington never knew that her little girl had seen her murder him. When the morning came, men in black coats and hats arrived at the house and Jo sat on the stairs eavesdropping on them talking with her mother. She didn't understand what they were saying in their gruff, grown-up voices but it was something to do with the word 'misadventure'. Her mother didn't get arrested and didn't go to prison. Nobody mentioned the pillow and people talked about how much Bob Darlington had had to drink that night, as he could barely walk home across the iron bridge and vomited over the side into the fast-flowing River Severn beneath, a witness had said. A doctor mentioned something about his liver and everyone said he'd lived a bad life. Jo watched her mother talk to Jo's Aunt Stella and all the neighbours and friends and never shed a tear. Jo wondered if she'd dreamt the whole thing. But deep down she knew she hadn't. She knew her mother – after years of beatings at the broad fists of her husband – had killed him in his bed. Jo carried the knowledge of it around in her belly like a stone and never told a soul. All she knew for sure was that it was a lot more peaceful at home without her father. And her mother looked peaceful too. Until she got sick.

Two years after her father's death, her mother was by this time bed-bound and her skin turned yellow. The doctors couldn't help her. She was looked after by Aunt Stella, who had a job as a nurse in the town, so was good at it. Jo stayed with her aunt's three daughters, to keep out of the way. Jo's cousins were all girls, all whiny and troublesome. Jo didn't like them much, or their father, Jo's uncle by marriage, who made his children call him 'sir'. Jo wasn't allowed to call him Uncle Ned and had to call him Mr Andrews instead. One day, when Mr Andrews came back from factory work, he told Jo, 'Your mother's dead. Go on home now.' Men in black coats came to the house again and Aunt Stella was there. She came down the stairs and hugged Jo tightly. Jo hadn't cried yet, just like her mother hadn't cried for her father. Jo hadn't cried for him either. She never found it easy to show her feelings to others. But now, what she mostly felt was fear.

Jo said to her Aunt Stella, 'I dunna wanna live in this empty house alone. There are ghosts at night and now there'll be one more.'

'Oh, child,' said her Aunt Stella, and a single tear rolled down her aunt's cheek. Jo wished she could cry. But the tears just wouldn't come. 'Dunna fret. You're to live with us now, little Jo.'

Jo was smaller than the average, she supposed. In every other way she felt completely average (apart from the fact that her mother had killed her father, but then nobody knew that but her). She had brown hair which she described to herself as being the colour of a rat or, if she were being charitable with herself, perhaps a mouse. They were both vermin, however you looked at it. Aunt Stella helped her pack a few clothes and knick-knacks and that was all she was allowed to bring from her old home to her new one. When she was taken in by Aunt Stella, the first thing her aunt did was cut all of Jo's hair off to a bob just below her ears, because it was so knotty from the months of neglect when Jo was without her mother or aunt, while Aunt Stella had been nursing her mother half the time and the other half with her patients. The only adult more present in her life at that time had been Mr Andrews, who would rather skin an elephant than brush his niece-by-marriage's hair. Once Jo's hair was chopped off, she felt peculiar, the back of her neck suddenly cold and her head lighter than air. She felt like a new person and, she supposed, she was a new person now, in a new life. Everything she'd known before, every comfort of her childhood and her home, was gone, never to return.

And that was how, in the space of two years, Jo Darlington gratefully lost her father and sorrowfully lost her mother, and thus became an orphan at the age of eight and went to live with her aunt, uncle and three troublesome cousins.

Aunt Stella lived in a different neighbourhood and thus Jo started at a new school, the one on Church Hill in Ironbridge, the first day falling on a cloudy and cool spring morning. The night before she had had nightmares about looming dark things in the room she shared with her cousins. The three of them were all cuddled up together in a double bed, while Jo was on a narrow horsehair mattress on the floor in their room, beside a wooden doll's house whose dark windows seemed to watch Jo as she shuffled to get comfortable, unsuccessfully. The four walls of their bedroom were covered in pictures cut out of magazines pasted to the wallpaper, a curious collection of angels and cherubs, little girls in posh outfits and stars of the stage in the latest fashion. Jo's cousins fell asleep in seconds in their warm, soft bed, while Jo lay awake for ages, thinking of how her childhood bedroom had no doll's house and only one doll, which she realised she'd forgotten and left under the bed there. Her aunt had told her all the things left in the house were sold, to pay for her mother's funeral, or burnt, because the other items there were 'no good'. Jo scolded herself for forgetting to bring her doll with her; how could she be so careless with her own baby doll? Perhaps it had been burnt up, a ghastly thought. She believed herself then to be a bad mother to her forsaken dolly, to also be 'no good'.

She tried to sleep that night but ended up staring at the faces on the walls that soon turned ghoulish in her shattered mind. Jo kept waking up clutching at her face as if she couldn't breathe, so by the morning she was exhausted. She was given a piece of bread with a smear of jam and half a cup of condensed milk by Mr Andrews (his good wife delayed upstairs fashioning elaborate plaits in her eldest girl's hair), who complained when he was forced to mind his own children and 'the extra', as he called Jo. He gruffly went off to work, saying they'd made him late. Once the eldest had come downstairs, Jo was left with her three troublesome cousins. They were Sarah, seven, Sally, six, and Celia, five. It sorely vexed Jo that their three names sounded like they started with the same letter and yet Celia's didn't. Jo found it insupportable that her clever Aunt Stella had made such a careless mistake. It meant every time Jo found herself looking at Celia, she drew out an S shape on her palm as if to correct the error. Aunt Stella really was the cleverest person Jo knew, being the town nurse, a kind of unofficial one. Aunt Stella told Jo that she'd never had any proper training but nobody liked the young town doctor, a Mr Hale – especially the women – and so most of them called on Aunt Stella when they needed medical help, particularly if it involved 'lady parts', as Aunt Stella said in an undertone with a furtive look.

'What are lady parts?' asked Jo, but she never learnt the answer, as Aunt Stella hurried them out to school as she was late to see her first patient.

'Get a shift on,' said Aunt Stella, not unkindly. 'You're the eldest wench of the house now and all your cousins will do as you say. Get yourselves to school, my beauts, and mind your cousin, little Jo.'

Then her three cousins whooped and hollered at her half the way to school, calling her 'little Jo', quite decidedly meant unkindly. Jo shouted at them to shut their gobs and they did, momentarily, then whispered about her behind her back as she strode ahead. She couldn't pretend to herself that she was not desperately jealous of them, not only because they still had both a mother and a father (although she'd be quite happy if the grumpy Mr Andrews didn't come home from work one day, perhaps killed in a ghastly accident at the blast furnace at Blesser's Hill where he worked). But Jo was also extremely envious of their dark hair, almost black, just like their mother's, and how long their raven hair was and how pretty the hairstyles their loving mother had crafted for them were. Despite liking the lightness of her own new hairdo, Jo knew she looked like a boy compared to her pretty cousins, and a very little boy at that, as the eldest, Sarah, was two years younger and yet taller than her. She heard her cousin Sarah tell the others that Jo was little because she was an orphan and never got fed properly because her parents had been 'drunken degenerates'. Jo didn't know what the second word meant but it didn't sound good.

'Hush with your chinwagging,' Jo said.

'Yes, little Jo,' replied Sarah, with a fake smile. *Trouble-some*, Jo thought, and not for the first time. She tried to tell herself that her cousins' hair was boring and traditional, while her new haircut was daring.

She had persuaded herself to be quite delighted with it, until she got to school that first day and the first thing that was said to her when she joined the queue of girls outside, opposite the queue of boys, was one girl shouting: 'Wrong line, boy-hair!' And then a significant portion of the rest of them all began to chant 'Boy-hair! Boy-hair!' at her, even though some of the girls had quite short hair too – though not as short as hers, it had to be said. Even her cousins joined in, which felt particularly treacherous. Then, one of the boys stepped out of the queue and shouted everyone down.

'Shut your cakeholes!' he cried.

And everyone did. The boy didn't even look at Jo but she stared at him that whole time they waited in the insolent silence of a chastised mob. He had yellow hair and was dressed neatly in his shorts, long socks, waistcoat and jacket. Despite his neat appearance, his hands looked filthy and he picked dirt out of his nails.

Then, at long last, the queues began to move and in they went. Jo had never liked school much and had often succeeded in getting out of it for days on end when Mama was alive, under the pretence of some sort of ill-defined snuffle or helping out around the house, but they both knew it was just her mother being soft. Louise Darlington had been a kind and well-meaning person but was easily swayed by any point of view, always assuming that every other person living had a better argument than she did and, weighing up all the possibilities, she was most likely wrong about everything. Jo knew her letters and could do sums, so she knew she wasn't an idiot and thus couldn't see why she needed to learn anything else at school, about what lay beyond the China Sea or why lightning occurred and other mysteries. She was poor and thus destined for a 'life of toil', as Mama called it (her mother had taken in laundry and needlework and worked too hard). What good was such fancy knowledge when you were toiling?

However, once inside her new classroom, with the schoolmaster, Mr Woodvine, at the front, and everyone seated according to boys on one side and girls on the other, Jo listened to everything Mr Woodvine told them. He had a kind face, a kind smile, even kind hands, the way he held them before himself and gesticulated expressively during every speech he made about the interesting things of the world. That first day Jo learned about the bears of Canada, which awakened in her a sense of wonder she'd never felt before.

At playtime, they all trooped outside, the boys to the lower playground and the girls to the upper, the playground on a steep terraced slope. Jo's cousins ran off and played with their friends, who whispered about Jo and pointed at her. Jo stood by the low wall marking the top boundary of the school and pretended to be interested in a snail climbing up it. Before long, the pretence wasn't real and she did become fascinated by the snail and wondered how it would feel to move so slowly, as if through water, just like she had played in the shallows of the river downstream with her mother on sunny days when she was younger, the weight of the water pressing against her shins as she edged forward. Then, a tap on her shoulder made her look round and there was the kind face of Mr Woodvine looking down at her. He was tall, with brown hair shot through with streaks of grey.

'Did you know that snails and slugs are also called gastropods?'

Jo shook her head, not really understanding what Mr

Woodvine was talking about, something about peas in a pod, but just happy to be spoken to. Nobody really talked to her at her new home, except for Aunt Stella, who was rarely there. Her cousins looked at Jo as if she were a creature, not a person, and though she was used to it, she also knew you could never really get used to such a thing in your life. You could never get used to loneliness.

'You might imagine that there is a dearth of interesting wildlife in Shropshire, but you'd be wrong,' Mr Woodvine went on. 'If one has a keen observant eye, there are animals everywhere one might look. Look up into the sky and you'll see a plethora of birds and insects winging past you. Turn over a leaf or lift a rock and you'll find more, scurrying away. And there, over there behind the town, you see?'

The school was up a hill and when you stood in the playground you could see across the town of grey boxes of houses and shops of Ironbridge nestled in the valley, fringed on each side by thick swathes of deeply green trees.

'Within those copses of trees you'll find all manner of wildlife, from rabbits to foxes to badgers and more.'

Jo worried about those trees, as they looked dark and brooding that day, the sky overcast. She asked Mr Woodvine, 'Do those forests have bears in them, like in Canada?'

'No bears, little Jo,' said Mr Woodvine, and smiled at her.

And then he left her, striding away to break up a fight between two boys in the lower part of the playground. She watched him go and felt bereft. She looked out for the blond boy from earlier who had saved her from the cruel chanting. She saw him playing at soldiers with his many friends, running around shooting at an invisible enemy. The blond boy was leading them all in the chase, and led them again in a breakout of cheering when they had beaten their foe. Jo wondered why he had been so kind to her, a stranger, a girl with hair like a boy. Or maybe he wasn't being kind and was somehow responsible for keeping law and order in the school. But why? Why that boy?

She watched as Mr Woodvine suddenly went over to the blond boy and took him aside, away from the other boys, and had a quiet word with him. He wasn't telling the boy off, Jo could tell. She watched as the boy ran his fingers through his blond hair, looking puffed, with pink cheeks from his recent soldiering exertions. He nodded at Mr Woodvine, then peered around the schoolmaster's back and pointed at Jo, straight at her. She felt glued to the spot. What was she being accused of? Then, Mr Woodvine nodded too and patted the boy on the shoulder and the boy ran off as the bell rang for the end of playtime. This vignette remained a mystery that Jo pondered until the end of the school day, when they were all dismissed and she was about to leave with her cousins, the three of them running ahead so they didn't have to be seen with her. And the blond boy came up beside her and tapped her on the shoulder, just as Mr Woodvine had.

Jo turned and gazed at the boy in wonder.

'My dad said you're the same age as me and you might need a friend, being so alone in the world as you are.'

'Your . . . dad?' said Jo, confused as to why this boy's father might know anything at all about her, let alone her deepest shame, that of being a blighted orphan.

'Mr Woodvine, the schoolmaster. He's my dad.'

'Oh!' she replied.

This was news indeed. And now it all made sense, how he shouted at the others and they listened to him with begrudging respect. How he led his platoon of boys in their war games in the playground. And why Mr Woodvine had taken him aside to have a word with him. She imagined that the child of a teacher might've taken some stick for that particular parentage, but instead it seemed to lend the blond boy a position of esteem in the school hierarchy.

'Sorry, I didna mean to draw attention to . . . well, you being alone. Sorry if that hurt your feelings.'

'It didna,' she said, amazed that anyone was talking to her so kindly, let alone a boy (who, in her experience from her last school, were usually cruel and mucky things who despised girls mostly, especially one that was not conventionally pretty, like herself).

'Good,' he said, and nodded. 'I'd walk you home for a bit of company but I live here.'

'You live in the school?' Jo imagined him and Mr Woodvine, and whoever else was in their family, sleeping all squished up together in a tight cwtch in the stationery cupboard at the back of the classroom.

The boy laughed and it was infectious. Jo actually smiled, the first time she'd done that in weeks, months even.

'Nay, nay! We live in the cottage there, beside the school, see? My parents have a garden behind it where we grow all sorts of fruit and veg. You should see it. I'm gonna be a gardener one day. Dad wants me to be a teacher like him, but I'd rather die than be cooped up in a classroom all day, wouldna you?'

She nodded ferociously. She agreed with everything he said, whatever it was.

'I'll be a gardener in a big fancy garden next to a big fancy house, you'll see.'

'I believe you,' she said, reverently.

'Anyway, must get off or we'll miss our tea. See you tomorrow. Tara-a-bit.'

He turned to go, then stopped and added, 'Oh, and I'm Alfie, by the way. Alfie Woodvine, of course.'

And off he went, with a skip and a hop, back through the school archway for boys. She heard his booted steps recede as he went around the school, then saw the blond top of his head above the school wall as he ran up to the cottage beside the school, his head bobbing out of sight.

She stood absolutely still for a minute, her feet unwilling to move from the spot where he'd stood just moments before.

'And I'm Jo,' she said quietly, to herself alone.

Chapter 2

Jo

April 1902 to December 1911

Alfie Woodvine became her champion. As Alfie's dad was the schoolmaster, nobody gave her any open trouble after that, nothing that Mr Woodvine could see, at any rate. He protected her in a particular manner, as she'd lost her parents, just as his kindly soul protected all orphans in a particular manner, but with Jo being Alfie's favourite, he seemed to keep a special eye out for the Darlington girl, to the chagrin of the other girls. Outside of school, the girls, including Jo's cousins, either ignored her obviously, turning their heads dramatically away when she was nearby, or openly bullied her with taunts. There were rumours in town about her parents that never left her throughout her school years.

Walking to and from school became a trial. She noticed that grown-ups often commented on gangs of boys ranging around as trouble. Yet Jo was rarely bothered by boys. It was coteries of girls that gave her the tight sensation of fear in her chest when she heard a group coming up behind her as she walked quickly, alone, always alone. She never understood what it was that girls pinpointed about her that made them hone in on her so accurately. But they did.

'Drunk,' one would say, and giggle.

'Drunk, drunk, drunk!' another would chime in.

Mostly she would walk faster to try to evade them. Sometimes they'd wander off after that, tired of the pursuit. Other times, they wouldn't. Instead, they'd speed up and surround her, forcing her to stop.

'Yer father was a proper bezzler, drunk every day of his life!' a girl would crow.

'He drunk himself to death,' another would add, jabbing Jo in the chest.

'And yer mother!'

Some days Jo would shove her way free and other days she'd stand her ground.

'That's old news,' she'd say, her voice riven with contempt. 'Keep up.'

But whether she answered or not, whether she was clever or not, whether she was angry or pleading or silent, nothing worked.

'They say yer mother was yellow as marsh marigolds when she went! What a sight!'

'You're a disgrace. Everyone says so. My mother says the Darlingtons are as bad as crow carrion pecked on the road.'

One time Jo shouted, 'Nobody gives a stuff what you or yer mother think! Everybody knows yer mother did it under a hedge with the ironmonger!'

But however witty or defiant Jo was, it never earnt her enough kudos for the bullying to stop. She could tell some of her classmates did have a grudging respect for her, but they showed it by giving her a wide berth, or a solemn nod when she passed. Nothing akin to friendship. The others simply hated her with a ferocity that Jo never understood.

Why did they care so much? Why was it Jo's disgrace to carry, that her father was a bezzler, a heavy drinker who'd drunk himself to death, and her mother had too? Why didn't it elicit pity from them, instead of scorn? She never found the answer but wondered sometimes if some people on this earth made themselves feel better about their own mean and mediocre lives by stamping down others, forcing others down further, to elevate their rotten selves. But the worst of it was that only Jo knew the terrible truth about her parents was a thousand times worse.

And so, she turned to Alfie, who never teased her, or turned his head away, or ignored her. He'd bring extra food for her from his parents' garden and talked with her of many disparate things, of the geography of Shropshire and the wars in southern Africa and how to be a goalkeeper at football and the mysteries of prime numbers. He was good at everything and yet people weren't hateful towards him and no one called him a swot, mostly because his dad was such a fair man and Alfie himself was a good sport and fun to be with. Everyone liked Alfie Woodvine.

But for Jo, it was quite different. She loved Alfie from the top of her head to the soles of her feet. She loved that boy with all the love she'd had to save after her mother had died. Jo poured it all into the new vessel of Alfie Woodvine. Firstly, he was kind to her always, which was like heaven to hell compared with the girls who taunted her and the boys who ignored her. He didn't care a jot about her parentage. He was interested in the world, in nature and science and the night sky, showing her insects he'd caught, why flowers had a certain number of petals, and the names of constellations. She fretted quite regularly that if, by some dreadful twist of circumstance, Alfie Woodvine died too, she'd throw herself off the iron bridge with a hand-iron roped to her ankle and let it drag her to the riverbed and drown rather than live even a day without him.

Jo grew accustomed to her life with her cousins, though they settled into an ill-tempered truce more than anything akin to friendship, let alone familial love. Once Jo's hair had grown out, it proved to be lustrous with a long bouncy curl. This made her cousins green with envy, as their raven hair was a lovely colour but straight as a rod and greasy as a bag of chips. They used cotton rags to curl their hair every night, which Jo's magnificent head of waves never needed. So, Jo flowered as she grew, much to the annoyance of her cousins. Time passed and Jo and Alfie left school at twelve, Alfie apprenticed to the Head Gardener at Rowland Hall, just as he'd told Jo he would be, all those years before. Jo was told by Mr Andrews to make her living doing the same kind of needlework at home as her mother had. The best thing about her post-schooling life was that her cousins were still at school, and so she spent whole days away from them, at last, thank heavens, which almost made up for the fact that her hands hurt from the constant sewing and she grew a little forlorn, alone in the Andrews' home all day (she never thought of it as her own).

As much as she was happy to have a break from her tiresome cousins, she missed school, and its sense of purpose and the importance it placed on learning for learning's sake. She missed Mr Woodvine and his fascinating facts. And most of all, she missed seeing Alfie every day. But he still made time out of his long work hours to come and see her, and they went for long walks by the River Severn or they sat in his garden at the schoolmaster's cottage, playing with the Woodvine family dog, a good-natured black-and-white collie called Snap. The happy hours she spent chatting aimlessly with Alfie, or his father, or his mother too, the beautiful Mrs Woodvine with the white-blonde hair, from where Alfie had clearly inherited his colouring.

Jo got to know Mrs Woodvine in those many visits to the cottage and liked her very much. Aunt Stella loved Jo, she knew that, but she had the brusqueness of a nurse about her, which meant hugs were quick and kisses were sparse. What Jo felt most keenly was how Aunt Stella's voice was subtly different when she talked to her own daughters compared to when she talked to Jo. Her aunt probably didn't even notice it, but Jo did. She knew it wasn't intentional, so she didn't resent it, but she still felt it viscerally, every time she heard the contrasting tones. There was a warmth in her voice that she used with her own children that cooled ever so slightly when she addressed her niece. But Mrs Woodvine – or Maria, as she insisted Jo call her, though Jo swore to herself she never would, out of respect – spoke to Jo with such fondness that somehow it made up for her aunt's failings in that quarter. Mrs Woodvine would call Jo simply 'Jo', unlike everyone else, who called her 'little Jo', even Alfie, and still Mr Woodvine, who Jo now knew was called 'Charlie' by his wife. Yet everybody else on earth called him 'Mr Woodvine' or 'Schoolmaster', except Alfie, who called him 'Dad', or sometimes 'Pa-*pah*', when he was teasing him and pretending to be a rich boy. Jo wondered sometimes if Maria Woodvine had wanted a daughter to go with her son. Maybe Jo filled that gap, who knows? Whatever the reason, the love that was shown to Jo by the Woodvine family saved her, in every way an orphan with a terrible, dark secret could be saved.

Mrs Woodvine was unerringly kind to Jo, in a manner in which no other females had been since her mother passed. And Maria was extraordinary in another way: she ran her own business. Alfie told Jo about this early on, that his mother took photographs for folk, at weddings and christenings mostly. Every so often when Jo was there, she'd see Maria go into the shed in the corner of the garden and close the door behind her, staying in there for ages. All she knew was that it had something to do with her photographs.

One day, when Jo was thirteen, she asked, 'Could I see what's in that shed you work in, Mrs Woodvine?'

'Course you can,' said Maria, 'but only if you call me Maria. You're nearly a lady yourself and it's time we became friends.'

'Thank'ee . . .' Jo hesitated. 'Maria,' she added, since she'd been asked, in particular.

Maria smiled and beckoned her inside. The walls were lined with black cloth, which made everything feel snug. There were trays on worktops, bottles of liquids and tins of chemicals on shelves, strings strung up across the space with photographs pegged on to dry. It was a treasure trove of a room. And only Maria went in here. It belonged to her.

'Here's the red lamp I need to develop the photographs,' said Maria, showing Jo an oil lamp housed in red glass.

'Why red?' asked Jo, fascinated by all of the paraphernalia.

'Photographs are sensitive to blue and green light, so because red light is the far length of the spectrum, it doesn't affect the photographic paper.'

Maria lit the oil lamp and pulled the shed door to, so that the room was bathed in the soft, scarlet light.

Jo looked at Alfie's mother in wonder. How on earth did she become so clever, so accomplished, so independent?

Maria smiled at her. 'I feel as if you have a thousand questions in your mind, Jo.'

Jo loved the way that Maria seemed to somehow read her mind, even though Jo didn't know herself precisely what she wanted to ask.

'I do. I wonder . . . how a woman can become . . .'

She wasn't even sure what she was asking. She just knew her mind was suffused with an urgent curiosity she'd felt most of her life but had never felt it so strongly until this moment.

'Can become what?'

'Become . . . just become. Herself, I mean. Become *herself*. Oh, I dunna know what I'm saying!' Jo laughed awkwardly, annoyed that she had not the words to describe what she meant.

Maria looked at Jo very seriously. 'I think I know what you're asking. How a woman becomes something other than all the things we've been told all our lives that we *should* become.'

'Yes!' cried Jo. 'That's it. Like you. You're a woman of business. Most women I know sew like me, or take on washing, or shop work, or they're in service or the factories. I dunna wanna do any of those things.'

'What do you wanna be?' Maria asked kindly.

Now, there was a question, one she'd asked herself many times and never found an answer.

'I . . . dunna know yet. I just know what I dunna wanna be, if that makes sense.'

Maria smiled. 'Makes perfect sense. First, I was a scivvy for my uncle as a girl.'

'Me too!'

'I know, Jo. We have more in common than you think. I lost my parents too, at a young age, in a driving accident.'

This was news to Jo. Alfie had never spoken of it to her. To see an orphan becoming something as marvellous as Mrs Woodvine suddenly gave Jo an injection of hope. But, of course, the key difference was that Maria would be a legitimate orphan by a tragic accident, whereas Jo's parents . . . she didn't want to think on it at that moment. 'I'm sorry to hear of it. I didna know that.'

'I too was brought up by family. I dunna know about you, Jo, but my uncle's family wasna nice to live with.'

'Mine neither,' said Jo, then, feeling guilty about including Aunt Stella in this, she added, 'Except my Aunt Stella. She's kind to me, when she has the time for it.'

'Now, there's a woman with a career for you. Trained herself in nursing, Stella Andrews.'

Jo had never thought of her aunt that way. She'd only thought of nursing as an extension of the work her aunt already did at home, keeping everyone well and happy.

'I dunna think I wanna be a nurse,' said Jo.

'Then dunna be one. Listen, Jo. It's not Victorian times any more. It's 1906 and change is in the air. For years now, there's been a growing movement, to emancipate women.'

'To *what-i-pate* women?'

Maria laughed. 'Emancipate. Emancipation. It means freedom. For women. From all that's expected of us.'

'I like the sound of that,' said Jo.

'We'll talk further on it, Jo. For now, I have darkroom work to do. Run along and see Alfie. He'll be impatient to talk with you. He loves your company, you know.'

Jo blushed. Alfie was her best friend. But in recent months, Jo began to feel they might be something more. When they'd both turned fourteen, they were walking Snap the dog along the river one day, Alfie telling Jo in great detail about all the things he was learning on the estate, about plants and weeds and pests and disease and other features of gardening. Jo listened but she didn't really understand much of it. Just the lulling sound of his voice caused her mind to drift off, falling to darker things, her loneliness and shame. Alfie had none of that. He'd grown up without any shadow upon him and she was drawn to him because of that. If her mind grew too gloomy, she'd turn to him and tune into his voice again. She'd turn to the light of him, shining from his eyes. He was always lit up by learning and wonder, which she admired so much it made her heart ache.

'I dunna know why you hang around with me, Alfie Woodvine. I dunna have your learning or your lightness. You love the world and I . . . well, I suppose I sort of hate the world really.'

As they walked along the river, the light falling through the willow leaves hazy and dappled across their bodies as they went, Alfie looked at her very seriously.

'I dunna like it when you do that, Jo. Putting yourself down like that.'

'But it's true,' she said. 'I get much more out of our friendship than you do.'

He stopped walking then and looked at her squarely. 'Stop doing that. You're the most . . . You are . . . Urgh, I inna good with words. I never was.'

'Try again,' she said, curious now.

'You're the most *alive* person I ever knew. The way you stood up to those stupid girls who had a go at you at school.'

'That wasna always true. Sometimes I ran away.'

'That's the sensible thing to do sometimes. Retreat, withdraw. Why face risk if you can be safe? It's not a defeat. It's strategic. Like in battles.'

'Well, I didna know I was *strategic*, I mun say,' replied Jo, laughing. 'I dunna even know what *strategic* means! I thought I were just a coward for running away.' But Alfie's face was still dead serious.

'Listen, Jo. I had it easy. All my life. Loving parents, a safe home. I'm the only one, so I get doted on. You never had that. But you've never let it stop you. You used to come to school every day, rain or shine. You never had a day off in years, do you remember that?'

'That's because it was rotten at the Andrews'. I liked school better. Because your dad was there. And you.'

'But another girl might run away, might turn to trouble and strife. You're brave, Jo. When those girls come at you, you never let them make you *small*.'

Jo stopped walking then. Her eyes had filled with tears. Not one single other person in the whole world made her feel like a person the way this boy did. Everybody else made her feel like a creature, an object, a nothing. 'Alfie, I dunna . . .'

'Nay,' he said firmly. 'You mun take a nice thing when it's meant nice, Jo. That's . . . well, it's one of the reasons why I hang around with you. Because you're brave and true. And you listen to me properly and dunna mind me rattling on about nonsense. Nobody listens to me like you do, Jo.'

At that moment, Alfie wrapped Snap's lead tightly around his left hand, as the dog was impatient to move on. Then he reached out and took Jo's hand, raising it to his lips, and kissed it. She stared at her hand, then at him. He leaned in, hesitantly, and she did too, then he turned his face and kissed her on the cheek.

Snap tugged hard on the lead and they carried on walking and did not speak of it again. For a month or so, Jo knew their friendship had blossomed into something new but she was too frightened of losing it to pursue that path. She sensed the same in Alfie. So, they were hesitant all through that year and the next, graduating slowly, over time, to hand-holding, to more cheek kisses, to a hug now and again. They kept talking, kept listening to each other's tales of their days, and now and again Jo would find him watching her intently, or he'd turn to her and see her doing the same. Then they'd use Snap as an excuse – even if he'd had two walks that day – and they'd slip out and walk him in the woods, snatching a kiss and a cuddle curled up beneath a tree as Snap dozed, or he would yank at his lead to stop this tiresome canoodling and get moving again, so he could follow his doggy nose to the next adventure.

By the time she had turned eighteen, in the autumn of 1911, Alfie Woodvine had proposed marriage to Jo Darlington and she gladly accepted, and they planned the wedding for a few months after Alfie turned eighteen at the beginning of December. As well as the delightful thought of living in their own house with the fine, handsome young chap that Alfie had become, Jo was also desperately excited about leaving the Andrews household, where she'd been an unpaid maid-of-all-work since the earliest days she'd lived there at age eight. She'd minded her cousins in the long hours when Aunt Stella and Mr Andrews were out at work, and she'd cooked and cleaned and scrubbed and mended and so on, while the cousins seemed to get away with doing very little around the house. There was a tacit understanding with Aunt Stella that Jo had to earn her keep as niece, in a way that her cousins, as the rightful heirs, never did. With Mr Andrews, there was nothing tacit about it, as he ordered her to do the many jobs that needed doing in their crowded family home, always scowling at her and pushing her aside when he entered the room. Nobody could say he was an overly loving father, but he did hug and kiss his girls from time to time, yet he barely looked at Jo in the nine years she'd spent living in his house. Sometimes she felt like an invisible person, almost a ghost, insubstantial and inconsequential in her own life. At the Woodvine house she was never made to feel that way.

As the day of her wedding approached, she knew that on that very night she would go with Alfie back to a little house on the hill right opposite the school, the house they'd spend their married lives in (helped by the Woodvines with the rent) – this place seemed like it would be heaven to Jo. Away from the cousins, away from the drudgery of the Andrews house, away from being the orphan alone in the world. Her house would be her kingdom. She'd no longer be sleeping on the floor in her cousins' room and instead she'd have her very own bed, with Alfie in it. What a delicious thought! She'd have dominion over each room in their tiny house. She'd take in sewing and Alfie would go to work at the garden where he was now an Assistant to the Head Gardener, and then he'd come home and she'd have his meals ready for him, and in between she'd fix the house up and it would be the same kind of jobs she'd always had to do around the house but this time it would be *her* house – her home, in fact – the first home she'd had since she was eight years old and was left all alone in the world. But she would never be lonely again. She'd be living right opposite her dear parents-in-law and maybe she'd even get a cat, though Snap the collie dog might chase it, so perhaps not. But no matter, for she would be her own woman at last. She would be Mrs Woodvine.

By mid-December, she was standing in St Luke's church on the same hill where the school was, where the Woodvines lived and now where she would be living too. In an unfussy white dress, empire line, with a shirt collar and a short veil that came down to her waist, she held silk flowers and wore the same as her headdress, as the month was mid-December, not a good one for fresh flowers. They had planned to marry the following summer but decided they couldn't wait; or, in truth, Jo had encouraged Alfie that they should bring the date forward, as her life in the Andrews' household had become insupportable. It was hard enough to fit into a house where you weren't wanted when you were a small child, but nowadays, as a grown woman, her feet extended far beyond the end of the mattress she still slept on down on the floor, and her cousins bickered with each other and took out their frustrations on her, the interloper, more than ever. Sometimes she'd hear them whispering that Jo wasn't good enough for the likes of Alfie

Woodvine. The sooner she could escape from that house, the better all round. And so, Jo and Alfie planned a winter wedding instead.

Present at the service were the Woodvines, Aunt Stella, and none of the cousins or Mr Andrews. Thus, as Jo's side of the church would be so minimal, it was quietly agreed that the Woodvines wouldn't invite anyone from their extensive local family, so as not to embarrass the bride. Jo was glad of it, as being the centre of attention was a new and unwelcome experience for her. She was relieved once the vows were done and Alfie was asked if he would take her as his wedded wife and he replied with a grin, 'That I do.'

Afterwards, the buffet lunch having been consumed, the photographs taken by her mother-in-law Maria, and everyone retired for the afternoon, Jo was glad of it. Jo and Alfie quietly left the schoolmaster's cottage, still done up in their finery. It was already dark, the days short, as they held hands and, without speaking, walked across the road to the little house the Woodvines had found for them. Maria had placed a pretty Christmas wreath upon the door, woven through with white silk roses to signify a seasonal wedding. At that moment, as they paused at the door, nerves suddenly getting the best of both of them, Jo felt the cold kiss of a snowflake upon her cheek and looked up into the sky to see a swirling mass of more snowflakes descending in flurries upon them both.

'Winter confetti for you, Jo,' said Alfie, and smiled at her.

She looked at her husband.

'I do love you, Alfie Woodvine.'

'And I love you, Mrs Woodvine.'

'That sounds nice.'

He opened the door and asked her if she wanted carrying over the threshold. He was polite that way, never assuming. She declined, as it felt ridiculous somehow. She walked in,

Alfie behind her, and pulled the door to. It was a two-up, two-down house, with the front door opening straight into the parlour. There was a minimal galley kitchen with a coal-fired range, and beyond it, a little square of cobbles in which resided the outdoor privy. Upstairs were two bedrooms, a larger one for the newlyweds and a small room for the hoped-for off-spring. Without a word, the house still in darkness, Alfie took Jo's hand and led her up the stairs to their bedroom. He turned up the gas lamp on the wall and they stood looking at each other.

He asked if he could kiss her and she said yes. He asked at every step after that, and so their wedding night was polite, and sweet, and tender. Afterwards, he opened the curtain for her so she could see the snow. They watched it together in companionable silence. Alfie was asleep within minutes, his head in her lap as she sat propped up against two pillows, watching the snowflakes dance. She knew that, in her eighteen years on this earth, no moment in her life could compare with her complete and pure happiness at that moment. It filled her from top to toe.

And yet, in the very same moment, the old fear returned, that anything she had would be taken from her, like her doll, like her home, like her father and mother. And she stayed awake for an hour or more, gripped by the dread of it.

Chapter 3

Jo

July 1913

Jo stirred her cup of tea, then gave the teaspoon a quick wash in the bowl of water in her little yellow sink with one tap. She put the teaspoon back into the cutlery drawer and noticed that her crockery, on a shelf above the drawer, was in the wrong order. One of the side plates was at the wrong end of the rack, where the dinner plates should go. She tutted while replacing it and could only imagine it was Alfie who'd put it there, as she'd know better than to muck up the arrangement. She briefly thought about all the jobs she was supposed to be doing that afternoon before the baby woke up. She was going to beat the peg rugs, scrub the kitchen floor and clean out the tin bath, as Alfie would need to bathe that night, and he'd end up making it all mucky again. Maybe she'd have a quick dip before him, so that the water was clean and fresh, before the earthy dirt of his job created another job for her to deal with. Before that, she'd need to clean the toasting fork from that morning that still lay forlorn by the fire from breakfast and make fresh toast to go with the kippers she'd purchased from the fish man that afternoon. She'd lay out the kippers on the coals and they'd cook a treat on there. Alfie loved kippers, though she wasn't so keen. She didn't much like their oily flesh or the smell. She had to air the house out after cooking fish, even in winter.

This reminded her that it was summer, and so she didn't need to stay cooped up in their tiny parlour, staring out of the window. She could go and sit outside in the cobbled back yard. The baby was there in the pram, sleeping, but if she was quiet she could sneak out and sit on the back step. The stink from the privy would waft across the yard if the wind came in that direction, but if not, sometimes it didn't smell so badly and she could sit out there and get a bit of peace. They had no flower-beds in the yard, but Alfie had used his green fingers to great effect with a cluster of pots against the east wall, all growing vegetables and flowers: peas and sweet peas at the back, with carrots and marigolds at the front. She'd have to water them in the cool of the evening, so the water didn't burn off under the sun, as it was a hot one that day. She seated herself on the step and eyed the pram. Her ears pricked as its little inhabitant shuffled about. Jo froze, awaiting the crescendo of a waking baby realising there'd been no milk for quite a while and it ought to be delivered from the nipple forthwith. Jo's breasts were so sore; she'd had no idea feeding would be so uncomfortable. Aunt Stella had checked in on her and said to watch out that her breasts didn't get all swollen and nasty, because that could be serious. She'd told Jo to buck up and keep smiling.

Smiling? When was the last time Jo smiled and actually meant it? Perhaps it was the day last year when she realised she was expecting. But it was a complicated smile, that one. She was glad, of course she was, because that's what wives did: they got married and then they had babies. She was relieved that she'd fulfilled her end of the bargain, while Alfie was out working hard all hours. She'd done her duty and Alfie was over the moon about it, as were his parents. Once she started to show, she walked through town and her old enemies – as yet unmarried young women with no proud baby bump like her own – glanced at her with envy. But was Jo happy about it, deep down? She wanted to be. But alongside her gladness that she'd pleased her nearest and dearest was something else, something deeper and darker, as ever with Jo. For she was gripped by the fear that she'd make a poor mother, like her own had done. That somehow it was lodged in her very bones, turning out a terrible parent and ruining her child for ever. She had no evidence to base this on except blood. But it haunted her nonetheless. Thus, her days of pregnancy were a mixture of pride and worry, fulfilment and trepidation. And the worst part of it all was that it only got worse when the baby came. So, she couldn't remember the last time she smiled and really meant it, which was a sad state of affairs to admit to herself.

These days, she forced her smiles at the baby all the time because she didn't want any child of hers to ever know that . . . know what? Her first thought was too terrible, so she swallowed it. She replaced it with another thought: she didn't want any child of hers to know she found motherhood . . . difficult. Even that word wasn't quite right. Not difficult but . . . impossible. Infuriating. Tedious. Miserable. That litany of woe made her eyes prick with tears. She couldn't cry again, not again, not today. That would be the third time, after bursting into tears the second Alfie left for work that morning, and again after she put the baby down for a nap and went to brew the tea. Her eyes were sore and red with it and she didn't want Alfie to come home to that. He asked her all the time: *Are you all right, love? Sure? Are you happy, love? Sure?* She couldn't admit the awful truth, the thing she'd averted her thoughts from just a minute ago, the thing that haunted her mind all day and night since she'd had the baby just eight weeks before:

Jo hated motherhood. The truth of that fell like a rock in her mind, landing with a sickening thud in the pit of her belly. And as dreadful as that was, it was only the latest in a series of realisations about her life: she hated her house too. And she hated married life on top of that. She shook her head to stop the tears coming, going over and over every moment of every day these heavy facts that made her want to scream some days, other days spurring her to put the baby down for a nap and walk down the narrow alleyway beside the house, up the hill, pass into Coalbrookdale, and keep walking, walking, walking, for ever. And never come back.

But of course, she'd never do that. She loved baby Harry. She adored him so much it made her belly ache. She loved her husband too, to distraction. He was kind and loving to her, always thinking of little things to help her and make her smile. True, he almost always forgot to take off his filthy boots before he stomped them into the house, either at the back door into the kitchen or the front door into the parlour. It drove her mad! Why couldn't he remember? She'd told him a thousand times! But yes, she had to keep reminding herself that he was a good man and she knew many girls about town were envious of her, snagging the schoolmaster's handsome son and having such a beautiful baby as Harry, his eyes a startling blue, his fine baby hair as yellow and soft as a duckling. She called him her little ducky sometimes, when she was feeling warm towards him, which wasn't often. She would die for baby Harry, in a heartbeat. No question. But she hated the job of mother and the role of wife. She despised the endless work around the house that wifedom and parenthood created, stuck at home while Alfie went off into the world six days a week. She envied him so sharply, when she watched him go off to work in the early mornings, to see other people, talk to people, do something purposeful, stand outside under the skies and feel the sweet-scented breeze that swept across the moneyed grounds of Rowland Hall. She envied him so much it made her feel bilious. Only eighteen months ago, before marriage, before motherhood, she was a free woman: eighteen years young, strong and healthy, out there in the world, her life holding its breath to see what first step she would take . . . and now she was here, cooped up, awash with desolation, trying to fathom every second of every minute why she felt this way about a life that to others would be their dream come true. It *was* her dream come true – her own house, husband and baby. Her own family, at last. So why on earth was she so utterly despondent? The tears came flooding out again and she slapped her own face to stop them, that moment being the exact time baby Harry decided to stir, then scream. And so the next trial began, of getting through late afternoon and evening before the exhausted embrace of sleep interrupted by interminable night feeds, before she'd have to start the whole damned process all over again tomorrow, and tomorrow, and tomorrow.

Maria & Charlie

'There's something wrong with Jo,' said Maria to her husband, Charlie, while he sat puffing on a pipe and avidly reading a newspaper, one of his favourite pastimes. He liked to complain about the politicians and their disastrous decisions that would send the country down the privy, as usual. He had just spotted a little article about an American politician who was complaining in public about his low wage and how he'd had to arrange a speaking tour to make ends meet.

'This chap, this American fellow, he's on twelve thousand dollars a year! And he canna make ends meet! I'll make his damned ends meet if I ever meet him.'

Maria sighed and glanced over at her husband. Normally, she'd find his political rants charming. From the first moments she'd fallen in love with him, all those years ago, she'd loved his political fire and sense of fairness. She looked forward to sitting by the fire in winter or sitting in the garden in summer and listening to his commentary on every infuriating story in *The Daily Herald.* But this afternoon there had been a thunderstorm, so they sat inside and her mind was as tumultuous as the weather; she had other taxing concerns on her mind. And one of them was her daughter-in-law.

'We need to talk about it.'

'Mm? What's that?' Charlie said with gritted teeth, holding his pipe in place. He peered over his reading glasses at his wife, sitting in her chair, knitting tiny socks for her beloved grandson. He snapped his newspaper to straighten it. His hearing wasn't what it used to be. He despised signs of his own aging, of which there were many these days, the reading glasses just the start of it. He didn't want to admit to his wife that his ears were faulty, as she was still as beautiful and vital as the day he saw her in Mr Boden's barber and tobacconist shop on Waterloo Street, back in 1892 – or was it 1891?

'Listen, cloth ears! This is important. Put your silly paper down.'

Charlie folded it carefully and placed it on the occasional table beside him, took his pipe out and placed it next to his tobacco tin. Then he rested his head on the antimacassar draped over the back of the chair and said, 'I'm all ears. What's up?'

'I've seen it before in other women, just after their babies are born,' Maria continued, finishing off a row of stitches and placing her knitting back in her quilted bag where she kept all of her wool and knitting needles. 'It inna good, Charlie. It's only a couple of months since the birth. I wish for her sake – for all of their sakes – that she was on cloud nine. But she inna that. Any mother at this stage would be tired, yes, of course. But not . . . not the way she's looked lately. She's struggling.'

Charlie pondered it. 'You know how little Jo can be, how she's always been. There's a touch of the night about her.'

He adored Jo, her sweetness, her quiet yet deep love for his son, Alfie. He'd thought he could love nobody as much as Maria until Alfie came. And then he'd thought he could love nobody as much as Alfie, until baby Henry came, who they all called Harry. And Jo was the girl who made his son happy and gave them all Harry. Charlie was extremely fond of Jo and protective of her, particularly as she seemed to find this whole business of life somewhat . . . what's the right word, he thought? Testing. Yes, Jo always seemed to find life testing. It was little wonder, considering her early years, and that violent father who brought her up, stinking of booze and smokes and filth every time Charlie passed him in the street, along with Jo's pleasant but utterly ineffectual mother. It was a blessed release for that child that they both died young, as cruel as that seemed. Charlie nodded to himself: he was right about that.

'Are you listening to me?' Maria raised her voice in frustration. He had such a butterfly mind, her Charlie, always flitting off to profound thoughts, or maybe just what they were going to have for tea. His tummy was protruding these days and she knew he didn't like that. He wanted to be young, fit and lean. But she loved his tummy. She had her own after childbirth and it never shifted. Now they had matching tummies and she liked it. At night, in bed, she'd lie behind him when he was sleeping and rest her hand on it, its roundness comforting. She'd make him a nice bit of liver tonight, fried just how he liked it, with runner beans and new potatoes from the garden. She'd need to start preparing it soon. But first, this.

'I am your servant,' said Charlie, flicking his eyes resolutely back from his little reverie and sitting forward. 'Tell me.'

'Jo inna herself. I know she's always been a bit quiet and watchful. But this is summat else. Every time she comes over here or I go over there, her eyes look red. She can barely look me in the eye some days. I've asked her if she's all right and she always nods and puts on this curious little laugh I've never heard her do before. It's a sham, not her laugh at all. And when she picks up Harry, she sighs, I mean, really sighs, deep from down in her . . . in her . . .'

'Belly? If she had one. She's thin as a rake is little Jo.'

'That's another thing. She inna eating properly. She eats like a bird. She needs to be feeding well for the milk. But I've seen her pick at her food. From her soul, that's what I was gonna say. She sighs from deep down in her soul.'

Charlie realised he hadn't really been paying much attention to Jo, to his shame. He'd been focused utterly on his delight of a grandson. He thought having a son was the best thing that could happen to a man. But a grandson! It was even better! All the joy and none of the bother. His son and his grandson were bright sparks in his life. But he knew also that they were illuminating the darkness he carried within himself, the secret he and Maria had had to bear for twenty years now, that Alfie was not truly Charlie's son and thus Harry was not his grandson either. Nobody else in the world knew . . . well, except the wicked bastard who got Maria in the family way, but Charlie did not want to think about Oskar von Schoen right now. He had barely thought of that madman and his creepy sister Lina for donkey's years now. But somehow, the birth of Harry had brought it all back. He didn't look like a von Schoen, Harry. He looked like Alfie, who looked like Maria. Harry was all Keay, all the way. But seeing Harry for the first time, it brought it back, the decision Charlie had made two decades ago, that his love for Maria and his desire to protect her from anything the world might throw at them would see them through, would let him love the child inside her. Gone were the days when he used to berate himself for telling her he was engaged to another, leaving her to it with her German lover. The truth was indeed that Charlie had been engaged to another; there was no lie on the face of it. But underneath, he'd known all along that Rosie Green was not for him, or he for her. He'd known it was a terrible mistake, but he was driven by the loss of Maria when she went away to Shrewsbury to that dreadful department store and they'd drifted apart, irrevocably, it had seemed. The sorrow of that had borne in him a kind of madness of his own, that drove him into the arms of Maria's jealous once-friend-then-enemy, Rosie. It was a disaster, their brief and ridiculous courtship. A random example popped into his head, when he'd been trying to discuss the trade unions with Rosie and she interrupted him to say she wanted a stuffed owl in a glass case on their sideboard when they wed. He recalled his disgust when she said it, a dead bird in a see-through coffin in his house, that he'd have to consider every day of his wedded life. He knew then it was hopeless. He had to see Maria and tell her that he'd been a fool, that it was she he adored. And he had found her, beaten, running away from the horror of that man, pregnant with his child. Charlie had never loved her more before that moment and he knew he loved the child inside her too, because it was hers, because it was a part of her.

Maria watched her husband, in his pondering aspect. She was used to it now, the way he'd go on these little journeys in his head, lost in thought, his profile focused on a spot in the middle distance. He'd always been a thinker, of course, clever Charlie Woodvine. But lately, she noticed his distraction was more common. But she wasn't worried. His mind was as sharp as ever – why, he could tell you all the rivers of Africa, in alphabetical order! She had barely noticed the ten years between them when they were first married, in absolute bliss over Alfie and all his little ways. They were just two people in love, with each other and with their child. Yes, *their* child. No matter where the child's origins lay: Alfie was Charlie's through and through. She wondered, though, in those early days of their grandson's life, whether Harry's birth had brought up thoughts of the past for Charlie, of things like provenance and inheritance, which he taught the children at school about in science lessons, Mendel's peas and so forth. It was a brand-new idea in the world and Charlie found out about it in a scientific journal an old schoolboy of his sent him from London, of how characteristics were passed on from generation to generation in peas, but how it could be used to explain inheritance in all living creatures. She saw how obsessed Charlie was with the idea, how he wrote letter after letter to his old pupil demanding more information. They had corresponded about it throughout 1910 and Charlie passed it on to his own pupils. She wondered if his obsession with it was sparked by their secret, about where Alfie had come from. She would never dare ask him; they simply never spoke of it. And why should they? Why should they give that horrible man any small portion of space in their lives? But it did make Maria wonder why her husband was so obsessed with the subject. She let him have his little daydream, whatever it was. But once he was fully gone into his imagination, his eyes glazed over, it was fun to shout and wake him up to the present world, which always made her smile, the way he leapt in his seat at her voice. But tonight, she did not feel like laughing. Tonight she was desperately worried about Jo's sadness.

'Charlie Woodvine!' came Maria's strident voice, shattering his memory. Oh yes, Jo. That was the topic of conversation.

He had to stop brooding on the past. Jo was in trouble, or so his wife said, and she was rarely, if ever, wrong. She added, 'What are we going to do about Jo?'

'We should . . . we should . . . take the baby more often. Give her a break.'

Maria smiled at him, which made him beam. Her beautiful smile could still fell him. And he was pleased with his idea also because it meant he got to spend more time with darling little Harry, his favourite small person to spend time with.

'You're a very wise man, Mr Woodvine.'

'I try, I try.'

'Jo does need a break. And we will offer to take Harry more often, so she can do her own thing. Even if it's just to sleep. But I'm wondering if she needs summat more than that, summat to focus on, summat that inna home, or family, or anything to do with that. I feel like she needs an interest, summat to – what's that word, when the old scientist feller made dead frogs jump?'

'Galvanising,' said Charlie. 'Named after Galvani. And they didn't jump. They twitched.'

'Galvanise, that's it! She needs summat to galvanise her. And, hang on . . . I've an idea brewing. And I think it's a good'un.'

'Dunna over-exert yourself, my love,' said Charlie, his wit dry as a cracker.

'Hush now, Woodvine, and let me think . . . hold on, it's Wednesday. I'm off out later tonight.'

'Yes, the meeting.'

'Right, I know what I'm gonna do. Leave it with me.'

'What is it, then?'

'Mind your own beeswax.'

Charlie loved it when Maria had a plan in mind. She got all feisty and bright-eyed. He would quite like to take her upstairs right about now, but also his belly was grumbling and he really wanted his tea, perhaps even more than the proverbial roll in the hay with his wife. Later, yes, they could have a bit of that later, he smiled to himself. If she was in the mood, with any luck!

Maria saw Charlie was off dreaming again, this time with a sly look on his face. She knew that look of old. He's thinking about bedding me, she thought with a thrill. She'd look forward to that. But for now, her project was Jo. And Maria was going to pop over there after tea and offer her a suggestion that she was sure even poor gloomy Jo could not refuse.

Chapter 4

Jo

That evening, after tea was made and done, and Jo was still airing the house out of the kipper stink with the windows flung open, she was outside bringing the washing in when she heard a knock on the front door and Alfie go to answer it. She came in the back door to the kitchen and placed the basket of washing on the kitchen table and went through to the parlour, curiously. Who could it be at this time of the evening? She was too tired to deal with visitors on top of everything else.

She walked in to see her husband Alfie going out of the front door, and his mother, Maria, standing in his stead.

'What's happened?' said Jo, a pall of catastrophe about her, as her ability to cope with any kind of crisis right now was around nil.

'Nothing's happened,' said Maria. 'I sent him over to his dad's for an emergency game of chess, because I wanted a quiet word with you.'

Jo didn't think she had the strength to deal with a talk, especially if it was to criticise her for how she wasn't looking after the Woodvines' precious son these days. Perhaps Alfie had been over there complaining about her and how she wasn't ironing regularly enough and it'd all built up in a wobbling stack and she didn't cut his hair like she normally did and Alfie's blond locks were getting long about the ears, and other such crimes. Baby Harry was fractious, grizzling about the world and everything in it. Jo picked him up from his basket and he immediately got worse, writhing and making little croaky cries that threatened to tip into full-blown bawling. Jo felt entirely at her wit's end. It was bad enough dealing with the endless whims of this baby alone, but with another person in the room it somehow felt a thousand times worse, as if they were watching and judging, wondering why Jo was such a poor mother who couldn't keep her baby from whining all day and night. It was all Jo's fault, she knew that in her bones. If only Maria would go, and Jo could be alone in her embarrassment. But Maria had seated herself comfortably on a chair, looking as if she intended to stay for a while. Then she suddenly stood up.

Maria said, 'Let me take him. You have a sit down.'

Jo wasn't about to argue. She was desperate to give up the wriggling bundle. Jo watched as Maria gently took him and snuggled him into the crook of her arm, bending her face close to his and kissing his nose. It had the effect of a kiss from a folk tale, as Harry immediately stopped griping. This was instantly understood by Jo as further proof that she truly was the world's worst mother. She let out a sob and tried desperately to hide it, running out to the kitchen. She tried to stifle her tears, as she didn't want Harry to hear her cry. It'd just set him off worse. It always did.

She listened as Maria cooed at him in the other room. He was completely quiet. Jo came to the doorway and watched as Maria popped him into his basket. Jo came back into the parlour. Even in that brief space of time, Harry was already fast asleep.

'You have the magic touch,' Jo said, miserably.

'I've no such thing,' Maria replied quietly. 'It's nothing to do with me. Or you. Babies can sense worry, or fear, or sadness. They absorb it like a sponge. I'm rested and calm and at ease with myself and Harry felt it. He gave himself up to the sleep he needs. You see, he loves his mother so much – he loves you so much, Jo – that he feels everything you feel, just like he did when he lived inside of you. That's how much he loves you, Jo.'

The tears came thick and fast, rolling uncontrollably down Jo's cheeks now.

'He dunna love me one bit,' she sobbed. 'He hates me.'

Maria simply said, 'I'll put the baby down in his pram outside, and then we can talk, all right?'

Jo nodded, unable to form words. How could she talk about her secret shame? But Maria seemed to understand, like she always did. She was the one person in the world who really seemed to know Jo. Not even Alfie understood her. He loved her, that was certain. But he did not understand her.

Maria returned from the back yard, where Harry lay in his pram sleeping, blissfully quiet. Maria said she'd make some tea. Jo helped her and they did it in a comfortable silence.

'I'm sorry I havna baked,' said Jo, as she sat down on the settee and Maria sat in Alfie's chair opposite. 'I'd've made biscuits if I'd known you were coming over. I dunna have a thing to offer you. This house is full of ingredients, not finished things. And I dunna have the energy to make a thing these days. It's enough just to be awake and alive, to sort the baby and keep the house clean. Everything else feels . . . impossible.'

Maria smiled gently at her and replied, 'Nobody wants you to waste your time making biscuits for us, Jo. What we want is to help you. Charlie and I have been worried about you, about how hard things are for you.'

Jo scoffed, not at Maria, but driven instead by a grim sense of humiliation. 'Women have been having babies since Adam and Eve. And doing it alone and getting on with it. Why am I such a person that canna do it right? There's summat about me . . . summat . . . broken.'

She fell to sobbing again, really letting it out this time. Her hands covered her face, to hide that shame, while she sensed Maria waiting silently, without judgement. Jo realised she didn't want Maria to leave. Instead, it was a great comfort to have her there. She wished at that moment that Maria were there all the time. Jo had never needed her mother like she needed her now. But Louise Darlington, a drunk and a murderer, was long gone. And Mama was never much of a parent anyway. Yet Maria was here. If only she could move in and Alfie could move across the road and the two of them could raise Harry together and Jo would have help, proper female help, the kind she needed now more than anything. But it was ridiculous. She couldn't ask such a thing. But sometimes she dreamt about it and it seemed like heaven on earth to Jo.

When Jo had cried it all out and quietened down, Maria came to sit beside her on the settee and took her hand.

'Fetch your coat, Jo. I've summat on tonight and you and baby Harry are coming with me.'

Jo glanced at her watch to see it was just gone seven. She didn't take the baby out at night and rarely during the day. And she felt so shattered, as she did every evening about this time, she couldn't fathom why Maria would think it was good for her to have to go out, baby and all.

'Thank'ee but I dunna think so, I'm sorry. Baby's finally gone down, though I'll need to move him to his cot upstairs later. I just wanna sleep, myself. And I never take him out in the evenings.'

Maria stood up. 'Well, tonight, you are. I've a photography

job and you're coming with me, like I said. Hop to it. I'll pop a nice blankie over Harry and off we'll go. I can see you're standing there with your mouth hanging open but you're just gonna have to trust me on this one, Jo. Get your coat. We're going out.'

Maria added she'd see Jo in the yard when she was ready. Despite Jo feeling like everything inside her was screaming that she was in no fit state to be seen by a soul, she felt her legs move and, mechanically, she gathered her pale green summer coat, her straw boater and her handbag. She met Maria in the yard, where Jo held the back gate open for her as she pushed the pram through into the alley. Harry barely stirred. He loved movement anyway. When his sleeping during the day was really bad, Jo would take him out on a walk, which would send him right off, but then she wouldn't get any rest for herself, which was a mixed blessing. Tonight, she was glad of it, because she had Maria's companionship and not only her dark thoughts to keep her in uneasy company.

They walked down Church Hill, both keeping a hand on the pram to ensure it didn't run away with itself, baby Harry sleeping peacefully on, of course, despite waking if a pin dropped at home. Jo wondered, what was that all about? The way they'd doze off when being jiggled about like the washing in a tub, but when there was quiet they'd wake up for anything. She supposed the movement must feel like when they were in the womb and it was lulling. When she was pregnant with Harry, it was always once she'd sat down to rest that he'd get busy and start kicking around. At the bottom of the hill, Maria took over the pram and turned them back on themselves along High Street towards the Market Square. Jo and Maria nodded and said good evening to folks they were acquainted with on the street and Jo suddenly felt ten times better than she had done, cooped up in the little house that had become her prison these past weeks. She didn't even know what this photography work of Maria's was going to be about tonight, but she was just glad to be out and about, with Maria pushing the pram, and Jo feeling strangely light-headed. Even her body felt like she was walking on air, just to be free, away from the house for once. The evening sun shone on the river and made the brooding Severn sparkle in its summer garb. They paused in their walk when they reached Market Square and wandered over to the edge of the iron bridge, drawn to the water as so many are when they visit the little town of Ironbridge, the mighty old river flowing through it taking less traffic than it had in days of old when boats and ships were kings, before the days of the railways and now the motor car. Jo saw the river banks thronged with flowers that waved in the gentle breeze, with names that Alfie had taught her as a child and she still remembered: the tall purple spikes of loosestrife alongside sedge and bullrushes, with the little yellow stars of iris flowers dotting the green-brown wavy border of nature that loved to grow there in the damp conditions. *Oh my*, Jo mused, *it's good to be in the world again.*

'Time to go,' said Maria gently.

'Oh, I thought you'd come over here to take pictures of the river.'

'No, no,' said Maria, smiling. 'We are bound for the Tontine Hotel.'

Maria turned the pram and Jo followed, wondering what on earth was going on that needed photographing at seven-thirty at a hotel and public house. They crossed the road opposite the bridge to the Tontine, situated perfectly for tourists and the like who wanted to stay near to the visual attraction of the world's first iron bridge, around which the town had formed, blossomed and spread for over a hundred and thirty years. The Tontine had a bar and bedrooms, yet also a function room at the back, towards which Maria pushed the pram confidently, Jo behind her. Jo couldn't remember the last time she'd had a drink in a pub. Now and again, before the baby, Alfie and Jo would go for a beer – she'd have a half – or sometimes if they were flush she'd have a snifter of tawny port, which she loved, as it reminded her of cough syrup her Aunt Stella used to give them as kids, slipping down warm and easy. Sitting in a pub and listening to Alfie's jokes seemed like a whole other life that she no longer recognised. Again, she was hit with a pang of regret, for giving up her freedom for the package currently snoozing away in the pram Maria pushed down the corridor, now reaching the door to the function room, which Jo knew existed – some girls from school had had their wedding receptions there – but Jo herself had never been in.

Maria stopped the pram and went round it to hold the door open. Jo pushed the carriage through onto a hardwood floor and could hear the hubbub of many voices before she saw them. Once inside, she saw with surprise that the room was filled with women. And only women. Not a man in sight. It seemed baby Harry was the only male among them. But what on earth were they all doing there?

Chapter 5

Jo

Jo didn't know where to put herself, then Maria directed her to a row of chairs at the side where she could push the pram behind and still be close to it while taking a seat. There were several rows of chairs on each side of the room and a central set as well, with narrow corridors between them for people to find their seats. Women were sitting and talking, some turned around to talk to others in rows behind them, many women standing in the aisles talking earnestly too and pointing out friends and comrades across the room, nodding, smiling, frowning, utterly engaged with each other, hands clasped in friendship here and there, others patting friends on the arm or even held around their shoulders. Their clothes, hats and hairdos were evidence of their variety: some were working folk like her and Alfie with their plain dowdy dresses, others were clearly well-to-do with an ostrich-feathered hat or a velvet purse. To Jo, this was a foreign country. The girls she'd known en masse at school were characterised largely by their hatred for each other, a kind of peculiarly female breed of nastiness that was largely psychological. Boys who fell out at school often had a dust-up and then it was over. Girls would engage in mental warfare, ignoring other girls for long stretches or teasing them about their worst fears, admitted in a moment of weakness. Large groups of women had always made Jo feel itchy and a bit scared. She peered into the pram to check on Harry and he was still away with the fairies. How he could sleep through all this noise was beyond her. She did notice two more prams on the other side of the function room, lined up against the wall. And one woman a couple of rows in front of her was holding a bouncing baby boy in blue, a few months older than Harry, who was being jiggled, which met with copious giggles from him, delighting his mother, who showed him off to the others around her. Jo wondered if she'd ever feel like that about her own baby. She knew Harry was a beautiful boy, everyone who saw him said it. She knew that other people loved to hold him and stroke his soft yellow hair. When she looked at him, she was filled with love and pain and resentment and fear. It was all too complicated and too much. She turned away, looking for Maria.

At that moment, Maria was looking for Jo too, as Jo saw when she was beckoned over to the back of the room, where Maria was chatting with two women, one with grey hair who looked quite a bit older than Maria's age and another who looked younger, but still older than Jo. Both women were very well dressed, in light summer fabrics in the latest fashion colours of lilac and cherry red, which made Jo feel very underdressed in her chequered beige-and-grey house frock with not even a frill to enliven it. She felt annoyed at Maria for not telling her they were going somewhere where people were dressed up. She could've worn her nicest embroidered white blouse with her favourite long apple-green skirt. She was glad that she had her pale green summer coat on, because at least it wasn't brown and grey like most of her cheap clothes; instead the coat was pretty and suited her well, though it was warm in there with so many people and she'd rather have taken it off. When she reached the trio, both women smiled warmly at her.

Maria said, 'Jo, these are relatives in Charlie's family. This is Hettie Malone and her daughter, Martha Haywood. Ladies, this is my daughter-in-law, Jo Woodvine, and mother to our darling grandson Harry.'

Jo was quite overcome as both women put out their hands and gave Jo a joint handshake, holding tightly on and smiling, saying what a pleasure it was to meet her.

'And to meet the mother of our latest Woodvine, little Harry,' said Hettie, the older woman. She had the most extraordinary green eyes, the same bright green of the lush grass that grew alongside the river. 'The Woodvines are good people. My mother-in-law, Anny, was a Woodvine, before she married Peter Malone. That's how we're related to your father-in-law, through the late Anny Woodvine, God rest her soul.'

'Indeed,' said Maria. 'A wonderfully kind woman who saved my life, she truly did.'

Jo had known Anny Malone *née* Woodvine. Or more accurately, had known of her, as she was regularly mentioned at the Woodvine household when Jo was visiting there to see Alfie over the years of her childhood. Anny Malone was well thought of around those parts, as she'd started off life poor – her father had been an iron worker killed in a furnace explosion – and yet, later in life, she'd acquired money and used it mostly to help the poor of Ironbridge. Jo knew that until only a year or so before Jo joined the school where Charlie was schoolmaster, Anny had helped out teaching useful domestic skills to the children, but had become too elderly and retired quietly and very comfortably to her big house in the woods, along with her husband Peter. Anny had died a few years ago now, a year after her husband passed. Then, Jo suddenly recalled, the money had come from her daughter-in-law, Hettie Malone, the woman with the marvellous green eyes standing right there. Hettie was famous in Ironbridge for also starting out from humble beginnings as a maid and then inheriting a fortune, from which she established a foundation that gave charity, housing, training and education to many of the unfortunates of the area. She was a local legend, Hettie, now Jo remembered the name. Martha looked very like her and they both had the same smile, looking attentively at Jo, awaiting her first utterance. There was a long pause as they all waited for Jo to say something, anything.

'Charmed, I'm sure,' said Jo.

Was that all she could come up with? She should've thanked them for their kind words about Harry. She should've reciprocated what they said about the Woodvines being good people, as she was married to one of the best, Alfie Woodvine. All these polite things and more she could've said but she didn't. She realised at that moment how complete her removal from society had been these last few months, so much so that she'd forgotten how to speak in a civilised way with strangers. She felt like a fool.

Then, a woman's voice called out from the other end of the room that everyone should take their seats, saving Jo from more desperate attempts at small talk. She was relieved and went back to the pram, Harry still out for the count, thankfully. Maria motioned to Jo to sit down, as the room organised itself into seats and three women were revealed at the front of the room, alongside a poster that was pasted onto card resting on an easel. It read 'WSPU', with an illustration of women marching down a road, all wearing sashes striped in green, white and purple, while at the base of the poster was written DEEDS NOT WORDS. Jo suddenly realised exactly who these women were and why they were here. She craned her neck to see where Maria had gone. She was in the back corner, her newest camera – a lightweight pocket Kodak she'd shown off to Jo a few months ago – resting on her hand, its miniature bellows held in place by criss-cross struts, the lens pointed at the rows of women and the flowing carpet of their straw boaters on almost every head that led the eye to the three women standing at the front, waiting for silence. It would make a good photograph. Jo wasn't going to be able to grab Maria's attention while she was working, so she knew she'd better sit back in her seat and listen. Never would Jo have imagined that she'd end up at a meeting of the women she'd heard tell of but never paid much mind to until now: the scandalous, rebellious, law-breaking women who fought for the right of all women to vote, the infamous suffragettes.

'Women of Ironbridge!' said one of the speakers, in a rousing voice, deep and sonorous, that boomed across the room and filled it to its corners. 'Welcome to our first meeting here in the cradle of the industrial revolution, the historic town of Ironbridge. We're delighted to bring to you news of our cause across the land, represented here tonight by the Women's Social and Political Union, Shropshire Chapter.'

This led to a spontaneous round of applause. Jo saw that every pair of eyes in the room was trained on the speaker. She was a youngish woman, maybe in her twenties. She wore a skirt of midnight blue, a white blouse with subtly puffed sleeves and a man's tie at the collar. Her dark hair was full and wavy, pulled up into a loose yet neat bun. Jo was transfixed by her the moment she began to speak.

'Tonight's mood is, of course, a sombre one.'

The whole room moved as heads nodded or shook sadly from side to side. Jo's eyes flicked about, trying to decipher what was happening. She heard a woman sob.

'Tonight we pay homage to the one-month anniversary of

the death of our beloved sister, Emily. This woman, this queen, sacrificed herself for our noble cause. The first death for our cause. She approached her task with determination and absolute focus, as she edged her way through the crowds at the Epsom Derby. The task she had given herself was to take hold of the bridle of the King's horse Anmer, as it rushed past, to attach to it a flag of our beloved colours – white for purity, purple for loyalty and dignity, green for hope – bringing our cause to national and international attention. We all know what happened next.'

A flutter of muttering and more shaking of heads rippled through the audience.

'On that day, Emily Wilding Davison bought a return ticket to Epsom. Remember that, sisters, when the cruel lie is whispered that she meant to take her own life. Emily was a force of nature. She had been arrested many times, had been force-fed in prison many times. And still she prevailed. She died on June the 8th, four days after her actions at the Derby ensured our cause could never be ignored. On June the 14th last, the funeral of Emily Wilding Davis took place in London, attracting a crowd of tens of thousands.

'Emily once said of her work with the WSPU, "I have come into a fullness of joy and an interest in living which I never before experienced." We lost the brief candle of her life far too soon but let us take heart, that her steadfast work towards women's suffrage gave her an "interest in living" that illuminated not only her own life but – with her heroic death – fanned the flame of our torch of liberty, to light the way for women in the years to come as we fight on for the freedom of our very souls. We will now bend our heads and hold a minute's silence for our sister who fell in the line of duty. Let us never forget: she died for women.'

Jo watched as a swell of straw boaters across the room

tipped forward and a heavy hush descended on the room. She had been in church many a time as a child (though she didn't regularly go these days, as she was too busy and Alfie wasn't much interested in reverence, something he inherited from his parents). But nothing she'd ever experienced during times of prayer in church could match this. The sadness and empathy in the room was palpable. Jo knew little of this woman Emily – only the bare facts of what she had done – and knew less about suffragettes in general. What Jo mostly knew of gatherings of girls and women were that they were judgemental, unhelpful or downright nasty. And yet here was a group of women who, despite the wide range of ages and classes, had joined together for a common cause. Jo knew it was wrong that only rich men could vote. Charlie talked about things like this all the time and sometimes Alfie joined in, though her husband was far more interested in plants than politics, which Jo noticed often seemed to somewhat disappoint her father-in-law. But she'd never really been interested in whether or not she could vote, because parliament and its politicians seemed a thousand miles away and of little consequence to her life. She wasn't against the suffrage cause at all. But she had never been roused by it.

Jo had read about the woman Emily and the King's horse and Charlie had gone on about it, the tragedy of Emily crushed under the animal after being trampled. Jo had wondered what Emily could have thought would happen, trying to grab hold of a galloping racehorse like that. Either way, it was the first death of a woman who supported the suffrage cause and it caused a stir. Jo realised that she had heard tell of it but had not stopped to really consider it, not tried to think of her as a person, a woman, who died for something she believed in. Everyone in town and in the papers said that the suffragettes were madwomen, everyone except Charlie, that was, who sang their praises. Jo realised the whole argument had flowed over her head, so utterly caught up was she in her own misery. But now, she was interested. This was the first time in her life she'd seen a proper sense of camaraderie and purpose among women, rather than rivalry. And to think that a woman had given her own life to further it was astonishing to Jo. Alfie once told Jo she was the most alive person he'd ever known. What had she been doing all this time since? Sleepwalking through life in a haze of loneliness, blind to the movement of history all around her? And not just any old history, but women's history, a slice of existence she'd always seen as something to carry like a burden, not to rise up and fight for. Now, for the first time in months, if not years, she felt utterly awake.

After this minute of reverence, the speaker at the front continued. Her voice was like music, like one of those woodwind instruments Jo didn't know the name of, but they were mellow and sweet, yet rich and low. She could listen to this woman all day and never tire of it. Along with the other two speakers, the three of them continued with news of other recent happenings in the WSPU ranks, and ranks was the right word for it, as they talked of their cause as if it were a military campaign. They spoke of women being arrested for protesting for their rights, of women barricading themselves in their prison cells and being taught a lesson by having a high-powered water hose trained on them, or being forced to eat by a tube inserted into their nose, which caused excruciating pain. Jo had never read or heard of any of this. How could it be that a rubber tube could be fed into your nostrils and reach your stomach and milk be poured in? Who would do such a terrible thing? She shivered to think of it, in absolute horror. The prevailing attitude was that suffragettes were uncouth, unladylike troublemakers. The women in this room, all well-turned out, even the poorer ones, and all listening intently and humbly, could not be further from this rowdy image. Jo began to look forward to the end of the meeting, when she could get together with Maria and ask her all about it. Jo felt ignorant and scolded herself that she knew so little of events that impacted so clearly on her own womanhood. She glanced round to check that Harry was still there and he was, of course, and had not made a peep in all this time. Suffragettes seem to suit him, she thought, wryly.

And at that moment, the door behind her was flung open and a man's voice was heard arguing with a woman's voice, growing suddenly loud as someone entered the room. Chairs scraped as women turned to see what all the brouhaha was about. A short man marched into the room in a smart tweed suit that looked far too warm for this weather, his red face showing what an unwise choice it was. He stood at the back of the room and shouted, 'This is an illegal meeting. Everyone mun leave now, this instant. Come on, you women. Disperse, disperse. Or stay and be arrested. I've summoned the constables.'

The room erupted in sound, a heady mixture of anger and hilarity. Some women were shouting at the man, others were pointing at him and laughing. Someone called out, 'On whose authority, William Wall? You're just a registrar at the council!' Nobody made a single move to leave, as they'd been ordered to by this angry little man. Someone was shouting, 'Bugger off, Willy!', which caused great hilarity. Whatever the outcome of this bizarre spectacle, Jo's first thought was for baby Harry. She immediately got up to go to his pram. Seeing her as the first woman to stand up, the man called out to her, 'Yes, yes, good, good. That's right. See, women? Here's one of your number who does as she's told. Come with me, there's a good wench.'

Jo was incensed by this and immediately spat back, 'I'm

seeing to my baby, mon, and I'd never go an inch with the likes of you.'

This raised a giant laugh and a cheer, which further shocked Jo, as she'd never been the centre of attention, of positive attention at least. She moved quickly over to the pram and found Harry grizzling and waking up, the noise around him not comforting any longer. She grasped the pram handle and did her best to manoeuvre it past the man with the ridiculous name of Willy Wall, who was still shouting, and women were standing up now and shaking their fists, and pushing forwards, while Willy stood his ground and shouted back at them. Jo felt a shot of fear as she shoved onwards, trying to get out of the packed, close room, as women surged forwards in defence of the meeting and the man literally jumped up and down to attempt to have his voice heard, his rage obvious, as he'd never had to wait for a woman to do as he said in his life, no doubt. As Jo shoved onwards, she saw Maria was outside the room, arguing with another two men, who then pushed past her to get inside. In their hurry, they almost tipped up the pram and Jo cried out. She saw Maria move swiftly, come to her and grasp the hood of the pram and drag it out as Jo pushed onwards. Just before she finally left the room, Jo glanced at the two men who'd shoved her out of the way, to see they were grabbing at women's arms and one wrenched an older lady's hat off, which caught in her hair and hat pin, making her cry out in pain. This was madness. She had to get her baby out of there.

Seconds later, Jo and Maria were free of the room and trotting away down the corridor, as fast as they could with the pram to push, while they were passed by more men from the town piling on down to the meeting to do God knows what. When they got to the open door to the street, they pushed on past the Market Square, until they were far enough away to stop and take a breath. Little Harry was by this time half-crying and half in shock, as the pram had taken him on the ride of his life. As Maria held on to the pram to steady it, Harry's scream rose to the heavens. Jo went straight to him without a thought and bundled him up into her arms. She held the warm little package of his body to her chest, stroking the back of his head tenderly and crooning to him.

'It's all right, my little mon, my little lamb chop. Everything is all right now. Mama's here. Mama's here.'

And for the first time since he was born, baby Harry Woodvine actually stopped crying the moment he felt his mother's arms about him and heard her sweet voice. He settled immediately as his mother comforted him and he nestled his ear against her chest to better hear her racing heartbeat.

Chapter 6

Alfie

July 1913

Whenever Alfie felt he'd chosen his favourite season of the year in the garden at Rowland Hall, another season would unfurl and he'd declare this was the one he loved most of all. Now, in July, he was deadheading the sweet peas to encourage more flowers. Lady Rowland loved them in little jars about the house, particularly for their heady scent, which Alfie inhaled as he worked – a mixture of orange blossom and rose – and decided again that summer was the best season of the year. He liked the sun on his back as he worked. He liked the green frenzy overspilling the broad lines of beds in the walled garden. He even liked summer storms, that heavy expectancy in the air before the warm, fat drops of rain doused him and sent him running to the hothouses, where he'd check the peaches on the west wall and the grape vines laden with plump fruit hanging delicately from the glasshouse roof. His favourite job in the garden was always weeding. He was never annoyed with weeds, only felt they were a plant in the wrong place. Some gardeners hated weeding – back-breaking work, his boss called it, the wise old Mr Cork, the Head Gardener.

True, it wasn't easy on the back, though at nineteen and a half years of age, Alfie knew he didn't have to worry too much about his joints and bones just yet. Weeding didn't bother him, or any of his list of tasks in the garden, really. That was how he saw gardening: a list of tasks that must be done, some pleasurable, some not so much, but all necessary. He took pride in keeping his beds free of weeds, his rows of vegetables neat with no insects surviving his brutal and efficient reign of terror over their existence, keeping cabbages free of holes and strawberries free of slug slime. All of it left him with a profound sense of peace when he would stop for a moment, perhaps standing and sipping from a mug of tea under the brick archway that led to the Head Gardener's office and the potting sheds, where two stray cats named Apple and Crumble came and went to bowls of scraps that Mr Cork left out for them.

When Alfie had finished the deadheading, he noticed a very tall rosebay willowherb that had inexplicably grown to chest height hidden behind a sweet pea stalk. Although it had a pretty flower, he eased it out by the roots and walked over to the office archway and threw it to the spot in the sun by a south-facing wall where he left weeds to languish and die in the heat before composting them. It was not quite time for lunch yet but he was hungry. The other lads who worked on the estate were not back yet from their work in the other sections, such as down by the lake, in the formal flower gardens and over in the orchard. There were eight chaps from surrounding towns and villages who worked the estate alongside Alfie and Mr Cork, from one older man to men in their thirties to Alfie to a couple of sixteen-year-old apprentice boys who ran around after the others as he had done not so long ago. Alfie usually waited until they were all back to take his lunch, but his tummy was grumbling, so he went back into the office to the row of wooden pigeonholes where the gardeners kept their bits and bobs. He took his lunch tin and went out through an archway to the low wall behind the potting sheds where the sun shone diffusely through the overhanging trees, a good place to take the weight off your feet and eat. He found Mr Cork already there eating his lunch too and nodded to his boss.

'Alfred,' said Cork, nodding back.

'Mr Cork.'

Alfie sat down and opened up the tin.

'We're both a bit early today,' said Cork. 'Heat makes me hungry, I dunna know why.'

'Same here,' said Alfie, and bit a great chunk out of his sandwich.

'What's your lovely wench fixed for'ee today for your snap?'

Alfie held up his sandwich, then finished his mouthful before speaking.

'Corned beef and tomato. Jo knows my favourite.'

'Tomatoes from your father's garden?'

'Course. Sweet and flavourful. Runs rings around shop-bought rubbish.'

'Course,' agreed Mr Cork, the deep lines of his face crinkling in his appreciation, then turning into a frown as he looked down in distaste at his own offering for lunch, a Cheddar cheese sandwich. 'My wife thinks we eat too many animals. She's got all caught up in some fad or fashion for vegetarianism. I mean, I love a vegetable, me. How could I not when we grow such beauties here? But I dunna wanna live off the damn things. Or cheese, 'specially Cheddar. If she's gonna foist cheese on me, least she could do is give me a lump of Cheshire. But truly I wanna slab of meat for my snap and no mistake. You're lucky your wife dunna take on so with fads and fashions, Alfred. Since our girls are growed and long since left, Mrs Cork dunna have enough to do and cooks up fancy ideas in that aimless head of hers. You're lucky your wife inna like that, jockey. A good little wife you have there in Jo. A good wife and a little nipper in her arms at home is all the ingredients a mon needs for happiness, by my reckoning.'

Everything in Alfie wished to spill out the truth to Mr Cork. He wanted to tell him how wretched it was at home. How Jo might make him a nice lunch, but everything else was wrong, every single thing. When Alfie woke up in the mornings, Jo was more often than not silently weeping in bed, or silently weeping in the kitchen, or silently weeping in the yard. She hid it from Alfie every time, but he knew that she knew he'd seen it. He'd ask her, a hundred times – a thousand – *Are y'all right, my beaut? My love? My lass?* She'd nod and say she was fine. But she wasn't fine. She was as far from fine as a person could be. And he did not know what to do about it. Everything should've fallen into place when he married his own dear little Jo, moved into their own dear little home and had their own dear little baby. But nothing was in place; everything was crooked, and split, and broken.

For a man who was as good with his hands as Alfie Woodvine, he did not know how to fix it. It was not only his hands he had a talent with; he also loved to solve problems with his mind. He did not love letters as his father did. Instead Alfie loved numbers, measurements, calculations, shapes, symmetry, tessellation and other scientific notions. He liked to measure out the rows of dahlias precisely, so each plant and flower had the correct proportion of space. He enjoyed marking out the nails and strings in the walls that trained their fruit trees in neat patterns across the bricks. He loved to talk to Mr Cork about how plants can be bred to create new types with new colours, and about the latest forms of pesticide to keep the insects off the Lord and Lady's prize fruit and veg they used for their fancy dinner parties. But nothing, nothing he could measure or reckon with his brain, or make or fix with his hands, could mend whatever was wrong with Jo. His little boy, his baby Harry, lit up his soul every second he spent in his company. Alfie could not fathom why his Jo was not bowled over with joy as he was. Even when Harry was screaming, Alfie would think what good lungs he had, and he'd laugh about it and invent songs to make Jo laugh about what a little misery guts their baby was, but Jo wouldn't laugh. He couldn't remember the last time she laughed, before last night, that was, before his mother brought her home from that blasted meeting and all they could talk about was suffragettes this and suffragettes that. That fact alone brought a deep shame upon Alfie he could never tell old Cork, let alone his wife's never-ending abyss of sorrow at home.

'You inna wrong,' replied Alfie. That's all he said. That's all he felt permitted to say.

Then, the other gardeners started to wander back for their snap and the conversation ended. Alfie was glad. He couldn't say what he really wanted to say and it bothered him.

The truth was, he wasn't against women getting the vote, never was and never would be against it. He was his father's son, a devoutly left-leaning working lad who spoke up for the working classes and thought the rich had far too much say in how things went in the world. Mr Cork doffed his cap in humble supplication to the Lord and Lady but Alfie saw them differently, as a means to an end for him: a reason for him to work as he wanted, on the land, outside, off the settee and out under the skies. If the rich will keep vast kitchen gardens to fuel their lavish lifestyles, then Alfie Woodvine was only too happy to work in them and love that work. He didn't hate the rich, as some fellows down the pub did. He took people as they were, judging them by their behaviour. Acts not words was his mantra growing up, something his mother taught him.

Judge people by the way they acted and not by the things they said. Talk is cheap, his mother would say. It was how he fell in love with Jo, for she was a quiet one, a watchful one, of few words and deep thoughts, perhaps of dark thoughts from time to time, he wondered. The way her brown eyes would darken at times as she gazed into the distance; she'd had that trick since they were eight years old. But she had an ocean of love inside her to give and she gave it to him. She did not speak silly words of romance, instead showing her love by all the little things she did for him, day in and day out. But since the baby came, all those had gone, the same as their intimacy had gone. She hadn't let him touch her in weeks, and he understood it, of course he did, her body taken over by the baby, needed by the baby, day and night. The last thing she needed was him pawing on her too, he knew that. But he ached for her soft touch, the nape of her neck, the curve of her hip, as he used to pull her towards him in bed. Those happy days before the baby came, before everything went wrong when it should be so right. Weeks of desolation.

But now, last night, he saw Jo smiling, actually smiling and even laughing. He'd finished his chess game with his father and gone home, to sit on the back step and have a smoke, smell the jasmine he had growing up his fence, think about Jo and what he could do to fix things. His dad had wanted to talk about it but something in him was too proud, too humiliated to answer his father, and instead he pretended all was fine. Dad offered to take the baby more often and Alfie thanked him. He came home soon after, avoiding more talk of his problems, which he felt obscurely must somehow be his fault. He was surprised by the sound of voices chattering and laughing coming up the alley and shocked when he realised it was Jo and his mother.

They came in the house and told him the whole story, about the meeting being broken up and men piling in the room and getting Harry's pram out safe and what an outrage it all was. He agreed it was wrong, for men to interrupt like that and manhandle women. That was unforgiveable. And he thought he'd chop off his own right arm to see Jo laughing like that again, but all he felt was fear. She was bright-eyed and lit up from within, but it wasn't by Harry, and it wasn't by him. He'd seen her lit up like that in the old days, when he'd make her laugh or touch her the right way in bed. He lived to see her like that. But now, all she talked of all night were these women. It scared him. Nothing good could come of joining a group so universally derided and abhorred, especially in the pubs and street corners and homes of hardworking men like himself. No respectable woman would get herself mixed up with the likes of the suffragettes.

But he said nothing of it to Mr Cork, of course. No man would admit his wife had been to a suffragette meeting. He spent the rest of the afternoon cutting lavender bunches for drying, as well as planting out autumn bulbs in the borders. He walked the long trek home from Broseley to Ironbridge. Sometimes he would hop on an omnibus if it rained, gripping onto the pole at the back before climbing the spiral stairs to the top deck, the lower deck filled with folk hiding from the weather; he'd still get wet but he'd be out in it for less time leastways. But mostly he liked the walk. It gave him more thinking time, which he always enjoyed. He came down the alley to their back door and walked into the kitchen, his wife in the far doorway holding the baby, immediately shouting at him, 'Take those boots off, Alfie Woodvine, or I'll give you a slap in the face with a wet fish!'

He stopped, looked up at her and saw her smiling from ear to ear, jiggling Harry in her arms as he cooed at her.

'Yes, we will,' she joked with the baby. 'We'll slap Dada in the face with a smelly old kipper, eh?'

As he took off his boots, he wanted to say to her, 'But . . . you're . . . happy!' Instead, he did not want to break the spell so kept it to his thoughts, putting his boots by the back door. When he turned and saw her smiling down at their son, for the first time since the clearly faked smiles she'd put on in the hours after birth, he couldn't help himself.

'You look . . . beautiful,' he said, as he came through in his socks.

'Your socks inna beautiful. The right one has a hole in it. I'll darn it later.'

'Did you hear me, wench?' he cried, coming over to her, feeling for the first time in ages emboldened by her smiles to put his arm around her waist.

'It's our boy who's beautiful,' she said, and looked down at him. Alfie wasn't going to argue with that. And Jo never could take a compliment. She never could believe the good things he said to her. She always brushed them off.

'No argument from me,' said Alfie, and Jo passed Harry over to his father. Alfie went and stood before the window, the late sun behind him. Holding the precious bundle in his arms filled Alfie's eyes with tears. He knew it was a mixture of love for his son and also the sheer relief of seeing Jo looking happy when he came home, an occurrence he'd not seen since this little one showed his face to the world. Alfie blinked away his emotions, as he was determined not to scare away Jo's good mood, so tenuous it was these days.

'How was work?' said Jo, going over to the kitchen countertop to peel some carrots, fresh from the garden with frilly leaves that Jo pulled off and kept in a bundle on the side, as next door kept rabbits, and the rabbits loved their carrot tops.

'All right. Weather was kind to us. A bit of a breeze kept things pleasant. More to the point, though, my love, how was your day?'

'Good, good. Your mother came over and helped with Harry.'

He never thought he'd be annoyed to hear that, as he loved his mother, but he was still annoyed with her for taking his wife to that meeting. And not telling him that was where they were going. Would he have tried to stop them? Probably. Would his mother have let him? Absolutely not.

'That was nice,' he said, noncommittally, making faces at Harry, who looked up at him with utter seriousness.

'Oh, it was,' replied Jo, biting down on a bit of carrot and crunching it up. 'It was so different to have help. You know, before, I didn't want her or anyone to come round. I was too embarrassed.'

'Embarrassed about what?'

Jo stopped and crunched a bit more. 'Just . . . being a bad mother, I suppose.'

'You inna such a thing, Jo!' cried Alfie. 'You're the best mother. You do everything for this little'un. How can you say that about yourself?'

But, of course, he knew she didn't rate herself much as a person, let alone a mother; she never had.

'I dunno,' said Jo, looking away, over his shoulder, out of the kitchen window.

Alfie watched her eyes turn dark, that way they did. He feared it, to see that shadow so soon after the sunniness of her disposition when he'd come in. He wanted to distract her from it, with a bit of wry humour.

'I bet my mum loved it too, coming round. She keeps saying a grandson is the best thing that's ever happened to her, which I'll try not to take as an insult.'

'We talked and talked,' Jo said, continuing the carrot peeling, her shadow dissipated, for now. 'All about last night.'

Alfie sniffed trouble again. But she was in such a good

mood, he didn't want to ruin it. And he had to admit, it had done the trick and cheered his wife up and he was almost grateful to the suffragettes for that.

'What did you talk about?'

He looked down and Harry had nodded off. He could put the baby down, he supposed, but he didn't want to. The next best thing to holding Jo in his arms was holding this perfect little creature.

'Maria told me all about the history of women's suffrage and all the protests and pressure they've tried to put on the men in parliament. Years and years of it. And no progress. That's why the suffragettes formed their own group, that broke off from the main one. They knew that being nice and ladylike wasn't going to get their way, as it hadn't done before for so long, so why should it now? That's why they're a bit extreme, I suppose.'

'A *bit* extreme?' scoffed Alfie, before he'd checked himself.

'What?' replied Jo, quick as a whippet.

'Well, I'm just saying, it's no secret these suffragettes are . . . well, they dunna hold back, do they?'

'Why should they? When nobody listens to them?'

'Because there are ways and means . . .'

'What ways and means? Your mother told me they've presented so many bills to parliament they've lost count and still the men in power say nay to them. Why shouldna they fight for what they think is right?'

Now, Alfie warmed to his theme, as he could see Jo was spoiling for a fight and, to keep things sweet, he could let her win, but also, he was really worried about all this suffragette business.

'Look, my love, women's suffrage is a noble cause, like Mum says, and Dad. But these women . . . they *are* doing extreme things, like setting fire to pillar boxes and even houses.

And whipping cabinet ministers in the street and suchlike. And they've even started setting bombs! Think of the folk who could be hurt!'

'But Maria said that's mostly suffragettes in London, not round here. And those ones only set fire to empty houses. They're really careful that nobody innocent should get hurt. But those cabinet ministers, they inna innocent. They're deliberately stopping women from having the right to have a say in their own lives. And these women . . . well, they inna gonna take it from those men any longer. They mean to win, at any cost. Just think of that poor woman who threw herself at the King's horse.'

'Madwoman, more like,' said Alfie.

'Nay!' cried Jo, which made the baby stir and Alfie freeze. He didn't want Harry to start bawling and ruin Jo's previously good mood, although Alfie knew he was ruining it himself by arguing with her. But he couldn't let this suffragette business lie, could he? What kind of a respectable husband would?

Jo continued, 'Nay, she inna a madwoman. She was fuelled by rage, as they all are, I believe, from what your mother explained to me today. They wonna take it any longer. And I wanna help. If you'd been there last night and seen that pompous little upstart of a man burst into that meeting and try to tell off a bunch of us women like we were naughty schoolchildren, why it would make your blood boil. As it did mine. I didna realise it before last night, but I am one of them. I have that rage they have. And, my God, I understand it, I understand their rage so deep, deep inside me.'

'Why, though?' Alfie stepped forward, Harry settled again in his arms, thankfully. He could see this discussion escalating quickly into an argument and he didn't want to wake the baby, but also, he wanted more than anything to comprehend his wife better. 'Why would you understand it? I dunna see that rage in you. I never have.'

And then Jo's eyes darkened again and she looked away quickly, and sniffed away tears.

Alfie softened his tone. 'What is it, love? Please tell me. I just . . . I've been at such a loss these past weeks. I wanna understand. I wanna help. What is this rage you feel? Rage against what?'

Jo stood, turned away from him, for what seemed an age. Then she turned back, wiped her eyes and stared at the tiles on the kitchen floor.

'I dunna know, Alf . . . I . . . I suppose . . . I've felt trapped. By my life, by being a mother, being a housewife, the chores, the baby, everything. It wasna how . . . how I thought it would be. And it made me sad. So, so sad. But somehow . . . it was already there.'

'What was?' he said, gently. It was the most she'd said in weeks. It hurt him to hear it but that was assuaged by the relief of hearing her talk.

'The sadness. It's always been there. In me. Since I was a little'un . . . And the rage . . . of not being cared for. You know, Aunt Stella never noticed when I grew out of my shoes. She always noticed with her girls, always had the right shoes for them. But mine got too tight and nobody noticed but me. Things like that . . . a great sadness and rage was borne in me, like a deep well . . . but it went back further than that, to before. To my mother. And . . . father . . . and . . . and . . . the fear . . . the fear of . . .'

Jo looked terrified, her eyes wide open. Alfie and Jo never spoke of her early childhood. Alfie only knew about her parents from what his own had told him, that they were drunks and no good for Jo. But he'd never heard it from Jo herself.

'Fear of what, my love?'

'I was fearful . . . maybe I was like *her*. Maybe the sadness I felt was what my mother felt, when she had me. And that made her do what she did . . .'

'Made her do what?' he coaxed. Jo's face looked blanched with fear. Then she shook her head to rid herself of it, sniffed and shook her head again.

'Oh, I dunno, Alf. I think I thought maybe I'd be a rotten mother . . . like my own mother was.'

Alfie's heart was filled with pity for the woman he loved. Such a sweet, kind person she was and to see this change wrought in her since she'd become a mother, something he thought would multiply their happiness exponentially, but now he saw it had changed her life in ways he couldn't fathom.

He took a step towards her, closer, so she would tear her wide eyes away from the floor and look up at him.

'Look at this little mon. This perfect little chapper. You made him, Jo. In your own body, you built him, cell by cell. I had a slighting role in the matter at the off, but after that, it was all you. You made him, you birthed him, all by yourself. And you've been by his side, every moment of every day since then, feeding him, holding him, wrapping him up, washing his things, cleaning his shitty arse.'

Jo couldn't help but give out a little laugh at that, even as her eyes still glistened with tears.

Alfie went on. 'I canna pretend I understand how that feels, to be a woman, to be a mother. I'm just a mon and a dense one at that.'

'Nay, you inna dense, Alfie. You're the cleverest mon I know apart from your dad.'

'I may be good with figures and flowers and such but a woman's heart is a mystery to me and all men, I'd wager. But I want you to know that I'm here. I inna gonna pretend everything's fine. I've listened. And I've heard you. And look, I inna happy about this suffragette business. But I canna deny too that it's brought such a change in you since last night, I am glad of it. Glad to see you fired up. And best of all, smiling again. I've missed your smile, Jo Woodvine. I've missed it so much.'

Jo looked at him, her heart full, he could tell. Tears ran down her face and she didn't even wipe them away, just let them fall onto her blouse and cause wet blots that spread through the pale cotton.

'You are the best husband in the world, Alfie Woodvine.'

They went upstairs to put Harry down in his cot and afterwards, despite the tea still unmade in the kitchen and Alfie's poor stomach rumbling, he lay down with Jo on their bed and held her tightly, listening to her talk about how she was going to another suffragette meeting with his mother soon and how excited she was at the thought of it, which scared him. But at least it would keep her happy. Then, he kissed her full on the mouth and felt her body soften to him. And that evening, starving as he was from two long walks and a hard day's graft and no evening meal yet, he made love to his wife with such verve, she cried out in joy and woke the baby up.

Chapter 7
Jo
March 1914

Jo watched the fields whip past as she looked out of the train carriage window at the Shopshire countryside. She thought about her very first suffragette meeting, where she'd been caught unawares in her house dress and had been ashamed at how slovenly she looked. Since then, she'd been to several more meetings at the Tontine, each time accompanied by a gaggle of men trying to shut it down. But despite the complaints of such as Willy Wall who worked at the council, it had been proven that the meetings themselves were in fact not illegal, as long as the suffragettes kept themselves to themselves and didn't go around fomenting trouble. The order had been adhered to. There was some support from Ironbridge women, mostly upper-middle class it had to be said. Jo was one of the few working-class women among them. But having family via Charlie of the likes of Hettie Malone and Martha Haywood helped Jo not to feel too out of place, as they were so kind and welcoming of her that she tried not to worry about how she had to wear the same green skirt and embroidered blouse to every meeting as they were her only decent clothes. For this special meeting they were on their way to now, however, Maria had given Jo a few bob to buy a new outfit. Offered the choice, Jo had known precisely what she wanted to buy. She wore it now: a midnight blue skirt, a white shirtwaist and a man's tie, completed with a midnight-blue coat with a slight puff at the shoulder. Her hair was twisted up into a loose bun, with a broad-brimmed hat pinned to it made of midnight-blue felt topped with midnight-blue netting. Her inspiration had been the enigmatic speaker at that very first meeting, a woman it turned out who came from Shrewsbury, a chemist's daughter called Barbara Rose. She was only twenty-three but seemed much older, due to her articulate confidence in speaking to the assembly. She'd not come to every monthly Ironbridge meeting, as she toured the area going to different town gatherings, yet Jo saw her once more in that period speak in her own town. Barbara gave her speech inspiringly, filling Jo with an indefinable longing to do more for the cause. But with a growing baby there was little she could do but write letters to her MP, which she and Maria did every week to annoy the man.

When the local WSPU contingent arranged a trip to the county town of Shrewsbury to join a march and rally there in the spring, Jo had signed up for it in a flash, her father-in-law agreeing to take baby Harry for the day, who was by now ten months old and eating mashed-up food with alacrity. Jo had left Harry with Charlie before, if she had errands to run and Charlie was free when Maria was not, but Jo had not left the baby for this long before, that is, a whole day from morning to evening. Charlie had told her they'd be fine, two chaps together. 'And if he cries,' Charlie had said, holding Harry on his knee, who gaped adoringly at his grandfather, 'then I shall read him a bit of *Great Expectations*. Dickens always works for me, doesn't it, Harry? We have the same Christian name too, you know, Dickens and I.' Jo knew she'd left him in good hands and hurried off down to the Ironbridge and Broseley railway station with Maria.

On the train, dressed up, she felt like an utterly different person: a person who wears new outfits, a person who wears smart and soft materials, a person who wears midnight blue, just like Barbara Rose. With Maria beside her and Charlie's relations Hettie and Martha opposite (the wealthy ones with the green eyes), Jo gazed out of the window at the blurred rush of nature outside and mused on how much her life had changed in the last few months since that first meeting. Harry had settled down, particularly once she'd started weaning him, and was now sleeping so much better. Jo's mood had improved, and things would've been better at home if Alfie wasn't still so annoyed about 'all this suffragette fiddle-faddle' (his words). They didn't even discuss it these days, as Alfie complained of too much 'argufication at home' and he was right, that it always ended in cross words and neither had the energy or heart for it, so they left it alone and agreed to disagree. For most of the month, they got on fine, but as the monthly meeting approached, things got more tense at home. This sunny spring Saturday, Jo felt it was a relief to get away for the day, fairly bolting from the house once she was ready. Alfie had gone off to work even earlier than usual that Saturday morning, almost as if he was so annoyed with her he'd escaped the house sooner than he needed to. Jo just rolled her eyes when she saw him go. He'd get used to it. The women's suffrage movement had been around for decades and the suffragettes were here to stay. Men just needed to get used to it. Nothing could stop them now.

'Do you think Barbara Rose will be at this meeting?' Jo asked Maria quietly, when Hettie and Martha were having their own conversation.

'I dunna know but I suspect she will. She's getting quite a name across the county for her suffrage work.'

'Is she?' said Jo, intrigued. She'd not discussed Barbara Rose with Maria before. She'd been too shy to show an interest, because she didn't want her mother-in-law to think she had a crush on Barbara, in the way she knew girls did for other girls sometimes, though Jo never had, as all the women around her age she'd known were pretty unpleasant. And she didn't have a crush on Barbara Rose, not really. She just admired her. She wanted to be like her. And Jo hoped Maria hadn't noticed she'd copied her outfit.

'Yes, she's been active in Shrewsbury, where she lives, but also travels around the county a lot, so I've heard. She knows a lot of the Shropshire hierarchy in the WSPU.' Then Maria paused. 'You like her,' she added, smiling. Not in a teasing way, just in a factual way.

'I respect her,' corrected Jo. 'She's only a few years older than me and she . . .'

Jo wanted to say, *She has her own life. She's unmarried, with no children, and she's free.* But Jo couldn't say that, of course. She didn't want it to sound like she was wishing away her own life, not when her husband was Maria's son and her child was Maria's grandson, after all. The truth was that Jo was enjoying being a wife and mother these days, more than before. What had helped her settle into it was her new-found interest in women's politics. It gave her another avenue to explore, something that wasn't parenting or wifedom, something for herself. It made the rest of it manageable.

'She's a good speaker,' said Jo, instead. And with that, the conductor announced that they were approaching Shrewsbury.

Jo had been to Shrewsbury for a daytrip once with Alfie, before they had Harry. She liked the shops and the parks. She liked the feel of being anonymous. Everyone knew everyone in Ironbridge. Even walking to the station in her new outfit that morning she'd seen her cousin Sarah on the footpath giving her a look up and down, as if laughing at her audacity to wear something stylish. They didn't even nod at each other these days. Both knew there was no love lost between them. But as Jo alighted from the carriage and walked behind Maria, Hettie and Martha, along the platform into Shrewsbury Railway Station, she felt as if she could melt into the crowd and start again, recast herself in a new role beyond wife and mother, reinvented.

Passing through the station concourse and out into the street, Jo saw that a large group of women were standing together to the right of the station entrance. Some already had their white, purple and green sashes on. Jo and her companions had kept theirs in their bags on the journey, wishing to travel incognito. At this signal, they all reached into their bags and arranged the sashes over their outfits, this branding being welcomed by the waiting group of women, who beckoned them over to join their crowd. Some were holding banners that read 'Votes for Women' and 'Deeds Not Words', while others carried the purple, white and green tricolour flag. Everyone was proudly dressed up to the nines and Jo felt a swell of pride and togetherness that she was too. She wished she had a flag. Hettie, Martha and Maria made small talk with some of the other women, while Jo hung back, too shy. She had no talent for chatting. Instead, she was scanning the crowd. More women were joining the group as they arrived from the other platforms coming in from railway lines across Shropshire, as well as others walking onto the concourse from the town itself. Before long, there must have been a hundred of them, perhaps more. Jo watched as flags unfurled, lifted high above the crowd, then she saw a clutch of them moving through the crowd as they were handed out to women and she hoped whoever it was would come her way. And then, she saw who was handing out the flags.

'Would you like one?' said Barbara Rose to Jo, who was thrilled to see Barbara, let alone talk to her, and even more that Barbara had spoken to her directly.

'I would,' she said, and thought about the time she met Hettie and Martha and didn't say anything of use and had cursed herself for her social ineptitude. She was determined that this time she'd be braver.

'Miss Rose,' Jo said, as she was handed a flag furled about a white pole, which Jo popped on the ground to steady it.

'Yes, my dear,' said Barbara, smiling at her. She looked magnificent that day in a pure white coat, with green and purple embroidery across the lapels and at the cuffs, the three colours of the cause. Her face was covered with purple netting attached to her hat, which was topped with white, green and purple silk flowers. She must have had it custom-made.

'I wanted to say . . . that I . . . I admire your speaking very much.'

'That is very kind of you. Very kind of you indeed. Where do you hail from?'

'Ironbridge, miss.'

'Please, there's no need to call me "miss". Call me Barbara.'

Jo nodded and Barbara went on, 'And what may I call you?'

'Jo. Jo Woodvine.'

'It's a pleasure to meet you, Jo. I'd like to speak with you later if you have a moment. We dunna have many young women like yourself devoted to the cause in Ironbridge and Coalbrookdale. Could we have a word about it some other time?'

Jo nodded emphatically, and then they were interrupted by an older woman, calling Barbara up to the front of the group, as they were ready to start the march now. Barbara beamed at Jo and Jo beamed back, then was bustled away.

Jo felt a thrill go through her. Miss Barbara Rose wanted to talk to *her*? This was better than she could've hoped for on her first proper day out since having a child. A new outfit, a train ride and now this? She felt giddy. What other wonders would transpire this day? She couldn't wait to find out.

The crowd then moved by some unknown gesture and began to walk sedately away from the station. Jo took a deep breath and followed on, acutely aware this was her first ever suffragette march. Sitting in meetings hidden away at the back of the Tontine Hotel was one thing, but walking in the streets surrounded by the unwitting public was something else entirely.

As they made their way across to the broad thoroughfare called Castle Street, the crowd split into pairs, creating a long snake of suffragettes that wound its way along the pavement. Shrewsbury folk crossed over the road and gawped at them. People on the opposite pavement turned to look, some stopped to stare. Jo tried to focus on Maria beside her and on her flag, which she carried in her right hand and was heavier than it looked. But it did provide quite a useful accoutrement to almost hide behind as they proceeded along. Jo could hear some people booing them as they passed. As they turned into Pride Hill, she heard more boos coming from around and about, and if she glanced askance she saw a face here and there frowning, or sneering, or outright laughing. At one point, as they stopped at a jam up ahead, she heard a man stop close to her and say, 'Dumb flibberty-gibbet, yer quite pretty, you could get a husband if you wonna hanging around with these old witches.'

She turned to see a man in a flat cap smirking at her and she said, 'I am married, thank'ee very much, mon, and it's none of yer business who I hang around with.'

'Dunna talk to them, Jo,' said Maria and wrapped her hand

around Jo's arm, steering her away as the crowd moved onwards. 'It just riles them up.'

Jo was more amazed at herself than him, that she'd answered back a stranger in the street like that. But it was the same as when that pompous little Willy Wall spoke down to her in her first meeting. She wasn't going to let these insects tell her what to do. She'd been bullied all her childhood and retreated into herself in adult life, comfortable in the fold of the Woodvines and her own home, going out little, except with Alfie and the baby for a stroll now and again. Now, she felt stronger, and ready to be not only out in the world, but also to deal with idiots like these men. The cause of the suffragettes was noble and yet in the newspapers and magazines that Jo saw from time to time at the Woodvines' house (she had no time for reading at home), she saw disgusting cartoons of suffragettes shown as ugly old maids with gnashing teeth and either impossibly fat or impossibly skinny and always a vicious look on their faces. It made her blood boil. As the crowd moved from Pride Hill into the High Street, and thence into The Square where the rally was to congregate, she held her head up and pushed her flagpole higher into the sky. She was proud to be among this group of brave women, and no idiot in a flat cap or boater or whatever they wore would stop her now.

The crowd packed into The Square, behind which Jo could see the Old Market Hall, with its ancient plaque on the front from the sixteenth century, which made Jo feel that history was looking down upon them there that day. Around her was a sea of beautiful hats, topped with flowers and ribbons and silk and netting, all tipped back to look up to a scaffold upon which stood a number of women, one in a graduate's cap and gown, others in long skirts and bowler hats or boaters, all looking expectantly as the crowd gathered before them. Jo looked out for Barbara Rose but couldn't see her.

'This is marvellous,' Jo whispered to Maria.

'Oh, it is,' said Maria, and squeezed Jo's arm. 'I lived in Shrewsbury for a time as a young woman. I had a rough time of it here, for many reasons, but mostly due to the actions of men, truth be told. If you'd told me then that one day I'd be back and standing here in this very square I passed through then and I'd be wearing a sash that said "Votes for Women", surrounded by dozens of other brave women and linking arms with my beautiful daughter-in-law, I'd've never believed you!'

Jo wanted to ask Maria more, as to what actions men had undertaken against dear Maria back then that had given her such a hard time of it. But there was no time, as the speeches began.

Jo and Maria were to the right of the crowd, at the edge. From here, Jo could see that the square was lined with men in their flat caps, boaters and bowlers, looking on with interest. Some sneered like the other men had, while others listened solemnly. Some stood in twos and threes laughing together, though they did keep their voices down, showing a modicum of respect. There were one or two women, here and there, but not as many as Jo would've liked. The women who were there looked as uncomfortable as the men looked the opposite. Jo realised there was something about merely being a man that made him easy with his station in life and even his right to stop and stand in a street. The women Jo saw looked entirely uneasy with standing around to watch, glancing about them with nervous eyes. What was it in men and women that made them so different in the way they felt about their place in the world? Until she joined the suffragettes' movement, she had never really considered it. There was something invisible about being a man, that one could do as one liked and not be questioned on it. Jo realised that a woman could never be invisible, was always noticed, was always scrutinised and commented upon. She wished she could change that but it seemed so fundamental. She wondered if women would ever feel comfortable to simply stand in a street and just be themselves, be unworthy of scrutiny and just exist in the world as a person, like a man did.

Then, she heard a voice she recognised. Barbara Rose had come to the stage. Jo heard a few wolf-whistles from the men lining the square, which sent a ripple of laughter around its edges. The women in the centre weren't laughing, though. Barbara began her speech. It was all about bringing young women into the suffrage movement.

'It is often seen as the business of an older woman, since if any change were to come about now or soon, it would be likely that only women over thirty might be permitted to vote, if any. And yet I say now to my sisters in their twenties that you matter also. You are the new guard, the new recruits that we mistresses of suffrage need to enliven our number. For I promise you now, that even if we achieve the vote for women over thirty, we will fight on until all women are given the vote, of any adult age or any kind of property, so that the voices of all kinds of women in Britain – young or old, rich or poor, will be heard and will be counted.'

This elicited a round of applause that took some time to die down. Jo joined in and clapped ferociously, bowled over by Barbara Rose's elegant voice, which sailed over the crowd. While she clapped away, Jo noticed something in the corner of her eye. A group of three boys in flat caps emerged from the onlookers lining the square and rushed up to the scaffold where the speakers stood. Jo stepped out of the crowd to strain her neck and observe what the boys were up to, to see them hurl something from their pockets at the stage. A scream went up and another, as the boys dodged aside and ran away laughing riotously, one of them throwing another thing from his pocket as he fled. Jo could clearly see that it was a mouse, landing on the ground, righting itself and fleeing in terror. There must have been more mice flung onto the stage, as pandemonium had erupted all around Barbara Rose, as women on the stage itself and in the front row dodged the vermin. Yet Jo saw that Barbara did not move an inch, did not even flinch. Instead she leant down and picked up a mouse and held it in her hand and stroked it. The crowd hushed at this rare spectacle. She popped the mouse into the pocket of her coat and said loudly, 'Shall we continue?'

The crowd erupted in applause, even some of the men from the sides joining in. Barbara finished her speech to another round of whoops and cheers, as she stepped down from the scaffold and her place was taken with another speaker. Barbara joined the crowd at the front and Jo lost sight of her then. She wished it were Barbara Rose speaking all day. She'd never tire of the sound of that magnificent voice.

Chapter 8

Jo

As the next speech continued, about the rights of working women and the evil of keeping representation away from them, when everyone who worked, male or female, paid taxes, Jo noted that police officers were beginning to arrive in the square, threading through the onlookers in pairs. More and more arrived, until the edges of the square turned dark with their uniforms. The presence of police officers on the streets should make a person feel safer, under normal circumstances. Yet the faces of these men did not look friendly and did not fill Jo with confidence. Instead, they looked as if they were waiting for something, all glancing at each other. At that moment, the final speech was given and the crowd erupted in applause. The speaker said that, after the speeches, the march would make its way over to the park they called The Quarry and there would be music and snacks to buy from stalls. They'd give the signal soon to start the walk over there. The crowd fell into a loud hubbub of talking, as women discussed the speeches with great fervour. But all Jo could think about was the policemen now thickly lining the square on all sides.

'Maria,' she said, and lifted her hand to surreptitiously

point. 'Look at all the policemen. What do you think they're here for?'

Jo saw Maria's face blanch.

'We should leave and do it now,' said Maria hurriedly.

'But why? The march hasn't finished yet.'

'Take my word for it,' said Maria quietly. 'There's trouble on its way.'

'I dunna wanna go,' said Jo. 'We'll be on our own. I dunna feel safe without the crowd of us.'

Maria looked furtively at the policemen and replied, 'You're right. It might be safer to stay with the others. Oh God, I dunna know, Jo. Alfie will be so upset with me if I get you into trouble. Perhaps I shouldna brought you here, to that first meeting, to any of it.'

Jo saw Maria watching the policemen intently, as if they might pounce at any moment.

Jo grasped her arm and said, 'But surely the police are here to protect us, to protect women, in case there are any trouble-makers around us.'

'Nay, Jo. There inna an ounce of love lost between police-men and suffragettes, mark my words. They inna here to protect us. They're here to get us.'

Maria turned and spoke to some of the other women surrounding them. They'd lost sight of Hettie and Martha in the throng. The other women that Maria had been speaking to were craning their necks to look through the crowd at the policemen. An undercurrent began to rumble its way among the throng as, suddenly, the policemen stepped forward and approached the women.

'It's happening!' cried Maria. 'Jo, take my hand!'

But the moment she said it, Jo felt an almighty push from the right, as the crowd reacted like a shoal of fish darted at by a predator. The weight of it carried Jo away from Maria, and small as Jo was, it literally lifted her off the ground for a few feet. She lost her flag in the melee and could hear the shouts of women and the grunts and yells of policemen, with the sight of truncheons lifted and dropped above the women's hats. Once she found her footing, she stumbled and fell, curling up instinctively to protect her belly, then flinched at the kicks of boots and shoes in her back and sides as women unwittingly tried to flee the chaos. She managed to scramble back up and blindly run forward, to see that she was now over at the other side of the square and all around her was the madness of women running in terror or fighting back against policemen beating them down with truncheons and men standing around and cheering, some joining in and kicking at the backs and bellies of women sprawled on the ground, the curdled sounds of grunts and screams joined with the thumping of fists and truncheons into flesh and bones, a war between men and women being played out on the streets of Shrewsbury.

It was a scene of terror like nothing on earth she'd ever witnessed before. Jo stumbled forwards to flee, to be caught by strong hands that manhandled her over against the wall, face first. She could not see the face of her attacker, only smell the stink of cigarette smoke on his breath as he gruffly spat his words into her neck: 'Yer filthy little fussock, yer know what yer wanting.' And he grasped at her midnight blue skirt and yanked it up, higher and higher, as she fought to keep it down, knowing anyone could see her stockings and her slip beneath, which filled her with frantic horror and shame. How could this be happening to her? How could it go on in broad daylight, in the county town, in the historic square, in front of everyone? The stale breath of the man was hot on her neck and his hefty bulk against her back crushed her against the bricks of the wall.

Suddenly she felt light. The weight of the man had gone.

'Take your hands off her!' someone cried, and she turned, jerking her skirt down as she did so, to see Barbara Rose throwing punches at a policeman's back as he tried to fend her off, grabbing for his truncheon in his pocket.

'Leave her alone, you coward!' Barbara shouted at the policeman. Jo rushed over and flew at the man too, hurling her feet out to kick at the man's legs. He stumbled and fell, then scrambled up and away, leaving Jo and Barbara beside each other, breathless and wild-eyed.

'Come on!' Barbara shouted and grasped Jo's hand, pulling her out of the square and running on up the High Street, then swerving into a side road and up a narrow alleyway, where they were finally alone. They stood breathing heavily, Jo's hands on her ribs feeling her chest heaving up and down, while Barbara had her hands on her thighs, half bent over with the effort of getting her breath back.

'Thank . . . thank'ee,' gasped Jo.

Barbara nodded, getting her breathing under control. 'I couldna . . . I wouldna let that bastard molest you like that. I'm so sorry that happened to you, Jo.'

'It inna your fault!' cried Jo. 'It's his fault! Dunna apologise to me for men, ever!'

Jo felt wild, like an animal that had been in a cage all its life and only now was set free.

Barbara replied, 'You're right, you're right. I'm proud of you. Too many women blame themselves for the acts of men. Are you all right, though?'

'I am,' nodded Jo. 'I'll be grand. I'm just . . . shocked . . . shocked a policeman could act that way. I always thought of them as . . . you know . . . our guardians. To keep us safe, that's what policemen are for.'

'They're still men. And all men are capable of that,' said

Barbara, adjusting her hat that had been shoved to the side in the battle. The net that had covered her face before was rolled up now. Jo could see her pink cheeks and her eyes sparkling in the dim light of the alleyway. 'Mark my words, Jo. All men would do what that policeman did to you, if there were no laws, no checks and balances of society. All men.'

Jo thought of her Alfie. Of Charlie. Good men like them.

'No, they wouldna. Some men would never do that in a month of Sundays. Never, in their whole lives.'

Barbara finished adjusting her hat and rolled the netting down.

'We'll agree to disagree,' Barbara said, smiling at Jo, to show there were no hard feelings. Then she took off her sash, bundled it up and thrust it into a leather-strapped bag she had trained across her chest from the shoulder. The bag rested on her hip and looked stuffed full with something already. 'Take yours off too. It's not safe now.'

Jo saw the sense in this, took her sash off, folded it and pushed it into the pocket of her midnight-blue skirt. The material of her beautiful new skirt was scored with deep creases, reminding her of the policeman's rough hands ruching it up. She shuddered at the thought of it and cursed him inwardly.

'Ready for more trouble?' said Barbara, grinning behind her purple netting. She looked resplendent to Jo, this young, well-to-do woman who'd just been in a fistfight with a policeman and, once her hat was straightened, was ready for even more.

'I think I might follow you anywhere!' said Jo, laughing. 'But, I'll be honest and say, not if it involves policemen.'

'There shouldna be any policeman at first. Look, I'll take you up there and show you, then you can decide. There's one more deed I intend to carry out today and I need someone with me. I was gonna do it with another lass but lost sight of her. It's all planned. You wonna need to do much, just have a look out at summat for me. What do you say?'

'I've a baby at home,' said Jo, feeling torn. She wanted to go with Barbara but she was worried about her responsibilities.

'I understand. You can go now, and I wonna think any the worse of you for it. Go on to the station and get yourself home to your baby. It's for the best.'

And with that, Barbara turned and marched away up the alleyway.

Jo called out to her, 'Wait!'

She didn't stop to think about it. She was tired of thinking about things. She was tired of talking about things. Barbara looked round at her and grinned. Jo followed on.

They walked along High Street to Pride Hill and then up to the large Post Office on the corner, crossing the road to stand opposite it on the pavement. It was a beautiful building, with a rose window on the top floor and archways filled with windows on the floors below. Barbara turned to Jo.

'It's time for deeds, not words, as our slogan says. It's time to show them we are truly here for change. This is a government building and the government needs to know that we will not go quietly. I mean to be caught for this, Jo. I mean to be arrested. I want them to arrest me and take me to court and I want them to send me to the Dana for this. I mean to make trouble in that prison and no mistake.'

'What on earth are you gonna do?' said Jo, her mind boggling.

'Break the windows. I have rocks here in my bag. They're too high to reach with a hammer but I've a good throwing arm. I used to play cricket with my brother before he joined the army. But I dunna wanna hurt any innocent folk inside. All I need you to do is go to the entrance, take a quick look inside and tell me if there are any folk near the windows. Once it clears, you're to give me the nod and walk away. Walk away quickly, Jo. Dunna look back. I mean to do this deed and I dunna wanna hurt a soul, including you. Will you have a look for me?'

'I will,' said Jo.

'Thank'ee, sister.'

The sound of another woman she admired calling her sister filled Jo with pride. No other female in her life, besides Maria, had treated her with such camaraderie. Jo knew she'd do anything Barbara asked of her, whatever the consequences.

Barbara added, 'I might be away for a spell after this. So if I dunna see you for a few months, you'll know why. Ready?'

Jo nodded ardently. She'd never felt more ready for anything in her life. She walked up to the Post Office's entrance and took the few steps up. Once standing underneath the arched doorway, she took a peek inside. There were several people standing on the other side of the room, waiting in short queues where employees served them. On the wall beneath the front windows, there was a table with a male employee sitting down and a gentleman sitting opposite him, discussing some papers spread out on the table between them. She glanced back at Barbara across the street, who was watching her like a hawk, her hand already in her bag.

Jo shook her head subtly and Barbara nodded. Maybe Barbara Rose might not think that these men at the table were innocents. Maybe she might say that no men were innocent when it came to women's rights. But Jo did not think that. She had had kindness from boys and men in her life. But was Barbara right that all men could turn to savagery given the right conditions? Jo was confused about this. She didn't know the answer. But she wasn't prepared to risk it and she waited, as awkward as it felt to be standing there in the doorway alone. She waited until the two men finished their business, stood up, shook hands and left their chairs behind. The employee went into an office by a side door, while the gentleman approached her to leave.

'After you, miss,' he said, kindly, smiling beneath his substantial moustache.

'Nay, I'm waiting for a . . . for my husband,' said Jo, ill-prepared for this conversation.

'Ah, forgive me, madam,' he replied, nodded at her, and walked by her and out of the Post Office and onto the street. Jo looked back at the windows and the table beneath them and saw now that the area was empty. The inner hall would be big enough, she judged, that a rock flying through it would most likely land within the hall and not reach the customers on the other side, so wide was the area. It was time.

She looked back at Barbara and firmly nodded. Barbara nodded back, then stepped into the street to cross the road.

Jo knew what her orders were. She knew she must turn and walk away. But, by God, she wanted to see Barbara fling those rocks at the windows. She wanted to see the glass shatter and the police come running. She wanted to protect Barbara from being roughed about, as had happened to herself not half an hour since. She wanted to walk beside Barbara to the police station, to the courts, to the Dana itself, the prison that all Salopians feared.

But she had baby Harry at home. And as much as he doted on his father and his grandparents, Jo knew how much her baby needed her, now and for years to come, if not the rest of her life.

So, she turned and walked away down Pride Hill. She heard the sound of shattering glass and grinned. Barbara's bowling arm had done it. Jo's chest ached with pride as she walked, then she flinched as she heard the whistle of a policeman shrilly blowing nearby. She stopped in terror to see one running up the hill. A woman was shouting, 'One of them blasted suffragette girls!' and pointing. The policeman ran on in the direction of the Post Office.

Jo breathed out. She looked down at her skirt. Yes, it had been messed up by the assault. But it hadn't ripped or torn. It'd held true. And once she got it washed and ironed, it'd look as good as new. The policeman who'd grabbed her wouldn't ruin her skirt and he wouldn't ruin her, damn him. As she strode onwards to the railway station, hoping to find Maria there, safe, waiting for her, Jo looked up as she approached along Castle Street and saw, in the distance, firstly the small figures of Hettie and Martha pointing at her, and then Maria, whose smile she could see from all that way, so broad it was. Jo thought of the shouting woman's words: *one of them blasted suffragette girls*. As she hurried on to reunite with Maria and the others, Jo said to herself, 'That is what I am. A blasted suffragette girl. And proud of it.'

Chapter 9

Jo

March to June 1914

In the days following the Shrewsbury meeting, news came of Barbara Rose's fate. The information was filtered through the Malone women to Maria to Jo that Barbara was sentenced to six months at the Dana prison in Shrewsbury for wilful damage of government property, as well as the charge of fomenting unrest in her speech. Jo and Maria felt this was very unfair, as her speech did nothing of the sort. The damage, of course, was true, and Jo marvelled at how keen Barbara had been to go to prison. She wanted it, as many of the more risky suffragettes did, to bring publicity to the cause. Barbara would be out of prison in September, so they said. Jo counted up the weeks on the calendar, wondering when she would next see the unsinkable Barbara. She would rise from prison like a phoenix, Jo was certain. And perhaps Jo would see her at a meeting, and they might talk, and reminisce, and Barbara would thank her for her service. Jo relished the memory of the moment Barbara had asked her to help. Jo had felt a marvellous sense of purpose that day, akin to the moment when she was a child and heard about the bears of Canada from Charlie

Woodvine. Both had the sensation of revelation, of a door opening onto a world she'd had no idea existed.

It galvanised her. Until then, her contribution towards the cause locally had been to attend regular meetings, and she still intended to do that. But surely more could be done to involve local women. Only a small minority of Ironbridge women attended meetings and most of those were middle-class women and above. Jo wanted to reach out to working-class women like herself, from the same kind of backgrounds she came from, with parents like hers, neglect like hers, trauma like hers. She'd landed on her feet later in her life, married to the schoolmaster's son, but before that, before Aunt Stella taking her in and later the Woodvines, Jo's life could've ended up very differently, she knew that. Her relationship with her aunt had suffered over the years and they barely spoke these days but, as the unofficial town nurse, perhaps Aunt Stella could be a useful person to talk to. Firstly, Jo arranged with Hettie that she'd collect from her a stack of leaflets about the suffragette cause that were often given out to new attendees at meetings. One morning, Jo put a bunch of them in a canvas shoulder bag, left Harry with Maria, and set off.

With Aunt Stella in mind, and wanting to avoid seeing the cousins or Mr Andrews and having to make dreaded small talk with any of them, Jo walked over towards the Andrews' household at around the time she knew Stella generally left in the mornings. Jo saw her aunt come out of the house with her nurse's uniform on, dark hair scraped back into a severe bun, medical bag in hand, and followed along behind for a time, then called out to her. Stella stopped and turned, squinted and then realised who it was as Jo got nearer.

'Jo, lass. Good to see you.'

It wasn't effusive but it wasn't cold either. That was always the place she'd resided in Stella's heart, Jo believed.

'Aunt. It's good to see you too. Do you have a moment to talk?'

Stella looked confused. 'What about?' Since Jo had more or less ignored the family since marrying, it made sense that Stella might not see this as a normal occurrence.

'Various things. Can I walk with you?'

'Yes, I'm up going up your way, actually, past the hill. There's a lady up there needs some pain relief for women's troubles.'

They carried on through town, talking of family matters. As they caught up on each other's news, they stepped on and off the pavement to let busy townsfolk pass. By the time they were nearer Jo's hill, she decided it was time to begin her pitch.

'There's another reason I wanted to talk to you. Because you're a nurse.'

'Are you ill? Or Harry?' Stella frowned.

'Nay, it's about your position in the town, working with so many women. I believe you can help me. Help us. With the cause. The suffragettes.'

Jo was hesitant as she wasn't sure what Aunt Stella's thoughts might be. She knew Stella cared deeply about women, as she'd devoted her working life to them, often to the detriment of family life. But how she'd feel about this political matter was uncertain. Momentarily, Jo had her answer.

'Oh, not all that nonsense.'

Jo steeled herself. 'It inna nonsense and I need your help with it. Will you hear me out?'

'Well, I am walking, and you are walking in the same direction, so I canna stop you.'

Stella quickened her pace then and Jo had to hurry to keep up.

'Women need to know their rights, that they mun be allowed to vote alongside men. We work hard, just as men do.

We pay taxes, we do unpaid work at home at all hours, no breaks, no bonuses, no holiday. We deserve to have a say in who runs our country.'

'You always did take life so serious, Jo. Always a dark little sombre thing you were, lost in dark little thoughts.'

Jo sidestepped her aunt's rather damning conclusion about her.

'Life is serious, I believe, and your clients know that. They need their rights taking seriously. I was wondering, Aunt, if you might assist by handing out my suffrage leaflets to your women. I could even come with you some days and speak to the women myself. We need to reach out to poorer women, those who dunna have time for meetings or reading the newspapers. I want them to know they have rights too and mun demand to have more.'

'You'll do no such thing!' snorted her aunt. 'Shoving yourself in with my ladies where you're not wanted? You're right, they dunna have time to worry about the vote with mouths to feed. And neither do I. Politicians dunna care about us, any of us ordinary folk, and they never will. What difference does it make if we can put our X or our names on a piece of paper every few years? It dunna change a thing. Be off with you with your silly modern ideas. You havna got anything better to do? You've a husband and little'un to take care of for one. And if you wanna waste your time, take up the pianoforte or summat that brings people joy, not all this political rubbish. I canna say I'm surprised, though, Jo. These suffragettes are trouble and you've always been trouble.'

After that tirade, Jo actually stopped walking and watched her aunt bustle onwards. They'd reached the bottom of the hill where Jo lived. Her aunt suddenly realised Jo wasn't there any more, stopped and turned to look at Jo.

'What now?'

'What now? I dunna think I deserve such a dressing down. But I inna surprised, if I think on it. You never did like me much.'

Stella stomped forwards, to make her point but also so they wouldn't be raising their voices in the street to the passing audience, some of whom Stella gave quick reassuring glances, as a couple of passers-by were staring. She had her good nurse's reputation to keep, after all.

'How dare you say such a thing. I took you in! When your mother made a mess of her life in every which way, I was the one who took you and raised you.'

'My mother died! Anyone with half a heart would've taken their niece in. Dunna think yourself so special.'

'The ingratitude! And Louise didna just die. She drank herself to death. Just as her useless husband did. Louise was a simpleton, bordering on "subnormal". That's the word the teacher used. You didna realise that, did you? Well, she was. Couldna do a thing at school. Our mother kept her home from school after seven years old, as she wasna cut out for it. Got her sewing at home, just like you did. You get your quick wit from your father, as he tricked Louise into loving him, then treated her like a dog. She followed him everywhere, like a dog too. Even followed him into drinking and death from it. She was a fool and a terrible mother. And I was there to pick up the pieces.'

Jo was horrified at this speech. She'd never heard Stella talk so about her own sister. Jo never knew that her mother was considered 'subnormal'. What a terrible word it was.

'My mother was nothing but kind to me. She was everything to me. She would've died to protect me. And she . . . she . . .'

Jo stopped. She'd nearly said it out loud, what she'd seen her mother do. But she'd stopped herself in time. She couldn't allow her mother's legacy to be seen by Stella in even blacker terms than she already did.

'Ungrateful wench,' Stella spat. 'To think me and Mr Andrews showered you with affection and this is the repayment we get!'

'Mr Andrews was cruel to me. A person can be cruel without hitting a child. A person can be cold and icy and cruel by doing nothing.'

'You take that back! My husband is a saint! And you're an embarrassment to us, with all this suffragette business. The scandal of it! You're an embarrassment to the family, just like your mother was.'

'She was my mother,' said Jo, simply. 'And though you took me in and I'll always be grateful for that, the truth is you never loved me. You . . . you never noticed when my shoes were too small. The girls got new shoes but not me. I'll never forget that.'

Stella's face screwed up in disgust.

'I dunna have time for this. Throw your damned leaflets in the river for all I care.'

Chapter 10

Jo

And off Aunt Stella went. Jo was trembling with anger now. She turned and marched back into town, past the square, alongside the river towards the iron bridge. She went to stand at the entrance to it, grappled with the buckles on her canvas bag, her hands still shaking, and drew out a fistful of leaflets. Then she took a deep breath and shouted, 'Votes for women!'

Jo brandished the leaflets and called out again, 'Women, know your rights!'

Anger was fuelling her now, yet she was momentarily distracted by the responses she was getting already from the townsfolk passing by. She remembered those looks during the march in Shrewsbury: amusement, disapproval, blankness, antipathy, even downright repulsion. She couldn't just stand there and let them look. She had to keep talking.

'Women, take a leaflet and learn how you can change the fate of women like you. Take a leaflet and learn how important you are. Take a leaflet and find out how you can get involved. Votes for women!'

She held out a single leaflet in her hand, using it to emphasise her points.

'Women who work, you work doubly hard, as you mun work at home as well as bring in money. Why shouldna you have a say in who rules us, just the same as any man?'

Jo tried to ignore the men who laughed as they passed by in pairs, looking her up and down. Instead, she stepped forward to address women directly, some of whom gaped in surprise as they side-stepped her and carried on. Others, however, slowed their step to glance at the leaflet.

'Here, please take one,' said Jo to a woman who'd slowed, carrying a bundle of washing.

'Got nowhere to put it,' said the woman, politely.

'I can see you're interested. Come to our meetings, first Wednesday of every month, at the Tontine.'

The woman nodded vaguely and carried on. Another was loitering nearby, the hem of her dress ragged, no hat and her hair awry, a small girl holding her hand, sucking her thumb.

'Would you like a leaflet about votes for women?' said Jo, smiling at her.

The woman stepped closer and muttered, 'I canna read.'

Jo winced inwardly, annoyed at herself for assuming that every woman she was trying to reach had had the same privilege as herself of a decent education. Not everyone had been so lucky, including her own mother, it turned out.

'It doesna matter about that. Come to our meetings.' Jo explained when and where. The woman nodded.

'I like your hat,' said the woman.

'Thank'ee,' said Jo, smiling at her. 'How old is your little girl?'

'Oh, she inna mine. I mind her.'

'I see,' said Jo. 'It would be nice if one day she had the vote. We can work together now for that, in her lifetime and ours.'

'What's the vote?' said the woman.

Jo paused, another realisation hitting her that this woman's life had far greater priorities in its day-to-day struggles than what was going on at Westminster, hundreds of miles away. She geared herself up to start explaining it, hopefully in terms the woman would understand, when she felt a hand grasp her shoulder.

'That's enough of that!'

Jo saw the face of Willy Wall, the short, red-faced and angry man who had tried to break up her first suffragette meeting. He had no coat on and had clearly been summoned by some passer-by to come forthwith into the street from his office and deal with this troublesome woman.

'Take your hand off me, now,' said Jo, absolutely calmly. She had dealt with worse than him, much worse, at Shrewsbury.

'I wonna do such a thing when you're spreading insurrection in the streets of Ironbridge!'

'Insurrection?' Jo laughed. 'I am telling women their rights.'

'You have no right to do it! Who d'you think you are, you little slut?'

This raised a cheer, which Jo realised came from a gathering group of men standing about to watch nearby. Women walked on, glancing, but many keeping their heads down.

'You canna call me that!' said Jo, loudly. 'I am no such thing. I am a respectable married woman and mother. I am speaking to the women of Ironbridge, not to you. Let me be and take your damned hand off my shoulder, I tell you.'

'Can I touch your shoulder, then?' called a man nearby.

'And me!' called another.

'Can I touch your other bits?' said the first man, and this caused great hilarity.

Now, Willy Wall put two hands on her and was trying to manhandle her away from the bridge.

'Go home, woman!' he kept saying. 'Go home!'

'I inna going home!' cried Jo. She was grappling with this

man now, who despite being small, was still taller than Jo and had unlikely strength. He shoved her hard and she fell, sprawled on the ground, the leaflets going flying, flapping open and shut in the breeze where they fell. She got to her knees, her stockings ripped. She looked up to see the gaggle of men whooping with delight at this latest instalment in their unforeseen morning's entertainment. On her knees in the dirt, she said to those men, 'Would you laugh if I were your sister, your daughter, your mother or wife?'

One leant down to her and spat in her ear, 'No woman of mine would behave like the whore you are.'

Jo recoiled, dragged herself up and immediately set to picking up her leaflets. She was going nowhere, she decided, in that moment. They'd have to cart her off to prison. She stood upright, knowing her dress was streaked with mud, her hat skewed on her head. She righted it, held out a crumpled leaflet, looked Willy Wall right in the eye and shouted, 'Votes for women!'

The man had had enough and launched himself at her, yet within seconds someone stopped him. A man's back came between Jo and Wall, and Jo stepped back in surprise as the man blocked Wall's progress and placed a calming hand on his shoulder.

'What on earth, Mr Wall? Fighting women in the street? This is no way for a member of the council to conduct himself.'

As the man turned to one side, she could see now who it was. Dr Hale, the one who Aunt Stella had always complained about, and said none of the women in the town liked him either, which is how she'd made a living. But Jo had visited Dr Hale several times over the years, particularly now with Harry. She wondered if her aunt had invented the rumours about him not being liked, in order to fuel her own business and earnings. Jo had always found him a calming, polite man and a careful listener. And here he was, to her rescue. At the sight of him, some of the men around them began to disperse begrudgingly. Jo supposed they did not want to fall foul of the town doctor, as they might be in need of him from time to time, for themselves or their families. Jo put the ruined leaflets back in the bag and dusted herself down as Wall argued with the doctor, yet eventually Wall saw his side of it and went back to whatever stuffy room of self-importance he'd come from.

'Are you well, Mrs Woodvine?' said Dr Hale, as he came haltingly over to her. He limped on his left leg, a leftover from childhood polio. He was in his late thirties, with brown side-parted hair and he wore a neat moustache.

'I'm fine. And I wonna stop, if that's what you're gonna tell me to do.'

'I wouldna dream of such a thing,' said the doctor, smiling. 'But I'm wondering if the iron bridge is the best place to persuade the women of the town to follow your cause.'

'It is the best place, as everyone walks by it,' asserted Jo. She was grateful to Dr Hale but did not want to be lectured about her behaviour. But then she realised she was being impolite. 'And thank'ee. For stepping in. No others did. It was kind of you.'

'You're welcome. Do you perhaps have any fresh leaflets not muddied in the street in that bag there? I'd be happy to display a little pile of them in my surgery, if you'd like.'

Jo looked up at him, quite shocked. No man except Charlie had ever shown the slightest bit of interest in her suffragette doings and certainly no support.

'That would be marvellous,' said Jo, adding 'Thank'ee again' as she passed him the bundle of clean leaflets.

The doctor offered to walk her home, but Jo told him she

wasn't going home, to which Dr Hale raised his hat in farewell and nodded, his facial expression showing clearly how impressed he was with Jo. She straightened her hat and stood stock still exactly where she was and stayed there for another hour, trying to hand out leaflets, being laughed at by men, ignored by women, even barked at by a yappy stray dog. But she stood there nonetheless, with her torn stockings beneath her muddied skirt. She would move for no one. When she went home, she did not pick up Harry from Maria straight away. Instead, she went into her house with the intention of changing her stockings and skirt. Yet the moment the door closed, she broke down in tears. She sobbed for a few minutes, standing forlorn in the parlour, her hat in one hand. Then, she stopped crying just as abruptly and went to wash her face.

After that first day at the bridge, Jo continued to hand out leaflets once a week. The town got used to her, the laughing subsiding, with most of the passers-by ignoring her, with the odd taker of a leaflet from time to time but mostly none. At home, Jo read more reports in the *Wellington Journal and Shrewsbury News* that, firstly, Barbara Rose was hunger striking, and then had been released, only to break more windows and be returned, which made Jo clap her hands in delight with each new nugget of information about her heroine. Barbara was unstoppable! She quickly became infamous as a suffragette hero in the local area. Jo continued to admire her hugely from afar, but would not tell the others at the meetings or at home that she knew Barbara Rose a little better than any of them would guess. For the fact was that Jo had told no one of her role in Barbara's crime that day in Shrewsbury. It was a delicious secret she kept to herself, alongside her shameful secret from her childhood.

Recently, she had begun to think of that childhood crime

she'd witnessed differently, her mother's murder of her father. She had known her father had beaten her mother. He took her mother away into the kitchen to do it and Jo never saw it directly. But she knew it happened and saw the bruises on her mother's back more than once when her mother was undressing. She realised now that her father was always careful to beat her on the parts of her body that most people would never see. He never hit her in the face. The calculating bastard. And now she knew from Stella how vulnerable her mother had been, it riled Jo even more, how her clever father had taken advantage of that and used her poor, simple mother most cruelly.

Jo realised that perhaps what was done to her by the policeman – or rather, what that man might've continued to do if he had not been in the street and had instead been behind closed doors – maybe this had happened to her mother by her father's hands and worse, much worse. Maybe this was a regular occurrence. Maybe her mother had put up with it all for so long and no longer. Maybe she knew that, even if she went to the police and even if the courts became involved, perhaps they would side with the husband – as his wife was like his property, after all – and not lock him up and throw away the key as they should, but instead let him out again to go home and beat her for reporting him. Maybe Jo's mother took the only avenue left to her and she raised that pillow and ended the man who would one day most likely kill her, and even her daughter. Jo began to feel differently about her mother's crime then. Instead of the shame she'd held onto for years, Jo began to feel a grim kind of pride, that her mother had done the only thing she could, to save herself, and to save Jo. If only her mother had not turned to drink as her comfort, turned yellow and died, then she would be here today and Jo could tell her how proud she was of her for ending the nightmare of the wicked existence of Jo's father.

Jo knew she was lucky to have a sweet man at home, instead of the terror that her mother had had to live with. However, that didn't mean everything was rosy in the Woodvine household. Though Jo was finding motherhood easier than before, and felt she'd managed to shed some of the weight of sadness she'd been hauling around since Harry's birth, Alfie was still very disagreeable about what he called 'this suffragette nonsense'. After the Shrewsbury meeting, once Alfie had heard of what had gone on with the police (and he didn't know the half of it, Jo mused), he'd responded in anger. He'd raised his voice at Jo, telling her she was forbidden to go on any more suffragette gatherings. Jo had laughed in his face then, which annoyed him even more. And then once she'd started handing out leaflets, he was even more furious. He said the men at work teased him about it and he was sick of it. They argued, and she replied that she'd do what she liked and no husband of hers was going to tell her what she could and couldn't do. Alfie protested that he wasn't trying to control her, just keep her safe. She responded by saying she didn't trust any men any more.

Alfie said, 'All men? Including me? And my dad? And what about Harry? He's your son, for God's sake. He'll be a man one day. Will you think the same of him?'

Jo had been humbled by this and did not reply, stomping out of the room instead. Alfie was right, she knew he was, about himself, about Charlie, and about their son, of course. But was it possible that all men could be what Barbara Rose said they could be? Jo's head hurt with the thought of it. Throughout those months from spring to summer, Jo and Alfie managed an uneasy truce, but Jo knew that there was a war raging between women and men, and she knew whose side she was on.

Chapter 11

Alfie

July to October 1914

That summer, Ironbridge sweltered under the blanket of a heatwave, bringing sleepless nights from the heat and violent thunderstorms that rattled Jo and Alfie's little house on Church Hill. The town held river regattas in the sunshine, which Jo and Alfie attended with baby Harry, along with Charlie and Maria. Jo always worried about keeping Harry's head out of the direct sun as he was so fair. Alfie told his wife that he himself was fair and he never had any trouble getting burnt as a boy, instead went brown as a berry in the sun.

'Jo, you fret too much about that boy,' he said kindly, trying to ease her burden, but she only looked peeved with him. This was a look he was getting a lot recently. He rarely elicited a soft look from her these days. They'd moved on from the halcyon days of their childhood, to the honeymoon period of their early marriage, succeeded by the miserable days of Harry's first few weeks, and then to the lightening of Jo's mood, infuriatingly created not by him, but by all this suffragette rubbish. He was sick of hearing about it and wished everyone would find something better to gab about.

But then, he got his wish and not how he expected he might. The newspapers brought other dark clouds brooding on the horizon. Alfie's father would relay to him key points from the paper when he went round there, as Alfie always said he never had the time to read, what with his long hours and the baby.

'Things are afoot among the rich and powerful,' his father said. At the end of July, after the shooting of Archduke Ferdinand, Austria-Hungary declared war on Serbia. Alfie knew little to nothing of who any of these people were and assumed it was far away and therefore irrelevant. But then, in Germany, which he knew was closer to home, the Kaiser's brother went to Russia to talk about peace. And the Stock Exchange closed in London, which made everyone nervous. Then another day Alfie's dad said the King was intervening. People talked about hoping for a settlement. But then Germany declared war on Russia. And Alfie heard that the German army invaded France, Luxembourg and Belgium. Then, on the 4th of August 1914, King George VI declared war on the German Empire.

People were talking about it in the street, but when Alfie's dad showed it to him in the local newspaper, it was only on page seven, so Alfie figured it couldn't be that important. Mr Cork at work said it was a storm in a teacup. So, Alfie went on with the business of life, walking to work, chatting with the fellows at work about the football or their families or the hard graft required to keep the garden fresh in such heat, walking home from work and managing the tense mood at home while enjoying his time with his now fifteen-month-old little chap, Harry.

It did not occur to Alfie that he should enlist, not at all. It felt to him a foreign war, led by the rich, the powerful, of machinations caused by dukes and kings and emperors. What did their problems have to do with him and his kind, in little Ironbridge in Shropshire? He carried on as normal. Yet it didn't take long for things to begin changing, subtly at first, then, like a snowball rolling down Church Hill, gathering size and speed exponentially. Men he knew who were already in the Territorials were going off to the war and that seemed normal at first, that those who'd chosen to be involved with military matters would be keen to go away. But it wasn't long before chaps he knew who'd never had a military thought in their heads were also enlisting and going off. Then Alfie and Jo went to see a picture show at the cinema one time, his parents babysitting Harry, and at the end they showed a news reel with footage of the British fleet sailing in full glory, accompanied by a rendition of 'Hearts of Oak' on the piano. He felt something stir in him then, and witnessed a similar frisson move through the crowd, a kind of invisible activation that made every man seem to sit up straighter in his seat. The feeling stayed with Alfie and he couldn't shake it the following few weeks. One day at work, one of the apprentice boys at the ripe old age of sixteen said to Alfie, 'What are you doing about the war, then?'

'Nothing,' answered Alfie, and the boy looked disappointed and sloped off.

Then a couple of mates from work enlisted and off they went. Alfie began to feel that the apprentice boy, Terry, who'd asked him about the war, looked at him differently. The lad had always looked up to Alfie, as Assistant Head Gardener, but now he answered back and looked askance whenever Alfie approached him. Then one day, on the way home from work, he was walking along the street and a young pretty woman was walking towards him and beamed at him from a distance, as if she knew him. He glanced at her again out of curiosity, but once she was closer, her expression changed to pure disgust, so much so she looked as if she might spit at him.

'Where's your khaki?' she said, with intense scorn.

Alfie was nonplussed and could not think of a thing to say in reply, at which she shook her head and marched onwards.

This shook him up and he hurried home after that. He didn't tell a soul about it, as the shame it elicited in him was not easily explainable. He knew logically that the war had nothing to do with working-class lads like him, yet all around him folk were whipped up in patriotic fervour about doing your duty. Alfie's parents were appalled by the whole idea, as he was. They talked about the whole thing being criminal, and Alfie agreed. War was a rich man's game, his mother told him. He agreed with that too. But he and his parents were in the minority. He talked to Jo about it.

She said, 'It's a lot of rubbish. And it's succeeded in knocking suffragettes off the front page. I'm livid about it. All this flag-waving nonsense. And where is the news of our brave women in prison? Maria told me today that all Ironbridge WSPU meetings have been cancelled until further notice. To serve the war effort, they say. What war effort? Why should we make an effort for someone else's war all that way away? Makes me sick. What about the rights of women? War doesn't have anything to do with us.'

Alfie listened to her ranting on and felt peeved. The suffragette business was surely irrelevant in the face of the current crisis. He hadn't cared much about it before war broke out and now it felt more out of touch than ever for Jo to be going on about it. The fact was, however you felt about the rights and wrongs of the working man going off to fight a foreign war started by the rich, the majority of the country was all in favour of waving the flag, and rushing off to enlist, of lining the streets of towns and cities as the local men joined up and marched off to railway stations to depart for who knew where and for who knew how long. The general feeling was that the war would probably be over by November or so, if that, thus a chap should join up as soon as possible, so he didn't miss out on the show. Before August 1914, Alfie couldn't have imagined wanting to leave his beloved garden for any reason at all. But a couple more lads from work had gone and there was only a handful of them left.

Then one day in September that still acted like it was summer, the heat standing still in the air, the river Severn languid, Alfie was in town, looking in a shop window at the tobacconists as he knew his father wanted a new pipe and he had it in mind to buy him a nice one, as his dad always made do with the cheaper things in life and he wanted to treat him. He had one hand in his pocket and the other at his side. And suddenly, swiftly, another hand took his own – petite and warm – and before he'd barely registered it, something had been pressed into his palm and the hand removed. He opened his palm to find a white feather. He looked up to see which woman had done it, for surely it was a woman, but could see only the usual collection of hats bobbing up and down the street and couldn't work out who was the culprit. He'd heard about the white feathers women were using to represent cowardice, given out to shame men into action. Alfie felt nauseous and tried to throw the damn thing away, but it stuck to his damp palm and he couldn't get it off. He peeled it from his skin and threw it hard into the street, but of course, being a feather, it merely drifted on the warm air and lingered before him. It felt as if it were taunting him, gently, softly, yet insistently.

On a warm Saturday night in early October, Alfie's parents offered to take Harry so that he and Jo could have a nice night out. He took her to the Central Hall to watch a bit of music hall on the stage there. He was excited to go, to get out of the house, to see Jo dressed up in her nice midnight-blue skirt and hat. He was proud to be seen with her, out on the town. They went for drinks first at a couple of pubs, then walked over to the Hall, keen to see the acts on stage and escape from the real world for a time. Yet once they got in there and looked to find their seats, Alfie saw that the stage had been half taken up with tables and chairs, at which sat some army officers with piles of papers in front of them. Was it some sort of theatrical skit? Alfie realised quickly that it wasn't. It was all too real. These officers were recruiting. They sat there po-faced as the first number began with a beautiful singer known about these parts as Vesta, though in town she was a local girl and everyone knew her real name was Brenda. She was all dolled up in this sparkly gown and long white gloves and she had a nice enough voice and sang a song called 'We Don't Want To Lose You, But We Think You Ought To Go'. She came down off the stage while she was singing and started to walk up and down the aisles, pausing randomly then placing her hand on the shoulder of a young man. Then that young man would stand up and follow her up to the stage and approach the officers at the tables, who'd start the paperwork that would turn him into a soldier for the British Expeditionary Force. Was it real? Were these chaps all plants? Alfie couldn't tell, yet the sweat began to build on his forehead and he felt it trickle down by his ears as Vesta approached. Luckily, Jo was on the outer seat and the singer didn't reach across her, only touching those men who sat on the aisle. The whole thing seemed to last for ever and around ten men were signed up that night. Every man who got up to follow Vesta to the stage was accompanied by a ferocious roar of approval from the crowd that drowned out the music and caused the wooden floor to vibrate, such was the violent power of approbation surrounding Alfie that night, making his ears buzz and his head ache.

Chapter 12

Alfie

Alfie couldn't get out of that stifling hall soon enough. As he and Jo headed home, they walked in silence. The air felt heavy with meaning. What surprised Alfie most was how he watched those men walk up to the stage and – this shocked him rigid – felt a tremendous urge to follow them. Just that morning, the last of the other gardeners at work had not turned up, Mr Cork telling him that they'd all gone off to the war now, even the other apprentice boy, who was also sixteen and had lied about his age to enlist.

'You dunna have to show your birth certificate?' Alfie had asked Mr Cork.

Terry, the remaining apprentice, stood near them in the office, listening with great interest but pretending not to.

'They dunna care,' replied his boss, shrugging shoulders and letting out a huge sigh. 'They're taking all sorts, even boys, as long as they're fit for service.'

Mr Cork had been fretting about what on earth was going to happen to the garden since all the staff but the three of them had now gone.

'Thank heavens you're still here, Alfred. And you, Terry, my boy.'

Alfie had smiled wanly at Mr Cork, then glanced at Terry, who was looking straight at Alfie, that same look of scorn as the girl in the street had given him.

That night, walking home from the show with Jo, he suddenly turned to her and said, 'What do you think about it all, love?'

Alfie knew that look on her face, of barely controlled rage.

'You know what I think. And I thought you felt the same.'

'I did . . .' said Alfie, trailing off.

'I dunna want you to go anywhere. I need you here. Harry needs you here.'

Alfie found he couldn't reply. He didn't know how to. He only knew a great weight was on his back, getting heavier each day that passed in wartime. It burdened him and made thinking straight difficult.

That night, he lay awake for hours, listening to Jo's breathing and the odd moment of sleep-talking from Harry in the next room. The witching hour came and went and he slipped out of bed, a bright moon that night making it easier to find his way across the bedroom and across to his son's room. He stood by the side of his cot. Harry's yellow hair was sticking up at all angles, his arms flung backwards over his head, his little mouth open. His eyelashes were as long as a camel's, thought Alfie, as the moonlight caught them and made his son look painfully beautiful as he lay in the utter abandonment of a child's sleep. Alfie made a decision then, in that moment, watching the peacefulness of his son.

He had no sleep that night and left before his wife and son woke up. He went to the square in Ironbridge and waited for the others. Sunday mornings were becoming the norm for chaps to muster there. He didn't speak to anyone, kept himself to himself. Then Terry, the apprentice from work, turned up. Strangely, he was wearing a bowler hat, something Alfie had never seen him in. He came over to Alfie and looked keenly at him.

'Mr Woodvine,' he said, and doffed his hat nervously. He stood there in long trousers and an ironed shirt and jacket. Alfie had never seen Terry look so smart. He was tall for his age but with a baby face.

'Terry,' nodded Alfie, wondering if the boy had come to watch or something else. 'Nice hat that.'

Terry fingered the hat's brim nervously. 'It makes me look older.'

'I see,' said Alfie.

'Mr Woodvine, you . . .' the boy began, then hesitated. 'You wouldna tell them, would you?'

Alfie paused at looked at the boy. He had long eyelashes like Harry.

'I dunna even know you,' he said.

Terry grinned. 'Thank'ee, Mr Woodvine. Thank'ee.'

Before long, a recruiting sergeant arrived and led them all across to the Library House on Severn Bank, just off Wharfage. Alfie felt as if time slowed down as he walked down Wharfage, the old river rolling onwards to his left. He was walking in the opposite direction to its flow as he did. He felt disoriented by it, his head swimming. When they got to the Library House, they queued up outside, around fifteen or so of them. Inside were a couple more sergeants from the King's Shropshire Light Infantry, set up at tables with pens, pencils and paperwork. The walls were lined with shelves filled with books, watching over them as the new recruits queued up behind each other at the two tables.

A sergeant-major with a neat moustache called Alfie over.

'Age?'

'Twenty, sir. Twenty-one in December.'

'Are you here willingly?'

'Yes, sir,' Alfie replied.

'You know you may be sent overseas?'

'I assumed so, sir.'

'Right-ho. Sign here, please.'

It was as easy as that. He was told to be at the square at midday the next day. Alfie didn't hang around to see if Terry got in. On the walk home, Alfie considered how sick he was of the bickering at home. Perhaps Jo would be happier with him as her choice of husband once he came home on leave in his smart new uniform. She'd miss him while he was away and appreciate him more when he was back. Maybe then she'd cheer up and show him more love. It got a bit better after she started with the suffragettes and was happy for a while, but soon soured once he got annoyed she wasn't home to make his dinner or get his work clothes ready. He recalled how, earlier that year, everything had been about the scandal of Jo in the suffragettes. Now that seemed a thousand years ago. War overshadowed everything and none of that suffragette business mattered any more. Alfie reasoned it as follows: he was going to go off and become a war hero, and then nobody could tell him his wife was a disgrace any longer, nobody would dare. He was glad that the suffragettes themselves had agreed to put their cause to one side for the moment, to support the war effort. He was pleased their hold over Jo would wane with time, and once he'd come back from the war, they could start again. Everything would be like it was before, when they were happy. He realised that weight he'd been carrying only the night before was gone from his shoulders. He felt as light as that white feather that had been pressed into his hand.

He found Jo in the kitchen, Harry in his high chair, his face a mess of porridge. He laughed at his dada and squished porridge between his fingers.

Jo said nothing.

Alfie washed his hands at the sink, standing with a cloth to dry them, staring out of the window at the little back yard with his sweet pea plants still climbing the trellis he'd nailed to the wall. There were no flowers left yet the skeleton of the plants remained, hanging on grimly into autumn.

Alfie turned around and looked at Jo.

'Shall I finish?' he said, gesturing to his son.

'I'm done,' snapped Jo. 'Nothing here for you to do.'

Alfie nodded. Then paused, watching her wipe their son's mucky face.

'I had to do it,' he told his wife.

'Did you?' she quipped, heavy with sarcasm. It wasn't a question as much as an accusation.

'Yes,' said Alfie, firmly. 'It's the same as it is for you, with the suffragettes. You had to do it. You didn't care what I thought, what anyone thought. You did it because you knew it was right. It's the same for me. I canna stand by and watch my friends, my colleagues, even boys of sixteen queuing up to go, and stay here and do nothing. I mun go with them and stand beside them. It's not possible, to stand by, to watch, to turn away. It mun be done. As a man, I have to go.'

Jo looked at him then, cloth in hand, her eyes wide and dark. He saw then how frightened she was, that her rage was a thin veil over her fear. He went to her and took her hand, threw the cloth down and pulled her into his arms. As he pulled her close and she nestled her face into his chest, the scent of her hair and the warmth of her body filling him with love, the years fell away and he felt eighteen again, on his wedding night. She'd admired him then, was satisfied to be with him, was happy. He knew that this decision he'd made today would bring those days back again, would make her proud of him. Everything would be all right, when he came home from the war.

Jo

Jo didn't go with Alfie that evening to tell his parents. She could only imagine the scenes that would follow and she didn't want Harry hearing all that. When Alfie came home, he was quiet. She didn't ask him how it went. After she'd put Harry down for the night, she got out her husband's best suit and ironed his best shirt, polished his best shoes. She wouldn't have her Alf going off to war in his shabby gardening garb. He'd be smart as he walked to the railway station with the others.

That night in bed, their last night together for who knew how long, they held onto each other. Both were too keyed up to make love or anything like it. She just lay entwined in him, her head on his chest. They didn't sleep but they didn't talk either. There was nothing left to say. She could argue with him till the cows came home, but what would be the point? The war would still trundle on and she'd ruin his last night at home. She could throw all the arguments at him, things she'd learnt from listening to the women at the suffragette meetings, how they always said that a society where men ruled everything wasn't just bad for women, it was bad for men too. A world dominated by men was cruel to everyone, forcing boys to never cry or show their feelings, expecting men to be the strong ones at all times, when they were just as susceptible to stress and worry as any woman, forcing men into moulds they didn't fit, all in the name of power. And now, with the advent of this damned war, the men again had to do their duty, marching off willingly to defend their country. And women had to stay at home and cope. All of the urgency of the suffragette cause had dissipated almost immediately on the outbreak of war. The WSPU more or less disbanded locally, with all efforts turned towards organising women to help with the war effort. First Aid classes were put on, which the local suffrage supporters attended, but not Jo. She was furious about the whole thing. Why should a war created by men end the women's movement overnight? The problems caused by men enveloped those of women every time. That was the way of things. But it wasn't only women who'd suffer, it was men too, namely those who were coerced and cajoled into going off to fight. Jo had seen the fervour in local women, shouting at men in the street who weren't in uniform or handing out those ridiculous white feathers. The whole thing disgusted her. She was glad that Alfie had agreed with her about the war being someone else's concern and certainly not theirs. Or, at least, he used to agree with her. But Jo knew her Alf well enough to know that something in him had shifted. She had been too scared of what it all might mean to even mention it to him. But she had felt it happen, felt him pulling away from her influence. It seemed inevitable somehow, to give in to the strong current that flowed against them and everything they held dear.

When she'd woken up that morning and found her husband gone, she guessed immediately with a sinking heart where he'd be. There was only so much pressure a chap could take, she knew that. She hated the system they lived under more then than she ever had, the system that kept not only women but also men in their place, especially working-class men and women like themselves, those without capital or standing in society, those who had no say in what happened to their country or even to their own lives. It filled her with incandescent rage to think of it, rehearsing the ideas in her head, of how wrong it all was.

But as she lay in her husband's arms that night, listening to his breathing, knowing he was not sleeping, her rage melted into fear, that he would go and never come back.

'I'm sorry,' she whispered.

'What are you sorry about?'

'For causing you trouble.'

'You never have,' he said. She could tell by the sound of his words that he was smiling.

'Liar,' she said, smiling too.

He squeezed her closer and she held on tightly.

'It'll be all right,' he said.

She said nothing.

'Chaps say it'll be a short trip to France or Belgium and a bit of a show, then home. Maybe a month or so, nothing more. I'll be back before you know it.'

'All right,' she whispered, though she didn't believe him. Alfie Woodvine had been raised in an optimistic household with optimistic parents. He always saw the best in everything. Jo had been raised somewhat differently. As she lay there, listening to him as he drifted at last into a fitful sleep, she turned over onto her back and stared at the ceiling, feeling the strangest sensation, that the roof might buckle and collapse onto them at any moment.

Alfie turned over in his sleep and flopped his arm across her chest, curling himself up like a child, easing his head onto her lap.

She stroked his hair as he slept and listened to every breath he took, for hours.

Chapter 13

Charlie

The next morning, around a half hour before midday, Charlie took Snap by his lead and left the house. The dog was surprised to be getting a second walk of the day, as his master usually took him early before school. Today was different, though, as Charlie had arranged for his other teaching colleagues to be in charge of the children on this particular Monday, and to take them down to the town to see the new recruits off at noon. He himself would need to be with his family, as his son was going away today. Maria was already over at Alfie and Jo's, helping Jo with Harry. Charlie looked down at the dog, who gazed up at him with a look of purest trust and faith. Charlie felt his eyes filling with tears and sniffed them away. He needed to be the rock that everyone expected him to be that day.

After Alfie had left last night, having delivered the terrible yet inevitable news that he had enlisted, Maria had collapsed, sobbing. When war was whispered of earlier in the year, they'd talked about it and both knew it was likely this day would come. Anyone in the whole country who had a son of the right age (and many whose sons were far too young but were accepted anyway) would be thinking the same thing, that their sons would soon be required to give their service. Maria had said all the way through that she knew he'd go, that there was nothing they could do to stop it and that she was ready for it. She believed strongly in protecting the innocent. She'd said to her husband several times that she felt wars were wrong, but if one found oneself in a war, then the right thing to do was to face up to it and do your best to help. She'd been highly rational about it. But when she was faced with the reality of Alfie leaving, face to face with their beloved son, Charlie had glanced at her and knew she was fighting away tears with every ounce of strength she had. They'd both said they were proud of him and would join the crowd in town the next day to see him off. It was a short conversation, none of them really knowing what to say, as none of them had been in such a situation before. It wasn't every day your son went off to war.

The moment the front door closed behind Alfie, his mother collapsed, her legs giving way as she sank to the floor. She let out an almighty cry of sorrow, rending Charlie's heart in two as he rushed to her side. She fell into his arms, sobbing wetly against his shirt. Then came a frantic knocking on the door, as Alfie called through the wood to ask if his mother was all right. Charlie didn't want to leave her, so called back that everything was all right, to go home and they'd see him in the morning. He felt as if his son lingered there on the doorstep, listening, so he shushed Marie gently, trying to calm her down and reduce the effect on Alfie of hearing his mother weep so inconsolably. Charlie knew it was Alfie's job to be strong now and face this challenge with no reservation, as he would need that certainty as he marched off into whatever hell they'd throw at him. Charlie himself had never fought in a war, thankfully, but he read so much he knew enough to know that a soldier's life in the British army was never going to be an easy thing. He'd seen young men come back from the Boer War at the turn of the century, some with lost limbs, some haunted around the eyes, never to be the same again. There weren't so many of them as now, but it had stayed with him, that look. Now, it seemed as if the entire population of men from forty or so down to mere striplings were enlisting and abandoning their homes for the 'great adventure'. Now, it was to be his son, his own dear boy, his Alfie.

'Come on, Snap,' he said, and urged the dog forwards as they crossed the road over to Jo and Alfie's house. He met them coming out of the house, Maria and Jo in their best frocks, Harry sitting up in his baby carriage and babbling nonsense. Charlie had bought them this new lightweight carriage a few weeks before, as the pram was a bit of an old beast and very heavy. This one was much easier and had a better view for Harry, so he could sit up and see the world properly all around him, which he drank in with his inquisitive large blue eyes. Alfie came out of the house last and closed the front door behind him. He was very smartly turned out. Jo had done a lovely job with his suit. He would go off to war looking every inch the man he was. The five of them – six including Snap – ambled away rather awkwardly down the hill, both Jo and Maria holding firmly onto the pram as they always did.

As they descended, they could hear the hubbub already, before they'd even left Church Hill. As they turned the corner, a steady stream of onlookers were walking towards the square where the new recruits were to gather, the others fanning out along the Wharfage on both sides, to see them off. There was quite the air of celebration about it, which activated Snap, so he started panting and yapping at all the excitement. The atmosphere even heartened Charlie a little. His son was doing a brave and noble thing, despite Charlie's misgivings about the necessity for the war itself. As a Labour Party man, his own colleagues in the fight for working-class rights were generally split down the middle in their support or lack of it. Many Labour members felt war should always be the very last choice and that suing for peace should be taken as far as humanly possible. They also believed that it was the poor that suffered most in wars. But not many of them were pure pacifists either, Charlie included. He also loved his country and was proud to be an Englishman (despite the evils committed under the Empire, which generally disgusted him). Charlie was not immune to flag waving and even supporting the King, if it came to it. He wasn't a Communist, yet he also found the structure of society where the rich lorded it over the poor abhorrent. However, as he walked behind his little family alongside the River Severn to a spare spot opposite the square, his thoughts of the rights and wrongs of war faded into the reality of what was about to happen. It was easy, he thought, to have an opinion on war in a theoretical way, but however intellectually satisfying it might be to debate the whys and wherefores, when it came to your own son, everything changed.

The Woodvines gathered in their spot, Maria parking the pushchair between them, tickling Harry under his chin, who giggled uncontrollably. Jo stood stiffly beside them, wringing her hands obsessively. They were surrounded by hats of every kind, bobbing about beneath the wave of sound of many voices and approaching music, filling the air with the jangle and clank of celebration and soldiery. A band was playing some way away down the road, marching up past the pubs and warehouses upstream. It would stop near the iron bridge, no doubt, the central focus for all in the town. The brass instruments playing patriotic sounds jarred in Charlie's ears until he thought he might punch a cornet player if they didn't shut that noise up. Then Alfie turned around to face them and Charlie knew it was time.

Maria

Which order would the farewells take? She guessed Alfie would choose his dad first, the one who could take it most, or so Alfie imagined. Her son thought of his dad as a tower of strength and knew little of the worries and anxieties he'd shouldered silently through the years. Then, Alfie would say goodbye to her, leaving Jo and Harry till last. They would be the hardest goodbye for him. It was the right order of things. But she found herself suddenly torn apart by jealousy, that anyone at all in this world held more importance in her son's life than his mother, who had been through hell since the first glimmerings of him began inside of her. She'd had to fight off Oskar von Schoen, who hit her while she was pregnant. And she'd run away from that place and never looked back, beaten and bloodied, exhausted and frail. Maria thought then of how Alfie's blood-related father was a countryman of the enemies that now threatened their own. The Germans were now their enemies en masse and the irony of this was not lost on Maria as she considered how cruelly one of Germany's sons had treated her and their unborn child.

But she had survived it and made a life with her great love, Charlie, and her greatest love, her boy. To think of how a mother had to be vigilant every moment of every day and night from birth onwards, to simply keep her children alive, to keep them from harm, from accidents and threats. Then to prepare them to go out into the world and have enough about them so that they didn't succumb to the dangers of the adult world, now their parents were not dogging their every step. It was an eighteen-year battle, and then even beyond that, it never stopped, despite her son being a man now: the worry, the anxiety, the fear. As she watched Alfie shake his father's hand – neither of them were men known for showing their feelings in public – she thought blankly how all those years of keeping him safe had led to this, where the son she'd fought to protect was now being handed over to the most lethal situation a young man can find himself in: a wartime army. What was the point of all that vigilance, Maria thought, for these bloody men in their khaki and caps to take her son away from her? Her head felt like it was rattling, as if all the parts of her brain had frozen and shattered into pieces, driving her mad. Yet, all around them was laughter and waving and music and she had to smile, was compelled to smile by the bright fakery of happiness that surrounded her. Her son was looking at her now. He let her put her arms around him. The shape of him, the bulk of him, the muscles and sinews and bones of him, all here, all safe, in her arms.

He whispered in her ear, 'I'll come back to you, Mum. See if I dunna.'

Hearing his voice made it worse. She thought of the days she taught him to speak, oh, so long ago now and yet like yesterday, how quickly they grow up and away from you. She patted him on the back and squeezed his shoulders, facing him again and forcing a smile to reassure him. Then she looked away as he said his farewells to Jo and Harry. She simply could not bear to look upon it, Jo's haunted eyes and Harry's blissful ignorance of the father he was saying goodbye to. The very air felt heavy with significance, yet in that baby's mind, his inner world was concerned only with fun, and food, and what Snap was doing. Maria chastised herself for turning away, and turned back to see Alfie whispering in Harry's ear too. She wondered what he'd said to him. She'd ask him the next time she saw him, when he came back from the war, as he surely must.

Alfie left them then, striding across the road to join the other recruits, around thirty or forty or so, of all ages and sizes and classes and types. The band started up again, Madeley and Coalbrookdale Combined Bands, so their signs said, the soldiers encouraged to sing along to the tune of 'My Sweetheart Till I Die'. The sight of those fellows in every kind of clothing society could provide – from flat caps to top hats, morning coats to shabby jackets – proved that, despite their differences, these men were all bonded by their choice to fight. Soon they'd be in khaki and indistinguishable from one another. Maria found the higgledy-piggledy sight of them – a neat cross-section of Ironbridge society – intensely moving as they gathered themselves into lines, ready to go.

The march to the railway station began, the crowd moving as one to file in behind them as they went. The Woodvines followed on, none of them singing, none talking. The people ahead and behind waved flags, while the shops along Wharfage were bedecked with bunting of Union Jacks and the flag of Saint George, fluttering in the breeze coming in off the river, which ran the other way from the men marching. It took some time to make their way to the station. The air of festivity dulled somewhat as they walked on, and the crowd quietened down. As they passed a street coming down from the farmland beyond the town, a strange sight greeted the crowd, who all turned to observe it as they walked by. A motley crew of working folk were leading an array of horses by their bridles, walking steadily down the hill into the town, joining up alongside the procession. They came from other roads too as the crowd proceeded, a farm horse here, a carthorse there, beloved old nags who'd lived and worked with their owners for years, now demanded by the authorities to be turned over to the army for the war effort. Something about watching these men and women leading their cherished horses to an uncertain fate, it caught Maria unawares and the urge to sob was so hard to bear, she lifted a handkerchief to her mouth and pressed hard against it. Those equine beauties, unknowing, clip-clopping onwards into who knew what vision of hell. Somehow, the horses were the worst of it that day when Alfie left, the utter pathos of those innocent creatures. For Maria, it summed up the pointlessness of it all, for man and beast. The sacrifice of all those bodies, all that flesh, all those minds.

Chapter 14

Martine

August 1914

Two months before Alfie Woodvine left to go to war, Martine De Bakker and her four-year-old daughter, Brigitta, were at home in their apartment building in Leuven. Sitting by the bow window of their ground-floor flat, Martine sketched out a vase full of flowers in pencil that she handed over to Brigitta to colour in with her wax crayons. Martine was good at drawing, always had been. She opened up her sketchbook and found a drawing she'd done of her husband a couple of years back. She didn't want to look at that, not at that moment. She had to stay strong. But it was never easy, to shut out a thought. She was still thinking about Emiel's pale brown hair and hazel eyes when they heard the first shots outside.

Martine grasped her daughter's arm and pulled her under the table. There they sat, huddled together for a time, listening to more volleys of shots, increasing in volume. Martine's flat was in a nice district of Leuven, not too far from the railway station and the Grand Market Square, where the beautiful buildings of the town hall and the church of St Pierre stood. Her husband's family were well off and there had been money after Emiel died, enough to keep them living comfortably. At that moment, when she hid herself and her daughter under the table in their little apartment in a nice area of town, she cursed their situation being so near to the railway station, as that's where the Germans had gathered when they came. It was becoming clear that they were sweeping through town from there, and had started shooting in the streets, willy-nilly. As the shots grew louder, the sound of voices shouting in German came to them. And that prompted Martine to run. She scrambled out from under the table, keeping low, beckoning Brigitta to do the same. They crawled across the floor of the front room, Martine reaching up to the handle of the door to the hallway. She managed to open it and get them outside, whereupon she saw three other neighbours with the same thought. They nodded at each other and mounted the stairs, Martine pushing Brigitta to go faster, faster. A couple of weeks back, just after the Germans first entered Belgium, the residents of her building had had a meeting and decided that, if the Germans came to Leuven and started trouble, as they had in other places, everyone should go upstairs to the empty attic and wait out the chaos until it passed and it was safe to come down. They had cans of food and bottles of water and beer up there. There were three other flats in the building, yet since the German advance, one family had left, leaving only an old couple and a young man with a bad leg who worked in the library at the university. The five of them climbed the stairs nervously to the very top and shut the door behind them. The attic room was where boxes were stored belonging to the building's owner. There was a tall window that stretched from the skirting board to the ceiling, taller than Martine herself. On first entering the room, Martine went to the window to see if she could get a look at what was happening, and the old man shouted at her, 'Get away from there!'

She leapt back as if burnt. Her daughter, who had thought it all a bit of an adventure until that moment, burst into tears and flung herself against her mother's skirts and sobbed.

The old man, a retired clockmaker called Peter, who was usually perfectly pleasant, beckoned them to come and sit as far away from the window as possible.

'You weren't around in the war. Forty-four years ago, the French irregulars grouped together in plucky little bands, causing havoc for the Prussians. The *francs-tireurs*, they called them. Haven't you seen in the newspapers? The Germans are saying they're back, and in Belgium this time. But it's rubbish. It's just an excuse. They're shooting high up in the towns, shooting at the attic windows, lying and saying they've seen Belgian marksmen up there. Gives them the excuse to shoot civilians. So, don't go near the window, any of you. Stay this side of the room. If they come in the building, with any luck they'll stay on the lower floors and loot them first, getting bored before they reach up here. They'll be on to the next house to loot, you'll see. We'll be all right up here.'

Martine sat down, back against the wall, surrounded by boxes. The young man from the university, Noah, stood with shoulders hunched against the wall, looking scared. The old woman, Mila, found a box to sit on, her husband on another beside her. Then they all flinched as another volley of shots shattered the silence and was joined by many others. Even up there at the top of the building, the shouting was so loud that they could hear the German words. These were met with the screams of women and begging, pleading in Flemish. Men were shouting in Flemish too, some in French, when more shots rang out; one whizzed past the window and caught the eaves, a little puff of brick dust obscuring the window as they all stared at it. Then more came and the top four panes of the window shattered, splinters of glass being hurled across the room. Martine threw herself across her daughter's little body to shield her.

Brigitta asked her mother, white-faced and gasping, 'Will we die, Mama?'

'No, little one,' replied Martine.

Frail old Mila began to cry and Peter comforted her. Noah said nothing, eyes wide. More shots came, clearly aimed this time, shooting out the rest of the window panes, tatters of them hanging at the frame, yet most of the glass gone.

Then, banging came on the street door downstairs. Everyone froze. Banging came again, then more shots. They must've shot up the lock, because the sound of the boot on the door flung it open and they all heard it smash against the wall. Many heavy footsteps thumped through the building. They could hear doors opening and more gruff shouts, the sound of clanging, perhaps precious metal ornaments stolen and thrust into sacks, who knew? Martine and the old couple's flats were down there. Martine couldn't bear to think what they were doing in their dear little place. More thumping feet and they came to the first floor, where the empty apartment and Peter's flat were. More swinging of doors and no doubt looting. Would they come further? Was Peter right, that they'd tire of it and move on to the next house?

No, he was wrong, as the boots came stomping nearer and nearer. Stuck up in the attic, there was nowhere to run. What a stupid idea this was, Martine told herself, yet they'd all listened to Peter, as he'd always seemed wise and he'd fought in the old war back in the 1870s and seemed to know his stuff. Now, Martine cursed him and herself for listening to him. But she also had a moment to consider that there was little else they could've done but hide, as the Germans were all over her country now, spreading through it like a blaze out of control. The door was kicked open and in came two German soldiers.

Martine stood up and dragged Brigitta behind her, squished against the wall. The soldiers took stock of the room's inhabitants, one grinning. They both sported huge moustaches, their heads covered with the rounded helmets topped with the infamous spike. Their grey-green uniforms looked shabby and their faces were those of boys on a spree, drunk on cheap alcohol or power, or both. One had a mouth wide open, tongue lolling like an idiot dog, the other his eyes screwed up. The latter was the leader and he spotted Noah beside the wall and grabbed at his arm. He shook the poor man like a rag doll, screaming at him in German. Peter called out to him in French.

'No gun!' Peter shouted. 'He has no gun.'

The soldier wouldn't listen and shouted some order at his colleague, who grabbed Noah's other arm and they manhandled him over to the window-frame, now empty of glass.

What happened next was a moment in time that Martine knew would be etched into her mind for the rest of her life. Although the moment itself was fleeting and took no more than a handful of seconds to execute, her mother's instinct made her twist round and reach down, covering her daughter's eyes with her palms. She found she herself had to watch, though. She had to keep her eyes on those men. The two soldiers kicked at Noah's legs, to make them bend, to weaken the stiff frame of him that strained with all his might to escape his fate, his feet shoved up against the skirting board. But it was no good and they pushed him, his long arms flailing as he disappeared from view, and fell two storeys to the street below.

The soldiers turned and hitched their rifles back over their shoulders, where they had come loose, shouting more at the inhabitants before bustling out and back down the stairs. No one in the room moved, even Brigitta was frozen in place. But then she spoke.

'Can I see now?'

Martine removed her hands and looked down at her daughter's face. Brigitta was the image of her father, those hazel eyes, that fair, freckled complexion. She gazed up at her mother with the utmost trust.

'Have they gone?'

Martine nodded. She found she could not speak. She turned and looked at the old couple. Mila was shaking her head from side to side, unable to say anything either. Peter looked ashen grey, an unearthly colour.

'Where's Noah?' said Brigitta.

Then, Martine could smell burning. Tendrils of smoke appeared through the open door.

They've set the house on fire, she thought. She tore off her daughter's cardigan and told her to hold it over her head, like a hood.

'Hold it with one hand, then hold my hand with your other. Come with me, don't stop, don't look up, just follow my feet.'

Brigitta nodded and Martine rushed to the door, looking back at Mila and Peter who had not moved, still sitting on the boxes.

'Come on!' she cried at them.

But Peter simply shook his head.

Martine did not have time to argue with them. She rushed down the attic stairs, one hand on the banister, one grasping Brigitta's. The air was filling with smoke now, the sound of the flames crackling in the floors below. Martine coughed and coughed, her eyes watering. As they reached the first floor landing, she glanced back to see if Brigitta had kept her cardigan over her head, and she had, good girl. The roar of the fire was terrifying but Martine knew she had to get her daughter out of there. She headed to the stairs to the ground floor, to see that the fire was licking at the bannisters outside their apartment. No time to dither, she told herself, and plunged down the next flight, coughing all the way. She just had to get to the front door and then everything would be all right. Down the stairs they went, stumbling down the hallway and the front door was wide open.

Out in the street, the first thing that met Martine's eyes was the crumpled form of Noah, smashed bloody and inert by the fall. She looked away and focused on moving forwards. She made it to the other side, where she fell to her knees on the opposite pavement, coughing up a lung, as her father used to say in jest. How she wished she could see her father's kind face now. But he was dead, years ago now, her mother too, both from influenza when Martine was a younger woman. When she'd married, she'd found her new family. She thought of her parents-in-law, across on the other side of town. She'd go there. Hopefully the Germans had not reached them yet. Nobody expected the army to arrive at Leuven so quickly. And yet here they were. Brigitta was patting her mother on the back, as if she could cure the cough that way. Brave girl, thought Martine, whose coughing fit had now subsided, thank heavens, and she was able to stand up and look back at the building. Their flat must have been the place where the soldiers started the fire, as it was engulfed in flames now. The whole building would be destroyed. She thought of Peter and Mila, still upstairs. There was nothing she could do for them now. They had chosen their fate. Her ears were assaulted by the sound of snapping wood and splintering beams, the thunder of fire, and above it sailed the high cracks of gunshot that still rang through the streets.

Martine had to get her girl to safety, to the De Bekkers' house. First, she had to get her out of that street, as every other house in it was burning, the red roof tiles sliding off and smashing onto the ground as roofs collapsed. The whole street would be aflame soon, so she grabbed Brigitta's hand and they ran down the middle of the road and around the corner. Martine ploughed onwards, Brigitta struggling to keep up, as she led her daughter as far away as possible from the fires and the sounds of shooting. The beautiful town where she had made her home with her beloved Emiel was utterly changed. Along its narrow, twisting lanes, shops had their windows kicked in, looted goods spilling out across the pavements. Bundles of clothes had been dropped on the ground, beside people's earthly goods, from boxes of cigars to wooden clogs, scattered across roads. So many buildings were ablaze, there were people with sooty faces stumbling along streets, aimless and terrified, children crying, the unearthly sounds of voices wailing. Martine had been so intent on forward motion, she had taken them down several streets before she realised that there were dead people on the ground. The streets were littered with them. Bodies, in strange contortions, dead where they fell, a man with his eyes open and his head a bright red flower of flesh and blood. A woman flung across a wooden bench, her skirt ripped off. A baby, in its dead mother's arms, its eyes shut, looking peaceful in death. She wished she could hide these things from Brigitta, remove them from her sight. But there was no time for that. They simply had to carry on.

They reached the square and Martine looked up into the sky. For a moment of madness, she thought it was snowing in August, but her brain searched for an explanation and realised, these were not snowflakes, they were scraps of paper, their edges ringed in orange flame, of pages and pages of documents and scraps of books, floating on the hot air, all around them. The university library was on fire and these were the remnants of its centuries-old archives. Martine hurried on, no time to grieve either books or people as she did so. As the streets broadened out, horses hurtled past her, riderless and wild, some tethered to military wagons – free from their cruel masters, they fled in terror. One crashed its cart into a row of pear trees, the horse flung to its side, its dreadful whinny tearing the air as Martine turned away and led Brigitta down yet another road, the ground littered with bodies and sad tumbles of belongings with no owners to claim them.

Martine had run so blindly, she had to stop briefly to get her bearings. They weren't too far from the De Bekkers now. She'd lost her way a little, but could find her way back. Yet as she approached their part of town, Brigitta was flagging now, hanging off her mother's arm. Martine hauled her up onto her hip, not easy as she was slight but tall, her gangly legs kicking against Martine's as she struggled along. The fires had died down a bit in the last few streets, but as she got closer to her parents-in law's place – the idea of which felt like heaven to her now – the columns of smoke grew thicker here and brought back Martine's coughing. They were just two streets away now, but the air was becoming unbreathable. Martine stumbled on, Brigitta grasping on to her, yet Martine's legs sinking as she fought to escape the bad air and skirt the smoky parts and double back to the right street later. She put Brigitta down on the ground again and led her away. But when she tried to circle back, she saw from a distance that the end of the street where her parents-in-law lived, and every house in it, was on fire. At the entrance to the street lay a dead horse, splayed across it, gunshot wounds blooming across its flank.

There was nothing for them there now. Nothing for them anywhere in Leuven. Martine stopped in the street, just stopped and stared at the remains of the city she'd called home for these past few years, since her parents had gone and she'd found Emiel. Now he was gone, his parents too perhaps, their home, their city. There was nothing left for them here.

Brigitta tugged at her mother's hand. Martine looked down at her.

'Where will we go, Mama?'

Chapter 15

Jo

Mid-October 1914

Dear Jo,

Just a short one. You know I am not a man of letters. But I do apologise for leaving you letter-lacking for the first couple of weeks. We are kept busy in our training schedule here near Shrewsbury. We have to be up at 5.45 a.m. and must work until 7 p.m. at the earliest, so no change there for me. We are put through our paces with such things as section and company drills. We are also taught about what they call Field Engineering. That's all about trenches. I know a bit about digging, of course, and preserving things and myself in the face of the weather. The chaps around me are all good fellows. Not a dud among them. All Salopian men. A few days ago I was inoculated against typhoid and had a day off to get over it. My arm ached like billy-oh and my head felt as heavy as a medicine ball. But I survived. We don't know when we'll be heading out but they say it'll be the western front on the continent. People here say 'The Front' with voices full of awe, like it's a place from storybooks. I wonder what it'll be like. That's all to report for now. Sorry I'm not much good at writing letters. You could sow sweet peas and broad beans about now in our garden pots for next year, if you fancy that. Give the pater and mater a salute from me (they hate it when I call them that) and tell them I'm doing well. Give my sweet boy a kiss from me.

With love,
Your 'old man',
Alfie

This was the first letter Jo had received from Alfie since he'd left on the train, with the band playing and the crowd singing along and the women crying. She hadn't cried. Her sadness after the birth had made her cry, but she'd always found it hard to cry for people, however much she'd loved them. The first night after Alfie had gone, she went home and, once Harry was asleep, she sat up in bed with the curtains open and just stared at the darkness. The solitude was actually comforting somehow. She had listened to her own breathing and felt at peace for the first time in a long time. She had mused how much of a contradictory person she was, longing for company and longing for escape simultaneously, a tiresome character trait which meant she was often dissatisfied with her lot. This was proven once again when she'd eventually got to sleep and woke up in the middle of the night, reached out for Alfie, only to remember he'd gone. She curled up into herself and felt the loss of him terribly.

The days without him proceeded likewise, veering between gratitude for the lack of their bickering and a deep ache in her belly for his absence. And the old fear reared up again, of losing him for ever. And nowadays the old fears were replaced by new, real fears. This was no accident of fate, this was war and men were soldiers now, put in the way of danger as a matter of course. The newspapers were filled with pages of the dead. Charlie read them every day. Neither Maria nor Jo could bear to. If they were to receive the dreaded envelope, then they would face that if they had to. Jo could not stand the thought of her eyes trailing down the lists of names to the Ws, looking for Woodvine, Alfred. The thought made her bilious. At least he was still safe on English soil. For now.

Life was changing for everyone. Once so many men had gone from Ironbridge, there was the odd sensation of walking through town and seeing only women for streets on end. There would be the older men and a few young ones in khaki on leave. The surface of everyday life was altered in that way. Women in Ironbridge were being trained in first aid and joining up with voluntary groups for the war effort. None of it interested Jo. She wasn't required to do anything in particular since she had her little boy to care for. But the old feelings of unrest and dissatisfaction were creeping back and, oh, how she missed her suffragette work. The war breaking out knocked the whole thing on the head. It felt as if the WSPU had never existed. And the rage lifted in her, of the pointlessness of it all, this war. Some fellows far away on the other side of Europe had fallen out and now everyone in the rest of the whole damned world was mobilised and being carted off to who knew where. It was a war made by men for men, even the men who didn't want any part of it, men like her Alfie, a gardener, a peaceful man. It angered Jo that decisions made by men hundreds, if not thousands of miles away, were tearing at the fabric of her everyday life. And the casualties were not only real men, women and children but also ideals and hopes and dreams, like the suffragette cause itself. And women who had poured their hearts and souls into the movement now had to cast it aside. Women like Jo. And the wonderful Barbara Rose, who Jo still thought about often.

She wondered what Barbara was doing now. Jo had asked Maria, who hadn't heard anything, despite asking around. The latest seemed to be that Barbara had gone to ground after being released early from prison, so she hadn't been arrested again. It felt as if the authorities weren't interested in suffragettes any more, not with the war to deal with. Maria had stopped talking about it and so had the Malones, with both Hettie and Martha putting their efforts full tilt into supporting the war effort. Jo decided to write a letter to Barbara, to enquire after her welfare upon leaving prison. She wrote it formally but with warmth, as she wanted Barbara to remember her as a friend. Perhaps they would become correspondents and share their deepest secrets. Jo had never had a close female friend and could well imagine how marvellous it would be to have Barbara Rose as one. She sealed the envelope and wrote upon it the WSPU headquarters address in Shrewsbury, writing on the back of the envelope to please forward it to Miss Rose. She posted it with a frenetic anticipation. If she could link up with Barbara again, she might find a way through this war without going mad.

Then, one day a few weeks after Alfie had left, Jo was asked by Maria if she could pop round with Hettie Malone and her daughter Martha Haywood, as they had something interesting to discuss with her. Jo nearly refused, but didn't feel she could. Maria helped her so much with Harry and the house, it didn't feel right to turn her down. Once Alfie had gone, Maria had asked her if she had thought about going into wartime nursing and she'd look after Harry. Jo had replied absolutely not, as that's what her Aunt Stella did and she didn't want to work with her, as well as the fact that nursing was what everyone expected women to do and she was sick of doing what women were expected to do. Hopefully, Maria wasn't coming round to try to persuade her of that again. Or maybe, with any luck, it might be something to do with the suffragettes. So, she said yes, of course they could. They came on a weekend evening, Harry tucked up in his cot. Again, Jo was struck by the greenness of Hettie and Martha's eyes and the strange dichotomy between their clothes, that were finely made and in the latest fashions, and their down-to-earth demeanour and way of speaking. It made sense, Jo supposed, since Hettie had come from nothing, an orphan child adopted by the Malones, a poor family at the time, working with iron and down the mines. Hettie had been a lady's maid to the old King family when she was given her fortune. And she'd put it towards good works ever since. Jo was impressed with her, how easily she could've lived in luxury and done nothing for her fellow Salopians, yet instead she created a foundation that cared for the most vulnerable. Jo had dressed up a bit for their visit, not wanting to be caught out again in her house frock as she had for the first suffragette meeting. They sat on the settee and Jo brought through a tray of tea and biscuits, then sat on the chair she usually used for knitting and sewing (as it had good wide arms for putting bits and bobs on and pushing pins into), while Maria sat in Alfie's armchair.

The small talk began, of town life and news of Alfie. And then Hettie Malone, her green eyes focused on Jo, her grey-brown hair swept up into a modest, neat bun, spoke directly to Jo, as she said she had a favour to ask of her.

'Jo, do you follow the news much, news of the war, that is, of what's going on in mainland Europe?'

'I could lie to you kind ladies and pretend I do. But I think it's best if I dunna do that and tell the truth instead. I dunna read the newspapers, no. I dunna wanna know about the war.

It feels to me as if it's a war for men, made by men. I dunna want a thing to do with it.'

There was a pause, which made Jo feel self-conscious. Maybe she should've lied.

Hettie replied, 'I admire you, Jo. I like a woman who takes a stand. And, of course, as we were once in the ranks of the suffragettes, I agree with you. But sadly, this war becomes the war of women once civilians become involved. And unfortunately, in Europe, it's the innocents who are suffering most. You're familiar, I reckon, with the invasion of Belgium back in the summer?'

'I heard about that,' said Jo. Everybody knew about that, because it's what had brought her own country into the war. She remembered Charlie going on about it, how the Belgian king had refused to let the German army march through his country to get to France, and how that meant they were at war, and then Britain had declared war on Germany due to some treaty or other with Belgium.

'Well, there are terrible things going on in Belgium. The German army have committed atrocities against ordinary people. They set fire to houses, shoot civilians in large numbers. Even babies and children have been murdered. And women have been . . . attacked . . . by men . . . in the worst way. It is a catastrophe.'

Jo had had no idea. She felt embarrassed at her own ignorance. She'd heard mention of it, but not listened properly. It sounded horrendous, unthinkable. A modest little country like Belgium, torn apart like that. And for what? Because they just happened to be in the way of France? An accident of geography? It was dreadful.

'I'm . . . sorry. I feel rotten that I havna paid attention to what's going on. I just have a lot on my hands with Harry and now Alfie being away. It's wrong, though. I should read more.'

Martha sat forward in her seat then and smiled kindly at Jo.

'Dunna thrash yourself on our account, dear Jo. Life goes on and the work of us women is never done. My son David is fifteen and luckily too young to go to war, as yet. I'm praying the war will be over before he is. And even though he's a young man, there's still enough to be done at home, even with help, to keep me occupied. There's little time for current events unless you make the time. And I've been kept abreast of what's going on beyond our shores and let me tell you, Jo. It's shocking. What the Belgian people are going through is appalling. I only pray that Germany never reach our shores to do the same.'

Jo hadn't even really considered this. She thought of the war as being fought 'over there', far away from her own little life.

'They inna likely to, are they?' she asked Maria, with trepidation, always her source for the right opinion on things.

Maria hunched her shoulders. 'Nobody knows. Most people thought the war would be done by now, by the autumn. A storm in a teacup. But it's dragging on. And the Belgian people are bearing the brunt. In fact, they are fleeing the country in their tens of thousands, if not hundreds of thousands, streaming across the channel on boats and ships and anything they can get their hands on, leaving their homes and everything dear to them behind, to escape the German cruelty.'

Jo replied, 'Well, I'm very sorry to hear that. It's a terrible thing, to leave your home behind.'

And Jo knew something about that. She had had to leave her home when her mother died. She thought of how their things had been burnt. She thought of the little doll she'd left behind, lost for ever. Then, sensing that the women were not there for a run-of-the-mill social call, she gave them what she guessed they wanted and, after the horrible news from Belgium, what Jo found she wanted now too.

'What do you want me to do? I wanna help, in any way I can. You know from my suffragette days I'm handy in a battle. What can I do?'

The three women all visibly relaxed, glancing at each other.

Hettie replied, 'We want to recruit you for a new battle. A battle against tyranny. Belgian refugees are arriving at British ports in their thousands, day after day. A national refugee committee has been set up to help. And we have set up our own local committee to support the cause. The local committees are in constant contact with London in finding places all over the country for the refugees to go. We've set up our offices in an old empty barbershop in town.'

'I know the place,' said Jo. 'You used to work there, didna you, Maria?'

'A lifetime ago,' Maria said, looking wistful. 'I suggested it, as it's in the centre of town and has rooms upstairs as well. Enough room for a small band of ladies who wanna make a difference.'

'What do you need, then? You know I have Harry.'

'Of course,' Hettie replied. 'We need volunteers to help with the administration of the committee, reading and writing letters, helping with the reception of the refugees at the railway station, organising the offers of help and matching them with the refugees we have, helping the refugees to write home and find their relatives in other parts of our country. And much more. There's a lot to organise and a lot to do. There's the three of us and we'd like a fourth. You can bring Harry. All children are welcome. We'll take turns looking after them, summat that'd never happen in an office run by men! A proper women's collective. Are you up to it, Jo?'

Something to do again, something that wasn't home and motherhood and housewifery and boredom and isolation and rage. Something meaningful. Something good.

'I certainly am!'

A ripple of laughter went around the four of them and Jo felt a part of something again.

'There's more,' said Maria, and took Jo's hands in her own. 'And it's a lot to ask.'

'What is it?'

'Once we've received the first lot of refugees, all of us have agreed to have some to stay in our own homes. We want to show the town that we are willing to offer a place for these refugees, so that when we ask Ironbridge to help, we are already leading by example. So, would you take in a Belgian refugee, Jo? Welcome them in to stay in your home?'

Jo stared at Maria's earnest face. It was a lot to ask, she was right. And in their tiny house? She'd have to move Harry's cot in with her. They'd have to find a bed for the poor soul to sleep in, in Harry's room. But it'd be company, another adult in the world of baby needs and wants that a mother is heir to. She missed that keenly, since Alfie had left. But what do Belgian people eat? What do they wear? Do they speak English? Or do they only speak . . . Belgian, is it? What language do they speak in Belgium? She was ashamed of her utter ignorance. But whatever questions she had, there was one thing she knew for sure.

'Course I will. As long as it inna a man. I canna have Belgian boots dragging mud in all over my kitchen floor like Alfie does. It has to be a woman!'

Chapter 16

Brigitta

August to late October 1914

The journey was long. How long, Brigitta couldn't tell. She had nothing to compare it to, because her daily life had consisted of walking around town, or a ride to her grandparents' house, or a stroll to the park and back. That was a journey to Brigitta, only four years on this earth. On this trip, hours and days went past and blurred into one another. She slept when she could, often with her head in her mother's lap, on a milk cart, or in the house of a stranger. Or, more rarely, in a place that her mother called an inn, where the two of them could sometimes sleep for a night in the same bed, with the sounds of other people seeping through the walls, which was how it was in the apartment building back home, so Brigitta drifted off to sleep at the comforting sounds of other people's business, but mostly because she was so exhausted. Sometimes they slept secretly in buildings without telling anyone, like a farmer's hayloft, or one time in an abandoned church. The worst nights were sleeping under a tree or even just a hedge. Sometimes they were given food by kind people and other times they found scraps of food in the makeshift camps left behind by soldiers beside the roads. There were some days when they ate nothing and Brigitta's stomach would groan and twist and keep her awake. Those were the times when Brigitta cried.

They had nothing but the clothes they stood up in. Sometimes they washed from a jug and basin in a hostel or a stranger's house. Before now, Brigitta had never been interested in clothes and used to protest when her mother told her to change before visiting her grandparents or going to church. But now that she had only one set, and nothing to change into, she realised she missed the clothes she'd once had, like the little yellow pinafore she wore over her white dress. She missed that dress and wondered if any passing good Samaritan had saved it from the fire and might give it back to her one day. But she doubted it. And anyway, they were such a long way from home now, how would the Samaritan find her to give it to her?

Her mother did not have her purse. Brigitta knew that, in their normal life that they once had, before the bad men came, her mother had to give coins to strangers in shops and other inside places to buy things. Her mother had no coins now, so people would say no, or they'd say yes and they'd have a look on their face when they said yes, either annoyed or kindly. Some of them wore funny costumes and interesting hats. They looked like the bad men at first, but her mother assured her they were good men, on their side, good Belgian soldiers. Some asked lots of questions about why they didn't just go home. Brigitta wondered this too.

So, she asked her mother, 'When can we go home, Mama?'

Her mother said that their little apartment – with all of her books and her doll, her wooden blocks and her three puppets on strings – all were gone now, set on fire by the bad men, the German soldiers. This made Brigitta feel a medium-to-bad kind of sad, not the worst kind of sad, as that was reserved for when her father hadn't come home any more and she was told he was in heaven with God's angels, and Brigitta was angry with her father for choosing the angels over her and Mama, and with God for taking her father for Himself when Brigitta and her mother needed him the most. None of this seemed to matter any more, though, because only the journey mattered now, more than anything. They were going somewhere far away, like orphans in stories, walking through forests with bare feet and thorns prickling at their skin. At least Brigitta had shoes and socks. But her feet still hurt. Her bottom hurt too, from sitting on wooden carts where the big old horse or scruffy donkey would sway along so slowly, Brigitta thought it might be faster to walk. But also, she knew that poor sitting was better than good walking any day of the week.

Eventually, after a long time – definitely days, because there was dark and then light many, many times, but whether it was weeks or months or years, Brigitta wasn't sure – they reached the sea. Mama said it was called Ostend, and Brigitta guessed it was called that because it was the end of their journey.

'Are we going to live by the sea now, Mama?'

Brigitta quite liked this idea, though she missed her home in Leuven, a nice place of pear trees and red roofs. But the idea of the sea was exciting, although seeing it, churning greyly away by the docks they waited at, destroyed any ideas she might've had of the sea being somewhere she wanted to swim in. She couldn't even imagine a fish living in that water, with strange shimmering pools of oil on the surface, sometimes catching the light and making tiny rainbows, but still something she'd never dive into. Besides, her mother kept her away from the water. They were waiting for a big boat, apparently. Something to sail across the water to somewhere else, though she didn't know where.

There was another sea, next to the real one, and that was a

sea of people. Brigitta thought it looked like a sea because it had waves and was constantly moving. She had never seen so many people in such a small area in her short life. It felt as if a whole city had decamped and come to this corner of Belgium. It seemed as if everybody else in the country had had the same idea as her mother. The two of them waited at the docks for a long time, many more lights and darks proceeding, sometimes sleeping outside, sometimes at a house or inn, one where rowdy people shouted and drank beer from big glasses. They were from the ships, her mother said, which made Brigitta worry about going on the boat if there were rowdy people like that on them. For a few nights, they slept in a little wooden hut on the beach, where people used to change their bathing costumes. The town beyond the beach was heaving with Belgian soldiers, horses and wagons, and other people running away from the Germans. Many of them slept on the sand around their little wooden cabin. There were arguments outside and sometimes Brigitta couldn't sleep as she listened to people shouting. Everybody was scared and angry these days.

Finally, Mama told her they had a place on a boat. It was a fishing boat, with rough-looking men on board that once upon a time would've made Brigitta hide behind her mother's skirts, but nowadays she realised that nothing seemed to shock her any more. The things she'd seen in her city – the things on the streets, the dead things – all these had given her the strength of experience that meant she could look at scary things now and not look away. She wondered about this, if this was what it was like to be a grown-up. She knew it didn't matter whether she liked it or not, as it was just a fact. And after all, nobody cares what a little child wants when the whole world is on the road and everything has gone quite mad.

They went onto the fishing boat and the smell of dead fish was overwhelming. Brigitta thought she might faint. The stink filled every opening in her head, so much so that she would not only hold her nose and breathe through her mouth, but also shut her eyes and try to cover her ears by lying against Mama's belly or chest, to block it all out. She was sure she could stop the smell coming in if she did that. But it didn't work. There were lots of other people on the fishing boat who looked like them, with shabby clothes and no luggage, or perhaps a bundle of some things wrapped up in a blanket or bedsheet. Brigitta was annoyed with all these other people on what she saw as their boat. They'd waited such a long time for it. Why should they have to share?

'Will the boat sink with all these people?' whispered Brigitta to Mama, who shook her head and said not to worry, though Brigitta noticed that her mother eyed the others suspiciously.

They stayed on the boat for three days and two nights. Brigitta was sick over the side a number of times and there was little to eat or drink. She felt very weak and slept a lot. Her mother's face looked grey and she wondered if her mother would turn grey all over, grey hair, grey hands and feet and everything. But she didn't. The other people had babies who cried and men who looked like broken toys, hunched over. Brigitta hated to look at them. She hated the other people. They scared her. Sometimes, a man would yell about the bad soldiers back home, or point over the side of the boat and say there were German ships out there or bombs down there in the sea and they were all going to die. Brigitta's mother told her it wasn't true and not to fret. But maybe the men were right. They certainly seemed very sure of themselves, the way they shouted. Mostly, Brigitta hid inside her mother's arms and tried to pretend none of it was happening, picturing the way the sun would shine through the stained-glass windows in the cathedral, or the sound of her grandfather's voice reading her a story about a puppy, or the scent of her grandmother baking waffles. She didn't have many memories of her father, as they were fading away since he'd gone, which made her scold herself. It was wrong to forget him, surely.

When they eventually reached another place that looked like more docks, and her mother said it was England, and the boat slowed down and inched its way into port, Brigitta said to her mother, 'I will never eat fish again, not ever.'

After that, everything was even more strange. There were people at the port to meet them, as if they had invited them to a party they didn't know they'd been invited to. Everybody spoke a strange language where every single word was different from her own. Her mother said it was called English. It astounded Brigitta, that there could be a whole other country where everybody spoke this whole other language and didn't know a word of Flemish. Along with the other Belgian people from the boat, and snaking lines of many other Belgians, they wended their way through the streets of this English town to a railway station. Now, this was a thrilling prospect. Brigitta had been on a train only once, to visit friends of her mother in Antwerp, but that was all.

It was warm and comfortable on the railway carriage seat. She snuggled into her mother's side and slept the whole way there. When she woke up, she was desperately annoyed she'd missed it all. But needs must, as she was too tired to stay awake for anything. The train had taken them and all the other Belgians to a big city called London. When they got off the train, there were so many people waiting for them and cheering, she couldn't believe her eyes. Certainly more than ten, maybe a hundred, or a hundred times a hundred, she didn't know. But it took quite a long time to walk past all the cheering people, who were handing out gifts and her mother took some food for them, wrapped up in waxy paper, which Brigitta wolfed down, a kind of meaty pie. They also had bottles of drink, which she glugged down too, and that was fizzy and sweet and made her burp. Again, they had to walk a long way through the city and she was glad she'd slept in the train so that she wasn't too tired for yet another period of being on her feet. She thought that if she added up all the times in her head that she'd walked anywhere around Leuven in her whole life up to now, it wouldn't be as much or as long as all the walking she'd done in the last few weeks. Sometimes she thought her feet would simply fall off. She'd take a step one day and find her foot had been left behind her, rooted to the ground. But it hadn't happened yet.

The streets of London were sometimes shabby and full of shadows, other times bright and cheery, with avenues of trees. Eventually, the crowd slowed down and came to a halt, next to a huge building shaped like on oblong with a tall roof. Her mother said it was a warehouse and they were going to stay there for a few days. Filing in, Brigitta stood on tiptoes to try to see over the grown-up heads what a warehouse was and what their bedroom would be like, but it turned out there were no bedrooms, just one huge area, bigger than her favourite park at home, she reckoned. And laid out in rows as far as the eye could see were little, low beds with grey blankets on. Her mother was shown where to go and they found two beds together and sat on them. Her mother stroked her hair and she fell asleep again. They were there a few more days and nights and were given food and drink by kind people who her mother spoke to in English. Brigitta marvelled at how the foreign words came out of her mothers' mouth, like an incredible party trick. They gave them fresh clothes and a pillow case to keep them in. There was a bathroom with washbasins and toilets, but very few of them, so they'd have to wait a long time in queues to use them.

'Is this our new home?' Brigitta asked her mother.

The answer was no and Brigitta found that, not long after, they were taken to another railway station. This time there were two trains, one at London, and another at a place her mother told her was called Wellington. This time, Brigitta stayed awake some of the time and was delighted to find herself next to a window so she could see the world passing by. England was sometimes hilly and sometimes flat, sometimes green and sometimes brown. The sun shone quite a bit and then there was a brief yet dramatic rain storm, with water pelting against the windows. She saw a person in a field with square shoulders and no legs, just a coat flapping in the wind against a pole where its legs should be. Her mother said it was to scare away birds who'd eat the seeds. Brigitta found herself agreeing with the birds, as the legless body on a stick was rather terrifying. And then, finally, after half a day on the trains, her mother told her they were coming into the place they were going to stay for a while, a proper house, hopefully.

They were met by people again on the platform, not crowds cheering this time, as it was a much smaller railway station. But the faces of the women who greeted them were smiley and nice. As they walked from the railway station into a small town, Brigitta held tight to her mother's hand as they passed a huge metal bridge stretching across a deep, fast-moving river. They followed the smiley women to a little office, where Brigitta's mother was given bits of paper and wrote things down and spoke a while in English. One of the ladies had very green eyes and leant down to Brigitta and gave her a toy, a little teddy bear with stocky arms and legs sitting down, with black beads for eyes. His fur was soft and Brigitta held him tight to her chest. The lady with the green eyes said something kind to her mother, who stroked Brigitta's hair and looked proud.

Then the lady led them on a short walk away from the river and up a steep hill. Brigitta's little legs felt weak and shaky when they finally arrived at the door to someone's house. She had been on the longest journey that perhaps any explorer had ever made in the entire history of the world. She was so very tired, she thought she might actually fall asleep standing up, like horses do. Then she thought of the dead horses on the streets in Leuven and it made her want to cry. She wanted to go home. But she knew it was impossible. Home must be on the other side of the planet. And maybe her home wasn't even there any more. As the green-eyed lady knocked on the door of a little house on the hill, Brigitta tugged at her mother's sleeve.

'Where are we, Mama?'

Her mother looked down at her, licked her thumb and roughly removed a smudge from Brigitta's cheek.

Her mother replied, 'This place is called Ironbridge.'

Chapter 17

Jo

Late October 1914

Once Jo had been inducted into the Ironbridge Refugee Welfare Committee (IRWC for short) – as it was newly named by Hettie – she would take Harry with her to the old barber's shop and help out with their preparations for their first batch of Belgians, who were coming soon. There was so much to do, the four of them were run off their feet with it. Jo and Maria took it in turns to mind Harry, when he needed it, though he did have a good afternoon nap each day and they got plenty done then while he slumbered. Hettie did most of the typing as she was used to running her foundation, her fingers moving like a blur. Martha had a very clear speaking voice and bags of confidence, so she handled the telephone calls. They had to have a line connected in the old barber's shop specially.

Jo organised the filing of the paperwork by designing a good system of card folders in different drawers for different areas of the operation. Firstly, there was the organisation of offers from volunteers in Ironbridge, local people who'd offered a space in their home for a refugee or two. A pattern was developing: nobody wanted men. Most people wanted 'a young woman', or 'an orphan child', or even in one rather grisly example, 'any child who has been roughed up by the Hun'. Both Maria and Jo found themselves having to talk around people to the reality, that they couldn't guarantee any such thing and people were people and they all needed help, which didn't always go down well. Both Hettie and Martha ended up offering to take the bulk of male refugees that were going to come, as well as Charlie and Maria, who offered to take in any men with sons. But they were in the minority, though it had to be said, the number of people coming forwards offering their homes to strangers gladdened the heart.

Once the allocations were made, the other work involved finding ways to integrate the refugees into the community, so children could go to school, and perhaps employment could be found for the men, as well as the women without children. There was also the tricky matter of raising funds to buy extra food and drink to help the hosts, as well as items the guests would need, such as clothes and shoes, toys and books, pipes and tobacco and so forth, as they were told many would turn up with nothing on them, not a farthing to their name. Thus, with myriad responsibilities at the IRWC offices, there was always work to be done and, despite having their own roles, all of the four women mucked in with whatever needed doing at any given time. Despite their purpose having a deadly seriousness, Jo couldn't hide her joy at having something useful and interesting to do each day and she threw herself into the business with alacrity. She was having such a good time.

While Jo had been waiting for the first contingent of refugees to arrive in Ironbridge from London, she began to take note of what the newspapers reported about what was happening to 'plucky little Belgium', as it was so often called, in order to cure her previous ignorance. What she read appalled her. She couldn't actually believe what she was reading. It was the kind of thing that people read in those nasty little horror stories in 'penny dreadfuls' that her uncle, Mr Andrews, used to read when she was little. She had stolen some once and had quickly put them back, as they were ghastly and scared her. But this was no story. It was real life and it shocked her to the core. She had imagined arson and shootings, which were bad enough, but the details were barbaric. Belgian men tied up and forced to watch their wives and daughters ravished, after which all were bayonetted. Babies having their hands cut off and German soldiers even eating the choice cuts. And more . . . and more. It was all so . . . unthinkable. Did people really commit such horrors?

Jo asked Charlie, whose judgement in all matters of education she trusted more than anyone, if these horrific stories could possibly be true.

'I dunna doubt that the German army have been treating civilians badly as they make their way through Europe. Those accounts of setting fire to property and the lining up and shooting of civilians is happening all over, I wager. The same goes, sadly, for the . . . let's say, the compromising of women . . . which is often a casualty of war throughout the ages. However, I dunna reckon that the more, shall we say, colourful aspects of these stories are accurate. It smacks of propaganda. Governments will instruct, or allow, newspapers to cook up all these scandalous stories to bolster the war effort. If our country sees our enemy as monsters, then we'll keep on sending our sons to sort them out. And the newspapers sell more copies. The only people who really know what's going on over there are the Belgians themselves. And I would imagine that none of them want to talk about awful things like that, wouldna you?'

Jo agreed wholeheartedly. She had no intention of asking her refugees what had happened to them. It would be an appalling thing to do, somehow taking advantage, to force a person to talk about the greatest horror of their life. Perhaps Jo's guests would tell her something one day, perhaps not. It would be their choice, though, of course. Only if they would find it helpful. Jo knew all too well what it was to carry secret trauma around with you and how it burnt a hole in your soul.

When the day finally came that the first batch of refugees were to arrive at the railway station from London, Harry had a bit of a sniffle and Jo didn't want to risk taking him outside, so she agreed with the others that she would stay at home and wait for Hettie to bring her guests to the house. She was excited at the thought, though scolded herself for such a cheap emotion when these poor people had been through hell. She admitted to herself that she was pleased, though. Their tiny house had seemed positively cavernous since Alfie had left. She put Harry down for the night and waited. It was quite late in the evening when the knock came and she opened it to find Hettie and two others on her doorstep.

'This is Jo Woodvine, and she lives here with her baby son, Harry,' said Hettie, once Jo had welcomed the woman and her child into her parlour and closed the front door against the dark autumnal evening. 'Her husband Alfred is away at war.'

'Oh, everyone calls him Alfie,' said Jo, cheerfully. 'Whenever they let him come home on leave, you can call him Alfie, if you like. Oh, if you can speak English? Sorry, I didna think to ask.'

'I do speak English, thank you, Mrs Woodvine.'

The woman's English was impressive. She was very slight and small, while her daughter had long thin legs and was quite tall for a four-year-old. The child had sandy-brown hair in a bob, not unlike the short haircut Jo herself once had as a girl. The mother had her straight hair pulled up into a bun, a beautiful orangey-red, the colour of ripe pumpkin. Jo was often envious of other people's hair and this woman's was stunning. Both the mother and her child had deep dark rings underneath their eyes and their skin was pale. They looked as if they hadn't slept for a year. Jo's heart ached for them. She just wanted to tuck them both up in bed and give them steaming hot soup in mugs.

'It's an honour to have you here in my home, Martine, and to meet this lovely young lady, Brigitta. What pretty names.'

Jo smiled particularly at the little girl, who nestled into her mother's side, clutching a teddy bear and burying her face so that Jo couldn't see her. Brigitta's shyness resonated with Jo keenly. She hoped one day the child would get used to her.

'Brigitta speaks no English. I am sorry.'

'No need to be. Your English is proper good. I dunna know a word of Flemish!'

Jo had educated herself somewhat since knowing she would be having some refugees to stay from Flanders.

Hettie said her goodbyes and left, leaving the three of them alone. The mother and child stood stiffly in the middle of the parlour, Martine holding on to a pillow case that seemed to contain all their worldly goods. Jo showed them the kitchen and took them outside briefly to see where the privy was.

'Come with me upstairs to see your room,' said Jo, and kept smiling at them, as neither had managed a smile yet, so Jo felt she was smiling enough for all of them. She couldn't even begin to imagine what they'd been through.

The committee had helped Jo get two beds into the nursery: one adult and one child-sized. There wasn't much room for anything else in there, but Jo had found a cheap bedside table at a junk shop and popped that in there, so at least they had something to put a glass of water on. She'd left the framed pictures on the wall that Harry had looked at from his cot since he was old enough to see properly. One was the alphabet, given by Charlie, with every letter represented by a different colourful animal or object. The other picture was a reproduction of a painting of Peter Rabbit from the books by Beatrix Potter that had come out a few years before. Maria had bought the book for Harry and then Jo found a colour illustration of the bunny enjoying carrots while a red-breasted robin watched on, perched on a spade handle. She loved the image, as it made her think of Alfie at work in the garden. When she showed the child her bed, the girl sat down on it and stared at the painting.

'Rabbit,' said Jo to Brigitta, and smiled.

Brigitta glanced nervously at her mother, who nodded and said, '*Konijn* . . . rabbit.'

The girl drew her teddy bear up beneath her chin and held it there, saying nothing.

'I'm gonna fetch you two summat to eat and drink,' said Jo to Martine.

'Please do not. We are so tired. We wish to sleep only. But I thank you.'

'If you're sure? How about a glass of water each?'

Martine paused, then nodded.

'Water would be good.'

Before going to fetch them their drinks, Jo popped in to her bedroom to look into the cot, now placed beside her bed. Harry was fast asleep, unaware of their new visitors, one arm up above his head, the other across his little chest that rose and fell, rose and fell. The relief of seeing her child breathing in and out, in and out, never passed. Jo smiled down at him and, ever so gently, brushed a fingertip against his soft yellow fringe. Then, she found herself welling up, filled with an unexpected wave of emotion. She suddenly thought of what it would be like to have your child see the terrible things these poor people must have seen. From the moment of the quickening, when she'd first felt her baby move in the womb, she had a keen sense that her job on this earth was to keep it alive, whatever that took. To think of all the months, weeks, days and minutes she'd laboured over this, to keep Harry healthy and happy, and she'd found it hard, very hard at points. And this poor woman, Martine, had no doubt done the same, until history moved against her.

Jo sniffed and wiped her eyes, went downstairs and filled two glasses from the tap. She popped two apples into her apron pockets too, just in case the guests awoke in the night and felt hungry. She took them upstairs and the door was still open, so she waited outside and said, 'Knock knock', just in case they were changing.

'Enter,' said Martine and Jo did so, seeing that Brigitta was already changed into a plain shift and was sitting up in her bed.

Jo handed the water and apple to each of them and said, 'I'll wish you good night, then. We'll sort everything out tomorrow. Just get some rest for now and sleep as long as you like.'

Martine said, 'Thank you. With my heart. I thank you with my heart.' Her eyes were shining and Brigitta was watching her, her eyes wide with concern.

'Oh, dunna fret, please. It's naught. I'm so happy to help. You dunna know how much. It takes me . . . out of myself. I probably canna explain it properly. But please know that you're helping me just as much. We're so happy to have you both here. You'll meet Harry in the morning and he'll love having you both too. He's quite bored of his old mum, now that his dad's away. He'll be bowled over to see a pretty girl in his house. Anyway, I'll stop rattling on. Good night, Martine. Good night, Brigitta.'

Brigitta looked at Jo and took a sharp breath, then held it. Jo waited with bated breath. Was the shy little Belgian girl going to speak at last?

'Rab-bit,' said Brigitta.

Chapter 18

Jo

November 1914 to May 1915

Jo's work at the refugee office continued throughout the autumn, all while the town of Ironbridge got used to its new inhabitants and they got used to the town of Ironbridge. Many local families took in refugees, particularly those with farms, where they made no bones about welcoming cheap labour. Quite a few of the men went to stay on farms. Still, almost nobody else wanted men to stay with them, yet – true to their word – Maria and Charlie took in two men, a middle-aged man and his adult son, who found work at a local factory and spent a lot of their time there, coming and going from the schoolhouse mostly only to sleep. The IRWC organised for the children to go to Charlie's school, while English lessons for adults were put on two evenings a week by Charlie. Some of the poorest families who'd come needed significant financial help, as they possessed nothing at all, so the IRWC raised funds to provide them with an allowance, so that they could be self-supporting and thus not have to bother anyone in order to provide themselves with the essentials. Martha also set up a project to help some of the refugees try to find lost relatives, helping them to write letters in English to the British authorities in order to look for them. It seemed that the flight of the innocents from Belgium had been characterised by utter chaos, as so many had lost family members in the crush and commotion of a fleeing population.

Meanwhile, at home, Jo and Martine settled into a routine. Brigitta still didn't speak much, only whispering to her mother. She'd been through a lot, poor poppet, Jo reminded herself, knowing she'd just have to be patient. After they'd been there around a week or so, Charlie persuaded Martine that Brigitta should come to school. He'd look out for her and it would be good for her to have people her own age around, and give her an opportunity to speak English. Jo agreed and told Martine that she'd been a pupil at her father-in-law's school once upon a time, and Charlie had indeed looked out for her and, since she was shy and hadn't made friends easily, Charlie had made school bearable for her.

The two of them were sitting on the settee in the parlour drinking tea, while Brigitta played silently on the floor with some wooden blocks that Jo had given to her, and Harry sat in his play pen by the window, a book on zoo animals beside him totally ignored while he bashed his own blocks together and chewed on them too.

'Charlie is a good man,' said Martine to Jo.

'The best,' replied Jo, nodding. 'I've been very lucky to know the Woodvines.'

'You are a close family?'

'Very. We're always in and out of each other's houses.'

'Charlie and his wife, they are not . . . your blood?' asked Martine, clearly wondering if her English was correct.

'That's right. They're my husband's parents.'

Martine told her, 'The parents of my husband are still in

Leuven, my city, in Belgium. I do not know if they are alive. Their house was burnt. I do not know where to write to.'

'We can help you with that, at the IRWC, the office where you first came when you arrived. We write letters to try to find lost relatives. We can write to the council in your city and ask them to look into it. Would you like me to sort that for you?'

'Oh, yes, yes, please,' said Martine, looking energised and relieved. 'They are very good people. And they love my daughter very much. I want to know . . . I want them to know we are safe. And I want to know . . . if they . . .'

Martine paused and glanced at her daughter.

'She dunna understand you in English, remember? You can say things,' said Jo, gently.

'Yes, of course. I forget. Yes, I want to know if they are living.'

'I'm sure they are,' said Jo, and poured them both another cuppa, the tea leaves caught in a damp heap in the strainer.

Martine went on, 'Charlie and Maria are the parents of your husband, so where are your parents? Do they live away from here?'

'Oh, they're gone. Ever such a long time ago. Both gone before I was ten years old.'

A shadow passed over Jo, as it did every time she considered her parents.

'I am sorry. I know what it is to lose parents.'

'I'm sorry too,' said Jo, then hesitated. Should she ask her about it? Was that prying? She wanted Martine to know that she could tell her things if she wanted to but it felt too intrusive.

'They did not die in the war, if you are thinking this. They died a long time ago, when I was a young woman. They had the disease . . . in the chest . . .'

'The flu?'

'Yes? I think so?'

'Influenza.'

'Yes, yes. When I was only sixteen.'

'Something we've got in common, then,' said Jo, softly.

Martine smiled at her, her first. A small smile, but a smile nonetheless.

'Your English is so good, you know,' said Jo, wanting that smile to stay or even increase. It did the trick as Martine smiled broadly.

'You are kind but I am very certain it is not good.'

'Are you joking? You speak better than half the folk round here. You say "did not" instead of "didna", for a start!'

Martine sat up and said, 'Yes, yes, I have noticed this. It is very interesting. Here in Ironbridge you have a way of saying things. It is different from the English I learnt from my mother.'

'It's just the Shroppie way,' said Jo.

'What is this . . . Shroppie?'

'Ironbridge is in the county of Shropshire, so we have our own "Shroppie" way of saying things here. Someone in another part of England, a posh person, who speaks proper English, might say . . . let me think . . . they'd say, "I do not want to wait for my ham pie because I am very hungry." But a Shroppie would say, "I dunna wanna wait for me fidget pie as I'm proper clemmed!"'

Martine stared at her. Then laughed. Her first laugh in Ironbridge!

'This is not English. This is another foreign language!' said Martine, still laughing.

'It's just Shroppie talk! It's how we all speak. Me, Alfie. Even his dad, who's a schoolteacher and teaches proper English.'

'And your husband, Alfred, you met here at the school of Charlie?'

Jo grinned. 'Yes, I did. We've known each other since we were little'uns, me and Alfie. He took care of me, all my life since then. We married at eighteen.'

'The same for me!' said Martine, and then Jo saw that same shadow – the one she had felt following her all her life – fall across Martine's face too, wiping out the fun of the last minute or so. 'But he is dead now.'

It sounded so harsh. But Jo figured that was because of the language barrier, rather than Martine's feelings, as she was visibly moved.

'So many are lost to this war,' Jo replied. 'It's so wrong.'

'Oh, my husband was not dead in the war. He died last year. It was a stupid death.'

'Oh!' replied Jo, again trying to remember that the words came out differently when it wasn't your mother tongue.

'Yes, last year, he visited Brussels for work. He took a journey on an electric tram. It – how do you say . . . fell? On the side?'

'Tipped over?'

'Yes, the tram tipped over on a sharp bend and three people were killed. My husband was one of the three people. My daughter looks very like him. I see him in her face, her eyes, her hair. I see him all the time.'

To think, this war was killing people by the tens of thousands, military and civilian alike, and yet poor Martine had lost all her loved ones in twists of fate. It seemed so utterly unfair.

'Martine,' said Jo, at a loss for words yet knowing she must say something. 'I just want to say that I have lost people I've cared about too and I know we have had very different lives. But I want you to know that I can be a friend to you and I'm a good listener, if you ever need to talk about . . . things.'

Martine looked at Jo keenly then, her blue eyes quite wonderfully intense against the contrast of her red hair.

'You are the most kindest person of all of the English people,' said Martine.

Jo loved the way she talked, the funny little quirks she had. She realised she was growing very fond of Martine. Somehow they just . . . understood each other.

'What was your husband's name?' Jo asked her.

'Emiel.'

Martine's eyes were shining now.

'Let's raise a tea cup to Emiel. That's an English custom. Or at least, it's usually a pint of beer. Or a glass of wine. But tea will have to do.'

She lifted up her cup from the saucer and Martine did likewise.

'To Emiel,' said Jo.

'To Emiel,' said Martine, and Jo clinked her cup against Martine's and the moment was solemn, yet comforting. But it didn't last long, as Harry was suddenly bored of his games and wanted attention. The two women set to dealing with the children. It was lovely to have company around the clock. Who'd have thought, back when Harry was a few weeks old and Jo felt so utterly alone, that one day she'd be sitting in her parlour with a Belgian refugee who was making Harry laugh by pointing to the zoo animals in his book and making all the noises? Even Brigitta joined in, mooing and bleating. Some things transcended language. And it was so nice to be all girls together too. Except baby Harry, of course, but as a baby, he could be an honorary female for the time being, until he grew into a boy. Then Jo feared she would lose him to the world of men for ever. After sharing a house with only a husband and son, now the females were in the majority in her home, and Jo recalled how this was something she'd dreaded as a child with her cousins or at school. Now, it felt comforting and safe.

That didn't mean she didn't miss Alfie, though. She still curled up on her side of the bed every night and put out an arm, feeling the coolness of the sheet where he had not slept in months. She missed his body curled around hers as he slept, the weight of him on top of her as they made love, the solid presence of him in every room or pottering about with seeds in the back yard. The thought that he could be dead already assaulted her now and again but she would push it down and flatten it and stamp on it, as she would not entertain the idea. She would know if he were dead, she was sure of it. A person can't be that close to another person and not know if they're gone from the world. Surely he was still alive and the war simply kept them very, very busy.

Every now and again, she'd ask Charlie when they would let him come home on leave, but Charlie couldn't provide an answer. He said it'd probably happen suddenly, when they were least expecting it and to try not to think about it. Alfie's rare letters revealed so little, it remained a mystery. Jo wrote to him regularly and his parents also sent food parcels, wrapped in cloth. But none of them heard much back from him. Jo thought about how it would be, when Alfie came home, and how it might make Martine feel sad, about losing Emiel, and Brigitta, about losing her father. So Jo told herself she must remember to be circumspect and not go around flaunting her love for Alfie in front of their guests. She'd have to explain this quietly to Alfie when he arrived. Whenever, in God's name, that might be, as the months stretched on, past quite a jolly Christmas, which they all spent at the Woodvines' house, eating one of Charlie's chickens he now kept in the back garden. Spring came and still no sign, as the snowdrops came and went, the bluebells came and went, and then it was May, and the daffodils and jonquils were past their best, wilting and forlorn, the yellow petal edges crisping brown.

And then, quite late one evening, Alfie turned up at the door, out of the blue, just as Charlie had predicted.

Chapter 19

Jo

May to August 1915

The front door opened and Martine and Jo had literally jumped with fright, never expecting such a thing.

Then, there he was, Private Alfred Woodvine, in his khaki, standing in the parlour, large as life.

'Mrs Woodvine,' he said, and grinned at her. Oh, that smile!

Jo didn't even think. She lurched out of her chair and threw herself at him, burying herself in his embrace. Then, she remembered they were not alone and was mortified, not only from her lack of decorum but what she had promised to herself she wouldn't do: making Martine feel sad.

She extricated herself and turned to Martine.

'I'm so sorry,' she began. 'Alfie . . . erm . . . this is Martine De Bakker, our guest from Belgium. Her daughter Brigitta is sleeping upstairs. I did write and tell you about it but I've not heard a thing from you in months.'

Martine stood up immediately and held out her hand.

Alfie took it and shook it heartily.

'Alfie Woodvine.'

'It is my pleasure of meeting you,' said Martine. 'And please,

Jo, there is nothing for sorry about it. I find I am very tired and must join my daughter upstairs. I hope I am not being terribly rude to Mr Woodvine but I feel I must sleep a very long time.'

'Call me Alfie,' he said, smiling warmly.

'Thank you and I retire now. Goodnight, the Woodvines.'

They wished her goodnight too and went to the kitchen, hearing her steps recede up the stairs all the while.

Once alone, against the kitchen cupboards, they kissed and kissed and kissed for all they were worth, and held on to each other as if it were the last night on earth. Jo felt quite overwhelmed with her strength of feeling. She knew she loved Alfie but somehow she'd got used to not really having any physical contact with grown-ups and convinced herself she didn't miss it. But having her husband's body, here in front of her, willing and hungry for her, she gave herself up to it and was surprised and delighted at how much she wanted him, and he wanted her. They hadn't even spoken a word since Martine left them. They kept an ear out for any steps on the stairs as they manoeuvred themselves to carry out their conjugal rights up against the sink in the kitchen, gasping as quietly as they could manage, the kitchen curtains in a teapot print the only barrier to protect their modesty from the neighbours. And oh, it was bloody marvellous.

They did that a lot in the first couple of days. Not in the kitchen, heaven forbid (after the first time, when they physically could not stop themselves), but in their bedroom, even though it was right up against the room where Martine and Brigitta slept, and baby Harry was in with them. Every chance he got, Alfie was either wrapped up in her, or picking up Harry, who he took from his cot when he was sleeping, just to hold him, which normally Jo would highly disapprove of. But in the circumstances, she just let him, of course. He doted on his son and called him 'little chapper' over and over again. He marvelled out how much his son had grown and the things he could do now he hadn't been able to do before. At times like these, Alfie's face would fall into a glazed expression, as if he were a thousand miles away, Jo noted.

It turned out Alfie was only there for four days and five nights. Four days! It seemed criminal, to let a man come all the way home from France and then let him stay for such a paltry length. His parents wanted to spend a lot of time with him too, and Jo understood, of course, but she felt the days ticking away, second by second, as he helped his father in the garden, or went for a walk by the river with his mother and Snap, who was also thrilled to see Alfie, if Snap's wildly wagging tail was anything to go by.

The days went by far too quickly. Alfie was cheerful, chatting with Martine and even trying to make Brigitta smile, but she was frightened of him and hid behind her mother the whole time. Jo tried to explain it to him, what she must have been through, but she could tell it bothered Alfie.

'It's not you,' she said to him one night.

'I know,' he said. 'I know about fear.'

His voice was strange, low, strangled. She asked him then, about fear. She asked him to tell her about the war. But he wouldn't.

'There's nothing to tell. We dig a lot. We wait around a lot. Little flurries of activity and then naught. It's mostly mud and rain. It's chalk country where we are, but the chalk is a few feet down under the topsoil and it's clay on top, which makes for hard digging. We have these entrenching tools with a spade on one side and a pick on the other, and you use the pick to break up the chalk. And in wet weather, the clay mud gets very sticky and water-logged. You're swimming in it. I'd never choose a garden with clay soil. There are other bits where the chalk is nearer the surface and, if the fields weren't all ruined, you'd get chicory and juniper growing there maybe, or hawthorn, spindle bush or the wayfaring tree. And poppies, of course. Poppies love chalk. Before I came back just now, I'd see poppies springing up here and there in the churned-up soil. Those wild red poppies, the seeds stay in the ground for years, you know, decades even. And they start coming up when the soil is disturbed. That's why there are poppies on the battlefields.'

She let him talk. He clearly needed to. It was more like a treatise on gardening. And she knew him well enough to know that he spoke about that because he didn't want to speak about the other business, the war business. That was all he would say. She didn't want to push him but also she was acutely aware that he would be gone so soon and she'd have to wait again for a long time to hear more. She made him promise to write. He said he'd try. He was leaving the next day and his cheeriness was ebbing away as the night receded. They went to bed and didn't make love. He held on to her and slept for a while, then he woke up suddenly, and Jo woke too, and felt he was drenched in sweat.

'Are you ill?'

Alfie replied grimly, 'Unfortunately not.'

They went back to sleep. But later that night, she woke up again and saw he was out of bed. He was standing over Harry's cot and watching him sleep. Then, Alfie sobbed and stifled it, his hand over his mouth. Jo did not move a muscle. She didn't want him to know she was awake and had seen him, had heard him make that sound. She knew Alfie wouldn't want her to see him that way.

He turned and she closed her eyes quickly, feigning sleep. He went over to the window and opened it. It was a warm night and the cool breeze that came in was welcome. She opened her eyes again and watched him standing at the window, staring into the darkness.

Then, in the distance, softly and eerily, came the hoot of an owl. Alfie seemed transfixed by it. The sound came again, a little louder each time. It was coming closer.

Alfie turned quickly and looked at Jo. She kept her eyes open this time.

'An owl,' she said.

'Tawny owl,' he said. 'A male.'

'You know things,' she said, and smiled at him.

'What things?'

'Just things. About birds and such.'

'I know about birds because there's stacks of them at Rowland Hall. I'll teach them all to Harry one day, you'll see. When he's old enough. I'll tell him about the old heron at the hall. I'll bring him to see it one day.'

The uncertain outcome of that intention hovered between them, palpable as smoke.

'What old heron?' Jo said, to break the spell.

'He's been there years, so Cork says. Twenty years, he reckons.'

'Can birds live that long?'

'This one has. Young'uns are vulnerable and can die young. But if they survive to adulthood, a heron can live five years, or ten, or fifteen or more. He's a wise old bird, our heron. He keeps eating the fish in the ornamental pond. Wily old thing.'

Jo had a sudden fear that came upon her in a rush, that she didn't know Alfie knew so much about birds. How had she known him all these years and never knew that he knew so much about birds?

'There are so many things I dunna know about you,' she said, sitting up quickly.

'Nay, there inna. I'm a simple soul, me.'

'Nay, you inna. I didna know about you and birds.'

She felt an urgent need to find out everything about him she didn't know, as time was running out.

'What's your favourite bird?'

They heard the tawny owl hoot again outside, as if vying for the position.

'Not owls. They're like ghosts.' Alfie shuddered. 'Herons, I'd say. Herons are . . . majestic. And mysterious.'

'Come back to bed,' she said.

He did so and curled up in her arms as she sat up, his head on her chest.

They sat in silence for a time, listening to the owl, and to each other's breathing.

Then, she asked him, her voice low, 'What inna you telling me?'

'Naught,' he said.

'But it inna naught. You're away with the war and all you've told me is that you sit in a trench all day and get rained on and the men are nice and you play cards and it's mostly deadly dull. That canna be everything. There's more, I know there is.'

Alfie sighed, a long, deep sigh that made him suddenly seem much older than his twenty-one years. He extricated himself from her arms and sat up, looking her straight in the eye.

'I promise you there inna anything more to tell. War is . . . naught. It's naught. You know I can never keep secrets from you, just like you can never keep secrets from me. Dunna worry.'

'I dunna believe you. Tell me. It'll take a weight off,' she said, and he drew her in for a cuddle.

He was quiet for a time as they lay together. She couldn't see his face. She was buried in their embrace. Then he murmured, 'It's . . . too . . . awful.'

She sat very still. 'I can cope with awful things.'

'Not . . . like this. I've seen . . . awful things.'

'I've seen awful things too.'

He withdrew from her then and pushed himself up resting on an elbow. 'Not like this. Nobody has seen these things, ever. Only soldiers. It's . . . it inna for wives. It's too awful to tell.'

'I've seen the worst thing possible,' she said, as her heart started beating faster. She felt light-headed.

He frowned.

'But . . . what? What have you seen? Those newsreels? They dunna tell the truth of it. Nobody can understand, unless they've seen it in real life.'

'Nay, I've seen, in real life. The worst thing. I never told you. I never told anyone. If I can tell you that, you can tell me what you've seen. Then we'll be equal. And you'll have the weight taken from you.'

He pulled himself up to sitting cross-legged on the bed. 'Now I mun know. What is it? Are you all right? What's happened?'

She felt the room might spin if she said it. But she needed him to know, that she had been to dark places in her life. And now that he had too, after his golden childhood, she felt ready to share it. She wouldn't have wished his horror on him for one second, but at least now, she might be able to tell him and relieve her own burden, to persuade him to relieve his.

'I saw my mother murder my father when I was six years old.'

Jo tried to read Alfie's face, to see his reaction. Would it be horror? Disgust? Pity? Had she gone too far by telling him? There was killing in war. That was one thing. But this . . . was something altogether different.

'How?' he said quietly. His face betrayed little, but it wasn't appalled, at least.

'She put a pillow over his face and he struggled. Then he

wasna struggling any more. He was a drunk and he beat her before that. So, she ended him.'

She watched as Alfie's eyes filled with tears. She'd never seen him do that before. She felt a catch in her throat and wanted to cry too. She couldn't believe she'd finally told someone, after all these years. Told Alfie, her rock.

'I'm so sorry that happened to you,' he croaked, wiping away tears. 'Christ, what a baby I am.'

'Dunna be daft!' she cried, and reached out, brushed his cheek with her fingertips. The wet of his tears felt sacred to her.

'What a . . . terrible . . . dreadful thing for a child. And you held it inside, for all this time?'

'I did,' she said, with a grim smile. 'I had to, at first. I couldna get my mother in trouble. And then, once she'd gone, it didna seem right, to tell it. It wouldna do any good. And folk'd think she was a wrong'un.'

Alfie shook his head emphatically. 'Nay, not a wrong'un. She did it to save herself. And you.'

Jo nodded, the tears rolling down her face now.

'You went through all that,' he said, 'and came to our school. You were so alone. So small. Everyone called you little Jo.'

'I was little. I still am,' she said, and smiled through the tears.

'Nay. You were mighty, inside. I could see that early on. But you, you went through all that, alone. You held it in, all this time. It . . . oh, God, Jo, it breaks my heart.'

He took her in his arms and they both shuddered, trying to keep in the emotion that threatened to drown them, and to keep their sadness silent, so that Harry didn't wake up, and the others didn't hear them in the next room. When the wave had subsided somewhat, she sat back up and put her hand on his arm.

'Your turn now,' she managed to say.

Alfie stared straight ahead of him. She could tell he was seeing things in his mind. Terrible things.

'I dunna . . . I canna . . .' he muttered.

'You can.'

He blinked, twice, three times.

'It's like . . . naught on earth. Just . . . death. Death. Everywhere. Men. Reduced to . . . bodies. Body parts. Like butchery. People . . . a man, you just spoke to. And then . . . a shell. Or a rifle. A grenade. Or machine gun. And then . . . But after . . . not even . . . nowhere to rest. Nowhere to put him to rest, to honour . . . to honour him. And then . . .'

He hunched his shoulders and wiped his nose with the back of his hand, still staring into space.

'And then, you carry on. It's . . . a kind of . . . it's a sort of madness.'

He broke down then, but clamped his hand over his mouth, to do it silently. She tried to hold on to him, but he stayed sitting up stiffly.

He turned to her and said, 'And that's all I'll ever say about that. I said what I said . . . to honour you. Your pain. What you'd been through. But you'll never catch me speaking of it more. I dunna want those pictures in your head. Not in your head, or my son's, or my parents. Not in the heads of the innocent. That's the one thing I can do in this bloody mess. I can protect you, all of you. From the truth.'

She wanted him to unburden himself more, but she sensed, too, that it didn't help him, as she thought it would. It made it worse, somehow. She pulled him close to her and stroked his hair. They lay like that for a while, a time she wished would never end. Eventually they slept, fitfully.

When it was time to get up and ready, he smiled wanly at her and said, 'Dunna worry, Jo.'

But she did worry, of course, and she would worry, for

every moment that passed until he was in her arms again. The family went down to the railway station with him to see him off, Martine and Brigitta too. Charlie kept telling him he must take the train to Wellington via Ketley, and then he'd be taking the GWR route via Birmingham Snow Hill to Paddington and it'd take about four hours if he was lucky, and Alfie kept saying he knew that because he'd done it on the way down and his dad needed to stop fussing. But everyone knew it was Charlie's way of covering up his own worries. Maria said little. She was always like that when things were difficult. Martine led Brigitta away down the platform when the moment came for Jo to say goodbye, to give them and their family privacy. Jo held on to him too long and the conductor was calling for people to 'entrain presently', which Jo thought Martine would like as an example of the English language, but she knew her mind was racing because she could not bear to let her husband go.

But he did go. And the train went. And the months passed.

Before she knew it, summer came to Ironbridge and she took Harry, Martine and Brigitta to play in the shallows of the Severn. At times like that, Jo thought, it seemed impossible that only a hop and a skip away over the English Channel, Alfie and the King's Shropshire Light Infantry were sitting in trenches, at war with Germany, surrounded by death, while she held their son safe as they paddled in the river, the weight of the water surging against them, and the same summer sun shone down on all of their heads.

Chapter 20

Alfie

September 1915

Private Alfred Woodvine of the 6th (Service) Battalion, King's Shropshire Light Infantry, was engaged in that morning's stand-to, sitting next to the sentry on the fire-step, an affable chap from Yorkshire called Precious. The third of the three-man team in their bay was Chadwick, another Yorkshireman. They'd been drafted into this battalion due to losses in the KSLI. It started off with only Shropshire men, but not any longer. Too many had been killed and needed replacing. Alfie was resting up against Precious's leg, while Chadwick was trying to sleep. Precious was gazing through the box periscope and if he saw anything of note out there beyond the trench, he'd give Alfie a kick to come and double-check it for him, hence the close proximity. It occurred to Alfie that he'd spent more time nudged up against men in this regiment than he'd touched another human in his life, save his family. War certainly was a leveller in some ways. They had to carry out a stand-to twice a day, before dawn and dusk, because that was when the Hun would be most likely to launch an attack. He wondered why at first, then someone told him it was because at those times of dull light it would be damned hard to get a sight on the enemy with a rifle. Alfie looked up at the sky, willing the dawn to come and go sooner. A watched pot never boils, he remembered his mother saying to him as an impatient child. But Alfie was ravenous. He kept thinking about bacon and licking his lips. Precious hadn't shifted his feet in ages, so Alfie looked up at him and whispered, 'Anything?'

'Nowt,' whispered Precious.

Chadwick started snoring.

'Lucky bastard,' muttered Alfie, giving Chadwick a kick to quieten down.

As the sky eventually lightened, the order came to stand down. Alfie nudged Chadwick to wake him up. The three men were relieved and went to get their breakfasts. Walking down the trench, it occurred to Alfie how odd it was that men could make a hole in the ground look so homely: an overcoat hanging on a peg here, a blanket on a bed of sandbags there. Alfie and the other two collected their mess tins, three parts of which were filled with water. The water they were given always tasted of chlorine and petrol. They went back to their spot and put their tins on the hob, lit by chips of firewood, to get the water boiling. Tea and sugar were applied, then Precious went to the chap who had the milk and gave Alfie and Chadwick a bit, from the hole punched near the edge of the tin lid. You couldn't leave milk out or the rats would snaffle it. Now it was time to sizzle that bacon. Alfie lifted his mess tin lid and popped in his bacon and breathed in the delicious scent. Chadwick had some bread for them all and Alfie shoved a piece in to soak up the bacon fat.

Precious started to chat, about this girl he'd been seeing back in Yorkshire.

'Helena, her name is. Such a grand name, sounds posh. But she's a working-class lass, like me.'

'You're a lass, that's for sure,' said Chadwick.

Alfie grinned, wiping the tin with his bread for the last dregs of grease.

Precious ignored him and went on. 'She works at a big hall up in't little village of Ravenscar. You know those two officers, brothers?'

'Lazenby?' asked Alfie. He'd seen them around, both good chaps. Some of the officers acted like you were dirt, but they didn't. They talked to you and didn't talk down to you. They didn't act all high and mighty, like some of the hoity-toity ones did. Alfie thought how you'd imagine war would bring men together, make them all equal in the face of death. But the old divisions were still there, heightened if anything, the haves and have nots. Yet, he had to admit, the officers were killed just as easily and as often as ordinary blokes like him. Death didn't care how much money your parents had.

'Aye, the Lazenbys. That's their home, where my Helena works. Raven Hall. They signed up together, the Lazenby brothers, serving together. Big sweeping hall where they grew up. Views across the sea to Robin Hood's Bay. Stunning views, up there.'

'All right for some,' muttered Chadwick. Alfie mused that some days you wanted to hear about life back home. Some days you didn't.

'Helena likes it. It's a good job, good pay. Her mistress is nice, so Helena says. They call her by her last name, Bairstow. Bairstow, do this, do that, fetch my slippers. Seems wrong to call a pretty young thing by her last name. And she's pretty, by gum. The legs on her. All the way up to here. Never seen legs like that.'

'Playing with fire, Precious? What about thi wife?' said Chadwick.

Precious sniffed and replied, 'It's a time of war, gentleman. All t'rules are different. All bets are off.'

'You'd better watch thissen or your wife'll be chasing you up t'trench with a rolling pin. More deadly by far than t'Hun.'

Alfie laughed at that. Chadwick was always ribbing Precious, who got so high-handed about things, Chadwick couldn't resist and it made Alfie laugh. They all needed to laugh, amid all this.

'If you saw my Helena's legs, you'd understand. They should win prizes.'

Alfie shook his head. He couldn't imagine wanting anyone but Jo. He'd adored her since their school days and could never not love her. He missed everything about her, even her complaining. It all felt silly now, their old bickering. Alfie was sure it had all been just the strain of having a new babby in the house. Jo was so much brighter now and, the last time he'd seen her, it was like they were two young'uns again, all over each other like a rash. Alfie smiled at the thought of them in bed that last time, leaving the sheets all ruched up like that, even though Harry was in the room, fast asleep though, of course. At any thought of Harry, Alfie would feel a deep twinge inside. He missed his little son like a hole in his heart. He just hoped he could make his son proud. Sometimes, if he considered it too much, he'd feel himself getting desperate at the thought, that if he died that day, or any day in this bloody war, his son would never know him.

'Stop brooding, Woodvine,' said Chadwick, eyeing him knowingly.

'I inna brooding,' lied Alfie. 'I'm wondering what manner of prize would be awarded for the best legs, if you'd get a pound per leg or a guinea for both.'

'I wouldn't give that'un a penny,' said Chadwick, nodding at a boot sticking out of the trench wall behind them, attached to a bit of some poor chap's leg who'd had it blown off. It had been there for days. Nobody had the heart to pull it out.

That was often the way. Conversations in the trench veered between memories of home and the grim reality of their present situation. Humour helped, usually. Nobody laughed at the leg that day, though. They were tired. They'd been up at the front for nine days. They were all ready for a break.

Alfie had left a bit of tea in his tin and dipped in a cloth and used it to wipe his face. That was about the height of cleanliness when they were up at the front for a few days. After that, the last little bit of tea was used for shaving. The three of them got their brushes out, lathered up in the dregs of tea and shaved. With the barbarity of war around them, it seemed a quaint thing to keep up appearances this way, but Alfie supposed that if they didn't, after a few days, they'd all look like tramps sleeping under a hedge, which they actually were, in a way.

Precious went off in a huff and Chadwick grinned at Alfie. A nice fellow, Chadwick, from Bradford. He worked in the textiles industry and his fiancée was a nurse called Dorothy. He told Alfie yesterday that he couldn't wait to see her eyes again, so pretty they were. And trusting. That was the word he'd used, that she had 'trusting' eyes. Alfie knew exactly what Chadwick meant and thought about how important it was to keep them that way, keep them innocent, like he'd told Jo. Chadwick told Alfie little snippets of his life, said his father could play anything on the piano by ear. Anything, any song you like. Alfie thought of the old piano in the pub back home in Ironbridge. It sounded dreadful, hadn't been tuned in years. But he'd give a guinea now to hear it again, playing daft old songs, from before the war, when they were all innocent too. Chadwick ribbed Precious about going on about home comforts, but when Precious wasn't around, he'd tell Alfie things like that, about his ordinary existence, before all this. Alfie would let him talk. He could see it was a way of wishing it to life, wishing themselves back there and out of this hell.

'Time for a bit of kip,' said Chadwick.

Alfie nodded. After being on duty overnight, they were permitted to grab some sleep now, if they could. They went to a couple of dugouts in the side of the trench, only around three feet or so from the ground and maybe four feet deep. Someone told Alfie that the Germans had much more swanky dugouts that were ten times as deep and, if they were shelled, they'd sleep through it. It didn't seem fair that the Germans seemed so much more organised than them. They were the great British Empire, weren't they? It didn't feel that way, as Alfie crawled into his dugout and lay down on the groundsheet and closed his eyes. He was tired, but he couldn't switch off his brain.

To stop himself thinking about what had happened yesterday, he tried to talk to himself, silently, inside his mind, about things of no consequence. Some of the Belgian names were strange – like Ypres, without all the normal letters in. The Belgians called it 'Eepr', but everyone he knew called it 'Wipers'. He thought of the Belgian refugees, Martine and Brigitta, living in his house, right that minute. He was glad they were there, safe from the Germans. The stories from Belgium were grim. But despite trying to kill each other at every opportunity, he was finding he didn't have a deep hatred of them, the men across the way. Some bits of the line were so close, a chap could say 'Morning Fritz' and the Hun would answer from their trench, 'Hallo Tommy'. They didn't seem so bad, when you heard things like that.

Then, other days, he'd hate them with a rage that was incandescent. Like yesterday. They had to bury some men. The three of them, Alfie, Chadwick and Precious, had headed for the place where they'd been ordered to dig. On the way there, they were walking over recent graves. Whoever had dug these hadn't bothered to do it deep enough and the bodies were decomposing beneath their feet. It was like walking over warm gravy. Alfie numbed himself to it. He didn't want to vomit in front of his friends and he didn't want to vomit on these dead men, buried so unceremoniously. He knew about digging. It enraged him to see it done so badly, so lazily. When they got to the right spot, the digging was hard, just like he'd told Jo about – clay then chalk. The weather was warm, too warm. There was sweat pooling in the small of his back by the time he'd done. When it was time to put the corpses in there, it wasn't as bad if they were face down. One was lying the other way and his face was covered with flies, crawling all over it. Precious started to cry. Chadwick told him to take a break. To think, in their first days at the front, everyone new was nervy as hell. Alfie had heard machine-gun fire and had thrown himself flat on the floor of the trench, watery mud splashing into his eyes. But he'd not been the only one: all the new recruits had done it too, instinctively. The old hands had laughed at them. Now, though, Alfie realised he'd become almost immune to it, particularly when it was happening. In the moment, horrific things would be occurring and you'd look at it like a number nine bus, like nothing out of the ordinary. It was only afterwards you'd brood on it and the full horror of it would climb into your brain and squeeze, squeeze, until you felt as if your mind would explode from the pressure.

He tried to think of better things. He thought of Jo's hair, lusciously brown as a chestnut, flowing over his hands. The softness of her skin at the top of her inner thigh. She was pristine, clean of all this mud and madness. He was glad he'd told her a little of it. But he was more glad that he hadn't told her the full horror of it. He didn't want to ruin her mind. It'd be like cankers on cucumber leaves, every gruesome nugget of information causing another festering dark spot. He'd never do that to her. It was very important to him to keep her clear of it, to keep the truth from her and Harry for ever. He fell asleep thinking of this, making himself swear he never would tell her another word of the war, the daily truth of it, however much he wanted to get it out of his head.

He woke up later and dragged himself out of the hole. He was walking along the trench. Precious was there, talking to the Lazenby brothers about that Raven Hall he was always going on about. Alfie had to double back to fetch his entrenching tool. He called back to Precious to see if he needed his. A shell came whistling over and hit the trench full on.

In the split second before he hit the ground, he'd seen the three bodies of Precious and the two Lazenby brothers come apart at the seams, as their legs and arms flew off in different directions, sailing over the trench in arcs, free of it, their trunks landing with a thud on the duck boards below. Alfie fell, face first in the liquid mud, then scrambled up, choking, his greatest fear being drowned in it. The haze and smoke left by clouds of chalk dust, mud and human remains made it difficult to see and, as he staggered forwards, he could've sworn ahead of him he caught a glimpse of the Grim Reaper stalking along the trench, dark cloak, scythe and all.

Some days he welcomed Death. At least then it would be over.

Chapter 21

Brigitta

November 1915

Brigitta was five and a half years old by the winter of 1915. She'd been in England for just over a year. She was proud that she knew such a lot of English words, she'd lost count of how many. She was not as good as her mama at speaking English but she was not too bad. Nobody there at school spoke Flemish or even French. If she dared to speak a few words, they all looked at her in a kind of disgusted fascination. There were a few other Belgian children living locally, but the others were billeted across town and went to a different school. Brigitta was the only Belgian at this one, so she would make sure she didn't speak any Flemish or French around her classmates. Instead, she would do her best to talk in English all of the time, despite the fact that sometimes it was such an effort, it would give her a headache. But even if she tried to speak to the other children in English, often they would laugh at the funny way Brigitta would say things. Her English wasn't polished yet, though she tried her hardest. Whether she spoke in her own language or in English, she couldn't win either way. On some days, as she crossed the road from Jo and Harry's house to the school, Brigitta would close her eyes and wish that, when she opened them, the school would have disappeared, swallowed up by a tornado. Or the Germans would've have flown over Ironbridge in an airship and dropped one single solitary bomb on the school and blown it up, leaving dear Charlie and Maria's house and garden intact, of course. She loved going to see Charlie and Maria along with Jo and Harry. They had a pretty garden and she'd be given fresh carrots to munch on or a handful of raspberries a bit earlier in the year. It was lovely there. So the German bomb would need to be very careful to explode only the school building, preferably with none of the nice boys and girls in it, and only the ones who laughed at her or said cruel words left inside when the bomb hit. They could be despatched and make everyone happier.

Brigitta loved to stay at home with Mama, Jo and Harry too. Harry was her best friend. He was exactly two and a half years old now, about half her age, but it didn't matter that they weren't the same age because they were very, very good friends and liked each other better than some people who were the same age. It didn't really matter what age someone was. After all, Charlie and Maria were very old indeed and she always had a nice time with them, despite how ancient they were. Besides, with Harry, she liked being the older one. She liked showing him how to do things and patting him on the head and holding his hand. He loved building things and playing with sand and water most of all. She could sit with Harry for hours, pottering away in the garden, making mud pies. Harry never laughed at her. Harry didn't care about her funny accent or her funny Flemish words. She would actually teach him a few Flemish words now and again and he would say them to his mama and she would say he was speaking nonsense, but Brigitta would smile, because she knew the truth, that these weren't nonsense words: they were her secret language that only she and Mama knew. And everyone else in her part of Belgium. But maybe it wasn't there any more. Maybe the bad soldiers had burnt it all down and all that was left were embers, like the fire in the parlour at Jo's house. Maybe Brigitta would never go home again. Maybe there was nothing to go home to.

One day at school playtime, she was cornered in the playground by an older girl and a boy who were often mean to her. They were a brother and sister who'd laugh at her and call her this word 'refugee', which Brigitta had learnt from her mother was a word to be proud of, that they had survived the troubles in their own country and been brave enough to travel for thousands of miles to seek out a new life somewhere else. So Brigitta didn't understand why that brother and sister – Fred and Mabel – would taunt her with it. Most of the time, she avoided Fred and Mabel, though sometimes it was impossible to escape them, as the playground was so small.

Mabel started on at her first. 'My mum says there's a Belgian man in town and he's moved in with an Englishwoman who was married and her husband is at the front and there she was carrying on with a Belgian man and they'd gone to court and she'd had to pay a fine and he'd gone to prison.'

Fred piped up: 'And he seduced her and it was all his fault, these Belgians. Like you. I bet he was your dad or summat.'

Brigitta had no idea who this man was but she knew enough to know her father had died in an accident back in Belgium a long time ago and was definitely not living with a woman in town or in prison.

'He is not my dad,' she replied, calmly, knowing she had the truth on her side.

'Is not! Is not!' cried Fred, doing a little hoity-toity walk like a rich lady. 'Say "inna" like the rest of us. Who do you think you are?'

'I am Brigitta,' she said, confused as to why they would think she might not know her own name.

'Brigitta, Brigitta!' cried Mabel, laughing cruelly. 'What a stupid name. Why dunna you call yourself Bridget instead? That's a proper name.'

'Is it?' replied Brigitta, forlorn, as she'd always quite liked her name.

'Yes,' spat Fred. 'And my dad says folk like you from abroad are probably German spies come to spy on us and give all our secrets to the Germans!'

'What secrets?' asked Brigitta, genuinely interested, as she hadn't heard any but they sounded thrilling.

'Shut up!' added Mabel. 'That inna the point. My mum says you and your kind have overstayed your welcome. You came over for a bit and we let you because we're good and kind but now it's time for you lot to go home.'

Brigitta said, 'But our house is burnt with fire.'

'We dunna care about that!' cried Mabel. 'Go home!'

Fred piped up, 'And our next-door neighbour was talking with our dad and he said these bloody foreigners are all getting decent food and it's not fair and there's not enough to go around as it is, without these greedy foreigners.'

'Bloody foreigner!' yelled Mabel. Her voice was high-pitched and unhinged. 'Bugger off home!'

Fred bent down and picked up a pebble from beside the little perimeter wall of the playground, considered it in his hand for a moment, then looked at his sister, who gave him a nod. Brigitta watched all this with fascination. What was so special about this pebble? Then he threw it hard at Brigitta and it hit her in the chest. The next thing she knew, Mabel was doing it too. A little volley of pebbles came her way and she dodged them as best as she could and ran away down the playground, but they followed her, both screaming 'Go home! Go home!'

Brigitta ran but was cornered again by the school building, her back to the wall as Fred and Mabel bore down on her. And all of her frustration and anger at everything she'd seen in Leuven the day the Germans came and everything that had happened to her since and even her father never coming home after that trip and never seeing him again and the burnt up house and leaving all her toys and books behind and the dead horses in the street . . . all of it welled up inside her and she screamed at her persecutors at the top of her voice, '*You* bloody well bugger off home!'

Brigitta knew she'd used two terrible words in a terrible curse and she'd probably go to hell for it, but it would be worth it, to see that dumbfounded look on her bullies' faces, it would be well worth it. At that moment, Maria appeared, who Brigitta had to call Mrs Woodvine at school, of course. Mrs Woodvine helped out at the school sometimes when she wasn't taking photographs around the town and she was right there and heard every word of Brigitta's terrible curse and would send her to Charlie – who she had to call Mr Woodvine at school, of course – to be caned on the hand.

But Brigitta was flabbergasted to see that Mrs Woodvine yelled at Fred and Mabel instead, saying their mum and dad would be ashamed of them if they could see them now, stoning another child, and that there was no place for bullying at this school and that she'd told Fred and Mabel before and they hadn't stopped bullying Brigitta, so now it was time to see Mr Woodvine. Mabel stated crying and even Fred's bottom lip was wobbling, because they knew Mr Woodvine would give them a wallop with his cane, but, Brigitta thought, Mabel shouldn't really be crying because Mr Woodvine only did it on the hand and he never did it very hard for girls, whereas Fred would do well to cry because Mr Woodvine had to do it harder on boys because they never listened. Mrs

Woodvine sent Fred and Mabel off inside to see Mr Woodvine and his cane.

Maria then took Brigitta's hand and asked her if she wanted to go back into school or come home with her for a drink of milk and a bit of cake. Brigitta didn't think twice about that particular choice and together they went back to the schoolmaster's cottage for a bit, while she drank the milk and ate the fruit cake. It wasn't as good as her grandma's cakes, but it was still all right. Then Mrs Woodvine took her home to Mama at Jo's house and Brigitta heard her tell Mama all about the bullying. Mama turned to Brigitta, took her hand and leant down to her and told her in their own language that next time Brigitta should curse them in Flemish because then the idiots wouldn't know what hit them and nobody could prove what she'd said anyway as none of these idiots round here even knew a word of Flemish because they were so ignorant.

Afterwards, Brigitta was proud that she'd stood up to Fred and Mabel. But that evening, tucked up in bed in the tiny nursery upstairs in Jo's house, alone and unable to get to sleep, Brigitta realised that the truth was, deep down, she wanted to be friends with the boys and girls at school, with all of them. She was lonely. She missed playing with children her age who understood her. She missed her home, her family and her people. She wanted to find new ones here in Ironbridge. She wanted to be just like everyone else. Lying there in bed that night, she made an important decision. In the morning, at breakfast, she told her mama that she was not to call her Brigitta any more. Her name was Bridget now.

Chapter 22

Martine

July 1916

Martine was looking at the calendar hanging up on the wall in her hostess's kitchen. She saw that Jo had written small numbers in the corner of each day's square, counting back from October 1914. That was when her husband had left for the war. And it was the same month that Martine had arrived in Ironbridge. It was nearly two years now since the invasion of Leuven and, when she realised that, standing in the tiny but neat kitchen in Ironbridge, she felt a rush of nostalgia and an ache of loss for her old life. There was nothing wrong with Ironbridge, nothing wrong with Jo's house, nothing wrong with living here, not really. The River Severn was wide and majestic, the lush trees above it hugging the sides of the valley, the riverbank flowers blooming gaily in the summer. It was pretty and the iron bridge was iconic, a historical landmark, she could see that. The place oozed history, though it did not have quite the same grandeur as the architecture of Leuven – though, she thought with a pang, perhaps much of that was destroyed in its sacking by the Germans. The streets of Ironbridge were narrow and quaint, the houses higgledy-piggledy, the marketplace jolly and cheerful, with its fountain and stalls. But it wasn't home.

There was the kindness of people (some people), but there was only so much kindness one could take. Martine realised that one of the luxuries of living safely in your homeland was that you rarely relied on the kindness of strangers. Here, as an exile, that was all she did. One said please and thank you. One said thank you over and over again. How could a person ever thank another enough, for taking them into their home? Jo had told her to stop thanking her, as they were friends now and this was what friends did for each other. Jo had said she'd never really had friends, except Alfie, so Martine was doing her a favour, really, by being her friend and keeping her busy while she was missing her husband. Martine appreciated her saying this but she knew, too, that the status between them was unequal: giver and receiver, however much you sugar-coated it.

Ah, she missed sugar. She missed the sweet treats of her home country, the cakes and waffles, the brioche and buns. The food here was quite dreadful, Martine concluded. She knew it wasn't Jo's fault, as there were food shortages and Jo did what she could with the ingredients she could get hold of. The fruit in the late summer was good and they made some rich jam that lasted through the winter. Jo did make a lovely dish that the locals called Fidget Pie, with potatoes, onions and ham. Brigitta wolfed that down. But otherwise, Martine knew it wasn't the food's fault, it wasn't Shropshire's fault, or even England. It was simply not home. It was home she missed. She wanted to walk the streets and talk to people in her own language. Instead of being a source of curiosity for some, hostility for others, she wanted to be invisible.

Her daughter was fighting her own battles at school in the playground, yet Martine was fighting a silent battle of looks, stares, eyebrow raises and eye rolls from many of the locals. The ladies of the refugee committee and the Woodvines were kind and sweet, of course, and the local doctor was always polite and kind, very much so, in fact. Nothing was too much trouble for him, Martine mused. One day last winter when Brigitta had a chest infection, he brought medicine to the house and checked in twice more to monitor her recovery. Beyond them, certain shopkeepers were pleasant and one or two of the mothers at the school sometimes tried to make conversation, though one of them spoke loudly and slowly, as if Martine were an idiot. It was all exhausting. The truth was that she had been very lucky to arrive here and find a wonderful family to live with, a good school just opposite, alongside clothes, food and a warm bed. But it wasn't Leuven. It wasn't home.

One morning, she received a letter from the refugee committee, addressed to her via their office, sent from the local council in Leuven. Jo had given the letter to her.

'I hope it's good news,' Jo said, a hopeful smile on her face.

Martine nodded and thanked her, then took her leave and went upstairs to their tiny bedroom to open it. She did not know what the contents would be, but her hands shook as she gently eased the envelope open. She guessed that it would be an answer to the letter she'd sent many months ago now, to enquire after the De Bakkers, Emiel's parents and her daughter's beloved grandparents. She read it quickly, scanning through the opening pleasantries to the meat of it. Her parents-in-law were dead, the letter told her, with their condolences. The estate of the De Bakkers would be looked into by their lawyers as Martine was the beneficiary, but much of their capital was wrapped up in their home, which was now destroyed. However, the lawyers would be in touch whenever they could with more news on the matter.

Martine sat down on her bed with a thump. She felt light-headed. She put the letter down and held a hand to her forehead. So, it was true, then. The De Bakkers really were dead. Emiel's parents were good, kind people, who had always made her feel welcome and had doted on Brigitta, who adored them too. How on earth could she break the news to her daughter? She thought, with a sharp inner pain, of when she'd had to try to explain to a three-year-old Brigitta that her father wasn't coming home any more. There was an acceptance of it when she said it, but over the years since, Brigitta had asked her questions about it and cried when she truly understood that her father was dead and gone, once she was five and understood more fully the concept of death. But it had been nearly two years now since they'd left Leuven in flames and little children's minds did often move on swiftly. Would Brigitta remember her grandparents as clearly as she herself did? Brigitta had not mentioned them in a long time. Perhaps, Martine wondered, she wouldn't need to say anything at all to Brigitta. Perhaps she could just keep it quiet and, if her daughter ever asked her about them, she could fudge it and put her off, say she didn't know where they were and they'd find out some time how they were, probably when the war ended. Yes, that was the way to do it. Postpone and avoid, the time-honoured evasion of all parents.

Then, it hit Martine with a thud. Now everyone who was closest to her – her parents, her husband, his parents – they were all of them dead. She realised there was nothing to go back to Belgium for. Nobody awaited their return. It was a cold and hollow fact. But could she stay here, in this strange little town with the iron bridge? Could she make this her home? Some people were very kind, like the Woodvines and the ladies of the committee. Some people were very unkind and did not want them and their sort there. She wondered what would happen to her and her daughter whenever this damned war that dragged on and on finally came to an end. Martine had nothing, only what kind people had given them. What would they do back in Leuven? What would be left of Leuven when the Germans had finished with it? Everything seemed pointless about going back. She thought of all the things she missed about Belgium and how odd England was, their customs, their houses, their food. Could she make her home here? Even if she did, it would never be like her home country. But the Germans had ruined it. It'd never be the same again. Her life, her home, all had been destroyed by war. She was truly homeless, in every way a person can be.

She lay down on the bed and wept silently. She wept for her homeland but also she wept for how her daughter, Brigitta, had now become a different person. A few months ago, she'd changed her name at school and now everyone called her Bridget. Martine had had to prevent herself from screaming at her daughter, shouting that this was wrong, that no child of hers would leave her identity behind so fundamentally and change herself for these fools, these ignorant people who shouted at foreigners, who saw them as less than human. Why bow down to such as them? But then she realised that if Brigitta wanted to become Bridget, it was her way of dealing with the terrible place circumstance had left her in. She wanted to fit in, to embrace her new identity in an unfriendly world and, by doing so, become a part of it. Did she want her daughter to be forever an outsider here, or to find her own place in it and, hopefully, be happy? Martine felt humbled by this and stopped crying, sitting up, wiping her eyes. She nodded to herself, slowly, thoughtfully. She realised that her daughter was being brave and forging friendships despite the huge challenges this little poppet had faced, being burnt out of her home, seeing death and destruction on the streets of her home town, and coming all this way to start again, not knowing a word of English when she came, yet working at it day after day, asking questions about words and meanings and nuance, trying so hard to get it right and slot in to the new life her mother had brought her to. Martine was proud of her and saw that she had to show the same courage as her daughter. That was what survival was about, courage and grim determination.

Over the next few months, her daughter's English improved no end. It was always surprising how swiftly children learnt, like sponges and soapy water. Brigitta was assimilating into her new life, making it seem as easy as putting on a new coat. For Martine, an adult and thus set in her ways, it was harder, much harder. But her daughter inspired her. No more crying for a lost homeland, she told herself. Ironbridge was their home, both of them, for now, anyway.

After the letter had come and Martine had lain down on the bed and wept, she'd slept for a couple of hours, unexpectedly. She found it difficult to wake up, her body aching from head to toe. She knew it was the shock of the news and so struggled on, getting through the next day helping Jo with the chores around the house and aiding the refugee committee, meeting other refugees and talking about home and the old days. But she couldn't shake this aching heaviness in her limbs and, two days after the letter, she found herself going to bed and then, in the early morning, a Monday, she simply couldn't get up. She awoke with a tight throat, and started to cough, with no amount of sipping water taking away its soreness or dryness. She felt hot and shivery. She didn't want to wake Brigitta but felt quite desperately that she needed Jo. She called for Jo, several times, as Jo hadn't heard. She hoped Jo would hear without waking the child, but her six-year-old always responded to the sound of her mother's voice, even when asleep.

'Mama?'

'Fetch Jo,' Martine told her daughter in Flemish. 'Go now.'

Brigitta dragged herself out of bed, yawning luxuriously, too sleepy to notice how ill her mother must look.

Martine lay still, every bone in her body throbbing with pain, her head swimming. She felt as if the heat were coming off her in waves.

Soon enough, Jo came in to see her, a puzzled look on her face. Martine had to act quickly.

'Get Brigitta out of here. Get yourself out of here. I have the influenza.'

'Are you sure?' said Jo, urgently.

'Yes. My parents died from it. I know the signs.'

Jo nodded and Martine could hear her tell Brigitta to go downstairs and start breakfast, even though it was much earlier than usual and Brigitta complained in English that she wanted to go back to bed, but Jo was firm yet calm.

Jo came back to Martine and placed a hand on her forehead.

'Leave me,' croaked Martine.

'I wonna be leaving you,' said Jo gently. 'Except to send someone to fetch help. I'll ask a neighbour to go.'

Once Martine knew that Brigitta was safely downstairs and help was being sent for, she felt able to sink back into her sickness. All was in hand. She drifted between consciousness and dreaming, her fever rising. Later that day, Martine neither knew whether it was minutes or hours, she saw Brigitta being carried by Jo and placed carefully into her bed. She wanted to cry out that Jo must take Brigitta away, that she must be protected from her mother's sickness. But then she saw that Brigitta was flinging the covers off, saying she was too hot in Flemish, curling up and crying from the aching of her limbs. She knew then that they both had influenza, the worst outcome possible. Where was the town doctor? Why hadn't he come yet? She tried to reach for her daughter in the other bed, but then she passed out of consciousness again. She dreamt of home, the Belgium of her youth, before the soldiers came, before she was married, when she was a girl and ate her grandmother's delicacies in her kitchen, sweet treats like crisp, wafer-thin Lukken waffles with their buttery, caramel flavour, and Mattentaart, the crumbly pastry and curd filling that filled you up till dinner time. She could almost taste them in her mouth now. She spent the summers at her grandmother's house and the floors were stone and cool on her bare feet; she could feel the coolness on the soles of her feet at that moment, in her dreams. Home is all we want, really, she thought. All we really want, all of us, is to go back home.

Chapter 23

Jo

Jo went out into the street, knowing it was so early that there wouldn't be that many people about. She was in luck, as a couple of boys were up with the lark, walking down the hill towards town. Maybe they worked somewhere and started or finished in the small hours. She called them over but told them to keep their distance. She told them where to go, saying she'd give them both a penny for doing so. Back inside, she filled a bowl with water and took flannels from the laundry cupboard, as well as the old muslin cloths she'd used all the time when Harry was a baby. She placed a muslin over her nose and mouth and secured it at the back with a tight knot. It was perfectly possible she'd already contracted influenza. But just in case, she'd not take any more chances. She took a jug of water upstairs and two spoons. Then, she took the bowl of water up, fetched the flannels and opened the window in the nursery, where Martine and Brigitta lay in bed, Martine quiet and still except for the odd cough here and there, while Brigitta groaned and twisted her legs slowly, muttering.

Jo placed a wrung-out damp cloth on Martine's forehead

and another across her chest, under her shift. Martine moaned a little in response. She tried to calm Brigitta and get her to lie on her back, so she could put the damp cloths on her. She propped both of them up with an extra pillow each. Next she would give them both fluids. She knew about this from her childhood, as from time to time, her Aunt Stella, the unofficial town nurse, would treat influenza in households in town and would talk about it when she got home. Jo always took everything in that her Aunt Stella said, she realised now, because she was eager for her attention and love, which she never quite received unconditionally, so made an effort for it. Conversely, her cousins ignored their mother most of the time, as they knew innately they were loved. Jo remembered the things her aunt had said about caring for the sick, about keeping them cool, making sure they had enough fluids and putting a cloth over your face if it was an illness that spread quickly. It wasn't foolproof but it could help, her aunt had once said.

There was a knock on the front door and Jo rushed down and opened it, cloth still in place over her face. Aunt Stella stood there, her nurse's bag in hand, her dark hair with swathes of grey tied into a rough ponytail. She must've been at home when the call came, as her work attire was usually much neater. They hadn't spoken since their stand-up row in the street before the war. But the moment Jo had seen Martine and Brigitta's state, she'd known it was Aunt Stella she needed. And right now was not the time for discussion of past woes. This was urgent. This was life or death and, whatever their differences, Jo knew that Stella would understand that too.

Jo spoke first. 'Those boys who fetched you. They'll need a penny each. I dunna have pennies on me, I dunna think.'

'I'll sort them,' said Aunt Stella, with a wave of her hand. 'Are you ill?'

'Nay, it inna me. My two Belgians, Martine and Brigitta. Or Bridget, they call her now.'

'Is it influenza?' Aunt Stella asked.

'Yes, it mun be.'

'Sore throat, dry cough, aching, fever, lethargy?

'All of those.'

Aunt Stella stayed on the doorstep.

'Well done on the face cloth,' she added, and Jo nodded. 'You know you may well've already caught it?'

Jo nodded again.

'Where's Harry?'

'Still sleeping.'

'No symptoms?'

'No.'

Aunt Stella paused, then said, 'You're wanting to take care of these two?'

'I am.'

'You'll need to keep them cool, keep their fluids up, change their bedding regularly. Feed them broth, beef tea, milk when you can. Use spoons and take it slowly. There's naught to be done except rest and care, keeping them clean and hydrated with nourishment. Are you up to it?'

'I am.'

'I'll visit opposite. See if the Woodvines'll take Harry. We need to get him out of there. It'll be a risk to whoever takes him, though. Will they do it?'

'They will,' said Jo.

'All right, I'll go and see. Then I'll knock on the door and you're to bring him down and hand him over. Keep your face cloth on.'

Jo nodded, adding, 'I'm sorry, about . . . you know.'

Stella sniffed and replied, 'I'm sorry too. And I'm glad you called for me. We're family, after all.'

'Yes, we are,' said Jo.

Aunt Stella left.

Jo went back upstairs and the cloths on the invalids' bodies were nearly dry already. She doused them again and replaced them, before giving them spoons of water methodically. The front door knocker sounded again. She rushed back down.

It was Maria. She was looking at the face cloth and gave a little gasp at the strange sight of it.

'Darling, are you well?'

'I am, so far.'

'Stella asked if we'd take Harry. Of course we will.'

'It's a risk to you both,' Jo said. 'But I think Stella's right, that he should be out of this house.'

'We dunna care about the risk,' Maria said. Jo had hoped she would say that, but didn't want to answer for her.

'I'll fetch him. Stay there. Dunna come in.'

She found him still fast asleep in their bed. It was still only just past six in the morning. He looked so peaceful, lying on his back with his arms up, his perfect feathery blond fringe across his forehead, his little body flung back on the mattress as if he'd dropped there from the sky. Jo sometimes felt little Harry had done that very thing, dropped from heaven just for her and the Woodvines, he was so beautiful. He'd just turned three recently and was coming into that lovely age when he wanted to try everything, know everything, do everything: tiring but lovely.

Jo gathered up his floppy form in her arms. He clung to her still half asleep, his head on her shoulder. If he'd seen her, he'd have thought the cloth over her face was a game. She was glad he was still sleepy. She carefully walked down the stairs and through the parlour to the front door, where she handed him over to his grandmother, who took him into her arms with infinite care.

'Thank'ee,' said Jo, feeling choked up and ready to cry.

'It's naught,' Maria said. 'Be careful and be well, Jo.'

Jo nodded and watched Maria carry him across the way to the schoolhouse, Harry beginning to wake up at the fresh air surrounding him. He was perhaps most adorable when he'd just woken up, all stretchy and cuddly and sweet. Jo shut the front door on the sight. She had to hope he was all right, that the Woodvines would be all right, that she would be all right. Firstly, she had to deal with these two precious ones upstairs too. Since they'd come to stay with her last year, Martine and Brigitta had changed everything for Jo, taken her loneliness from her and given her a purpose. And in Martine, Jo had found her first proper friend, after Maria. The two of them would watch the children play and sit with cups of tea and talk, about their hopes and fears for their little ones, about the war, about their pasts. She had told Martine all about the suffragettes and could tell her friend was mightily impressed by it all. Martine was the first woman other than family that Jo had been able to talk to about anything. Jo knew she would do absolutely anything she could to save them.

She spent the day and night in their room, with quick breaks for air and rest. She kept their window open and their cloths damp, and kept them going with spoonfuls of water and beef tea. She dozed here and there in a chair in their room but did not want to leave them for long. On the second day, a Tuesday, she carried on until the afternoon, then fell asleep from exhaustion in the chair and woke up an hour later to the sound of the door knocker. She went down and stood behind the door without opening it.

'Who is it?' she called.

'Doctor Hale,' came the voice through the door.

Jo hadn't expected him to come. Everyone knew, once there was influenza in the house, there was little to be done except wait.

'We're all right, thank'ee, Dr Hale.'

'I'm sure you are, Mrs Woodvine. A very capable woman. But I know there's influenza in the house and I want to check on you all.'

'You mun wear a face cloth,' said Jo. 'We canna have the town doctor coming down with it.'

'Never fear, I have it on already.'

Jo couldn't think of another reason not to answer the door, so she let him in.

Dr Hale came over the threshold and into the parlour, his limp slowing his progress only slightly. It had kept him out of the war and at home in Ironbridge. Jo was so relieved to see another human being, she suddenly sobbed, completely involuntarily.

'Now then, Nurse Woodvine,' he said gently. 'You're shattered.'

'I inna Nurse Woodvine,' she said petulantly. She was annoyed at herself for breaking down, even a little, and had repressed it instantly.

'I know,' he said, with a small, kind smile. 'But you're doing a fine impression of one.'

'Have you seen Harry? Is he well?'

Dr Hale nodded. 'He's fine. I've been across there first. Your aunt told me everything.'

'Oh, thank God,' muttered Jo, and a sob caught in her throat again.

'He's fit as a fiddle,' added Dr Hale. 'How are the patients doing?'

'No better,' said Jo. 'I mean to change their bedding today. They're still feverish, still sleeping much of the time, except for the coughing. They're in pain. I give them spoons of water and beef broth throughout the day and night.'

'Do you have any little teapots, by any chance? Smaller than a normal one?'

'Brigitta has a little china one she uses for her tea parties. Why?'

'You can use that to give them water, and broth too, if the funnel isn't too wide. It's easier than a spoon perhaps, as long as you use it sparingly.'

'That inna a bad idea,' said Jo.

Dr Hale said, 'Go and get some sleep. I'll check in on them and come back later. You'll be no good to them if you inna rested too.'

Jo wasn't going to turn down an opportunity to rest. She crawled into her bed, shut the door and dragged off the face cloth. She was sick of wearing it. But the thought of putting herself at risk and thus risk Harry losing his mother was unthinkable. It was just how it had to be, as nobody else would volunteer to look after the refugees, and she didn't want anyone else to either. She just hoped Harry would be well and that she'd get through this in one piece too. The relief at hearing that Harry was all right was immense. She immediately passed into sleep without another thought.

When she awoke later, it was night time. She leapt up, pulled on her face cloth and rushed through. The doctor was asleep in the same chair she'd been sitting in. Jo was surprised to see him there. Doctors came and went from people's homes but rarely stayed. She didn't want to wake him, though. She went back to bed. She guessed he'd wake her when she was needed. She fell into a luxurious sleep again, yet with unsettled dreams of Alfie, trying to find him in a maze and failing, nightmares that made her toss and turn.

On the Wednesday morning, she awoke and went through again to find Dr Hale using the toy teapot to feed milk to Brigitta, while Martine slept.

'You found the teapot,' she said, quietly.

Dr Hale looked round and said, 'Everything is so tidy in this house, it took a while. But, yes, I found it stowed away in a little picnic hamper in the cupboard. It works well, see? Just right for the little one.'

'How are they?' Jo asked.

'The same. No worse, which is good news. This strain of influenza seems to take around three days to clear, if it's going to clear. We've got another night of this and then we'll know. If they're brighter by tomorrow morning, then they'll probably get through it all right. It's a waiting game. And they need to be hydrated and nourished, with plenty of rest, just as you've been doing. Well done, Jo. You're a good nurse.'

'I never wanted to be a nurse, I mun say.'

'But you'd make a very good one. It's a shame they rarely take married women or mothers of small children. Since you're both, they would never accept you, unfortunately. It's silly, really, as you'd be ideal. A local hospital has just been set up locally at Rowland Hall, did you know?'

'Alfie worked there,' said Jo, 'before the war.'

'I know he did. And they need nurses of good calibre to help with the recuperation of soldiers. Since you couldna train as a nurse, you could certainly volunteer to be a patient visitor. They need people to keep them company, talk to them, write letters for them and so on. I'd recommend you to think about it. You'd be valuable and sorely needed. As you were brought up by your aunt, the nurse, I thought you might be interested in spending time in a hospital. And maybe they'll change the rules one day and you could apply and become a nurse, who knows?'

'Thank'ee but nay,' she replied, shaking her head. 'I grew up thinking I wouldna want my aunt's life, toing and froing all over town at all hours. And then when I got interested in suffrage, I was certain I never wanted to be just another woman nursing. It's one of the few professions we're permitted to do, fetching and carrying and caring. All women are good for, so it seems. You know I was a suffragette before the war, of course, and it hasna left me. I'm still one at heart.'

'Everybody knows that, Jo. The Suffragette of Ironbridge, as I've heard you called.'

'Why me? I wonna the only one.'

'You were the youngest, I think, and perhaps the most vocal, certainly beside the iron bridge, as you so regularly stood. It was said by some with disapproval, and others with awe.'

Jo was surprised. She hadn't imagined that anyone in town had ever given her a second thought. She'd always felt utterly obscure in her own life.

'Well, I've lost all that now. The war has eaten up women's rights.'

'Or, one could say,' added the doctor, 'that it has propelled them forwards by decades. All these women doing men's jobs. It's made society see them in a different light.'

Jo mused on that for a moment, watching him finish off feeding Brigitta the little bit of milk left. Both patients were soon fast asleep again.

'Dr Hale . . .?' she asked hesitantly. 'May I ask you a question?'

'Of course.'

'Why've you been so kind to us, to me, to Martine and Brigitta?'

Dr Hale breathed out and thought for a moment.

'I hope I'm always kind to my patients, whoever they are. But the Belgian refugees have touched my heart more than the average patient in need. Some are quite well-to-do, that is true. But I know that Mrs De Bakker here and her child are quite alone in the world, with nothing to go back to. They've lost everything. Mrs De Bakker told me this herself during her first appointment when she arrived here. Ever since, I suppose I've felt a special responsibility towards them. After all, if we dunna do the right thing by these folk in need, who will?'

Jo thought to herself what a good man he was but was too shy to say it. She couldn't figure out why he was unmarried, as any girl in town would be a fool to turn him down. If she could think of a girl to recommend him to, she would. He needed a woman's touch, with his shirt not well ironed, and his hair needing cutting, just as she did for Alfie. But Jo never had had friends among the young women in town so couldn't recommend him to anyone. She was no matchmaker, that was certain. He ran his fingers through his hair after this speech and yawned. He looked exhausted.

'Why dunna you go home and get some sleep?'

'I canna do that, I'm afraid, as much as I'd like. I have my day appointments to do. What day is it, Wednesday?'

'I think so,' said Jo, but she wasn't sure. All the days and nights had melted into one.

He glanced at his watch and said, 'Yes, I better go. I've got my first appointment at nine.'

'But you havna slept.'

'I'll manage. I'm glad you slept, though. Ready to carry on?'

Jo nodded.

The doctor stood up and pulled on his jacket.

'I'll come back this evening. Well done on the nursing. Again, do think about what I've said about being a patient visitor. I know you canna forward your suffragette cause right now, but you're needed in another way, just as valid. And once this terrible waste of life is over on the continent, then you can take up arms again and show just how valued and necessary women were in this war, whatever job they were doing. Whatever happens about women's suffrage, the truth is our country needs women like you, so does Shropshire and so does Ironbridge. I'll leave it with you.'

The doctor showed himself out. Jo had a quick wash and changed clothes, then did the same for the patients, also managing to change their sheets around them, with great difficulty, but she was proud she managed it. Martine had barely spoken in three days. Brigitta said words in Flemish now and again. They both moaned in their sleep. They were both still hot. Tonight was the real test, then, Jo thought. If they didn't show signs of improvement soon, it might get worse. When Jo had finished her latest round of hydration and nourishment, she sat down on the chair again and did something she'd only done for Alfie until then. She prayed.

Chapter 24

Alfie

July 1916

Dear Alfie,

I hope this letter finds you well. As well as can be, that is, circumstances as they are.

We've had a difficult, dark time of it this week. Martine and Brigitta came down with influenza. I nursed them for three days and nights. They barely spoke and were gravely ill. But they survived, Alfie. They are alive. I was very scared there for a while, but they are recovering now, thank heavens. I know you will probably be angry at me for staying with them. I sent Harry straight across to your mum and dad's, don't worry. He's fine and so am I. But who else would there be to look after them? I was the only one and I was glad to do it. I covered my face with a cloth too. So don't be too angry with me. It was the right thing to do and I know that Martine would have done the same for me.

Doctor Hale helped me a lot and he also said I'd done an excellent job of nursing them. He told me Lord and Lady Rowland have set up a hospital in the big house. Can you imagine? I didn't think they had it in them. Dr Hale said I could be a good patient visitor to help out with the men. But I also found out they need cooks there, so I think that might suit me better, if I did do it. It might give me something useful to do. Now that many of the Belgian refugees have stopped coming and also many are going back home, that line of work has dried up for me now. I suppose it would be good to have a new focus, other than being a mum. What do you think?

I hope the weather is as good for you there as it is here. I do think it's healthful for you to get a bit of sun, when you can. I take Harry down to paddle in the shallows but he doesn't like the weed wrapping around his legs. He's learnt the word 'slimy' and now says it every time I say we should go down to the river and then points to his feet. He's such a sweet, funny thing. He's getting on fine and asks after you. I tell him that his daddy is saving the world, which of course is true.

Sending love and all the kisses.

Your Jo

The trench was absolutely heaving with men. Each one of them was loaded down and dressed up to the nines. Alfie had on his greatcoat, a pack with his blanket in, rifle, pick, ammo and Mills bombs, and his box respirator slung in a bag across his chest. It all weighed a ton. They had only found out the day before, but even that short amount of time felt like an age of waiting. Alfie felt browned off they'd told them in advance at all. It made everything worse. At least he'd had Jo's letter to read last night, which cheered him up. It also made him worse, in a way. Hearing from home had that double-edged quality here, of providing comfort and yet landing as if on another planet, where nothing made sense. Knowing that in the morning they were going over the top made the letter welcome.

He'd sat in his funk hole in the trench the previous night trying to compose a reply to hand in for posting before the morning. He'd had a little notepad he kept in his pocket and he'd tried to start the letter five times and given up each time. He did not know what words could ever sum up the maelstrom of feelings and thoughts in his mind. In the end, he'd decided not to write any sort of farewell letter because a thought crept into his brain that writing such a thing was asking for trouble, jinxing the battle.

Instead, he kept Jo's letter in his pocket and tapped it with his fingertips now he stood in the crowded trench. It was a thread of normality in the midst of this madness. To know that his son Harry asked after him had made him beam when he'd read it, smile at first and quickly his eyes had filled with tears, which he'd swiftly wiped away with a mucky fist. One of his perennial fears, and perhaps one of the worst, was that he would die and his son would forget him. He was so glad to think that Harry missed him, and surely that proved that he hadn't forgotten his dad. Alfie also knew that Jo wouldn't let him forget either. She was the best mother that way, and the best wife. They'd had their troubles, as all couples do, but wartime had changed them both, the trivialities they both used to argue about burnt away and only the bones of their love remained, purifying it. He loved her and she loved him, and she was the best mother for his son he could imagine. And she would make a marvellous helper at the Rowland Hall hospital. Now, why couldn't he have written all that down in a letter to her last night, he thought? Then other thoughts crowded in, the darkest kind, and even thoughts of Jo could not displace them. He stood in silence, waiting, waiting.

Some of the others around him were more vocal, openly

complaining about the wait. However, Chadwick was making jokes, as was his wont, while others stared vacantly into space. They weren't vacant, though; Alfie knew that. They were contemplating the immediate future and what the hell would be the end of it, as he was. He wanted to drown out the voices in his mind, the what ifs, the negative ones that told him he'd be dead in a matter of minutes. He wondered sometimes if the war was finally driving him to lose his mind. The army didn't put any stock in a soldier's mind. The army barely cared about a soldier's body, as long as it was just fit enough for sacrifice. On that note, the quartermaster made sure everyone had a few slugs of rum from a stone bottle. Then they offered more and some of the chaps around him were drunk, proper drunk. This got Alfie asking himself, why would they let us be blotto like that? Then a chill ran down to his bones, that the rum was a last kindness, an anaesthesia of sorts, that they were lining them up as some kind of fodder. He shook his head and closed his eyes to get rid of it, the effects of the rum making it seem as if the trench were tipped on its side, until he opened his eyes and everyone was still there, standing shoulder to shoulder, still waiting.

The time finally came and the trench fell quiet. The hush was thick with anticipation. Alfie focused on the sounds of the men, sniffing, coughing, shuffling. They were given last directions. The British wire had been cut in places for them to get through. The areas were marked out with tape. They were to walk, not run. There should be an arm's length between each man and the man in front. It all sounded reasonable. Would it be that simple when they got up there? Alfie glanced at Chadwick, who was looking at him. All of his customary humour had drained from his face. In the dim light, Chadwick's eyes looked huge and dark. The lieutenant shouted the time, counting down: 'Five minutes! . . . Four minutes! . . .' All the way to, 'Ten seconds! . . . Ready yourselves, men . . . Over!'

The whistle was blown. It was time.

Alfie and Chadwick were three rows back, edging forwards in the heaving lines.

Chadwick whispered to him, 'Might get a Blighty wound. Get ourselves sent home.'

Alfie nodded quickly, then swallowed a lump in his throat.

The first line thrust their makeshift ladders against the trench wall and climbed upwards. The moment they clambered up onto the parapet, Alfie watched as almost every last one of them was peppered brutally with gunshot and fell forward, or some fell back into the trench, causing chaos. The lines shifted like shoals of fish. The second line surged forwards and climbed up, where most met the same fate. It was insanity, to follow that, to walk into that, when you knew what was coming. But there was no choice. No time to think. He felt his boot on the first rung and forced the weight of himself upwards, so heavy with his pack dragging him down and his knees like jelly.

'C'mon, Alf, heave ho!' cried Chadwick, behind him.

Alfie pushed on and climbed onto the parapet, keeping his head as low as he could and crawling forwards. He would not stand up. He glanced to one side and saw anyone standing was immediately felled. They were falling like corn threshed by the scythe. Before him, men were on their bellies, inching forwards. All pretence of walking, of arm's length, all that was gone. They'd been told to hold their rifles at high port but that wasn't going to happen. It was pure survival now. Around him the cacophony – of bombs whistling, shells exploding, machine-gun fire whizzing overhead – was deafening and made his head swim. Alfie looked to the other side, to see where Chadwick was. There was no sight of him, no sight of anything except smoke in great billowing clouds and above it what Alfie thought at first was rain coming at them sideways as in storms driven by wind, yet instantly realised it was machine-gun fire, like deadly raindrops. He could hear the bullets hit bodies with a thump and then bodies would fall, groaning as they went. There were clouds of earth driven by shells hitting the ground all around him and rolls and strips of wire as far as the eye could see, a hellish jigsaw of sights that made every single thing around him capable of killing him. Then he spotted, in between gusts of smoke, men inching forwards, fixed bayonets, shouting and swearing and falling, as if the field were a stage and they were actors throwing themselves about in dramatic fashion. But they weren't acting, they were dying, or having a shoulder blown out, or an ear shot off, screaming and yelling and landing on the earth with a thud. Everything moved very slowly as if under water and yet at the same time it was all happening at top speed, too fast to comprehend, life becoming a blur.

Alfie screwed his eyes shut again. But he knew he couldn't lie there for ever or he'd catch a bullet or a shell eventually. He had to move forwards. He dragged up his knees and began to crawl, then saw a couple of his regiment run onwards, leaping into a shell hole and disappearing. That was the answer. There were shell-holes everywhere he looked, the battlefield polka-dotted by them. He clambered up, doubled-over, head down and rushed headlong towards the spot he'd seen the men go and found himself falling into it, skidding down the muddy side. The two men in there were shot dead. They must've caught it just as they jumped in. Alfie looked away and held on tight to his rifle, somehow for comfort, as he leant against the shell-hole wall and decided he never wanted to leave it. Maybe it'd be all right, if he just stayed here. Maybe he'd survive it. He sat there for a long time, alone, refusing to look at the faces of the two soldiers beside him, splayed out awkwardly against each other, surprised, caught unawares by death. He knew he ought to at least try to train his rifle on a German at the front, try to pick them off, one at a time. But he couldn't move. His body felt stuck in place, stiff as a scarecrow. After a while, the barrage of shells and gunfire thinned out a little, the sky clearer. Perhaps the madness was stopping. Had other lines reached the German trenches? Should he join them? Should he take a little look first?

He peeped out over the top and saw Germans shooting at his fellow soldiers, even sniping at the dead, over and over and over. If he went out there, he'd be dead in an instant. But if his officers knew he'd stayed in the shell-hole the whole time, would he be labelled a coward? How could anyone be brave against certain death, when it seemed to serve no purpose whatsoever? He could jump out and run at the Germans and be shot down instantly, and to what end?

He hesitated, torn by duty and scepticism, when the odour of something strong and musty was suddenly upon him. The smell was so particular, he froze, enchanted by it. It was the familiar scent of freshly cut hay. He knew it so well, because he helped out on the estate fields at harvest time back in Broseley and it was always one of his favourite scents in the world. He breathed in deeply and let it fill his nostrils and down, deep down, into his lungs. Was he hallucinating? Was he back in dear old Shropshire? Was he dreaming that he was back home, at work, at a job that he could not believe now he ever complained about on early rainy mornings? Just as he could not believe he ever complained about Jo's bad moods or Harry's crying in the middle of the night, when all of those things were heaven on earth compared to this hell? It couldn't be real, the smell of haymaking, the hot afternoons in the fields with old Cork and the others, the young lads, the other gardeners all abandoning the gardens of Shropshire for the fields of Flanders and France, destroyed by war, creating a new world of mud and wire and blood and bone. Alfie thought he was finally losing his mind. He breathed it in deeply again, to see if it were real or just a memory. The scent of freshly mown hay wafted closer and closer and was cloying now, thick and stultifying. It was real, all right.

Nearby, he heard a voice shouting, 'Gas! Gas! Quick, lads!'

And then it hit him. The smell. They'd been told about it. They were warned, about the new deadly phosgene gas that the Germans were using, that was colourless, which made it more deadly. There was no yellow cloud to spot now. It was invisible, creeping low and heavy, with the scent of hay. And no instant effects either. It wasn't like the yellow chlorine gas that made you gag and cough and sent you blind straight away. It insinuated itself into your lungs and rested there, sometimes for hours or even days until it'd kill you slowly, drowning in your own dissolved lungs. That's what they'd been told, that's what they'd heard when it was first used by the Hun a few months ago. How could he have been so stupid? He was furious with himself as he fumbled wildly for the box on his chest, in which sat his gas mask. His fingers felt fat and useless, his hands shaking so much, he couldn't open the damn thing. The moment he finally dragged it out of the box, he pulled on the goggles and the mouthpiece clamped over his face. Now he was safe. Or had the damage been done already? Only time would tell. There was a call by an officer to move forward and he knew it was time to go. He couldn't stay here for ever. After all, he'd need a medic to check him over. Perhaps the mask had caught it in time. Maybe he'd be all right. Before he was ready to clamber out of the shell-hole, he paused, listening to his ragged breathing through the respirator, the world around him restricted and fogged by the panes of his goggles. He was never a godly type, attending church more as a social event than for prayer. But at that moment, he prayed more than he'd ever prayed in church. He prayed to see Jo and Harry one more time. He'd do anything to see them just one more time.

Please, God, he said in his mind, from a humble gardener of Ironbridge: just let me see them one more time. One more time is so little to ask, in the grand scheme of things.

Chapter 25
Maria & Charlie

Army Form B104-82 was the manner in which the death of Private Alfred Woodvine was communicated to his family. It seemed such a dreadful thing to have such devastating news relayed in a printed letter with gaps for names and details. They all said that, when Jo brought the letter over that terrible evening. Jo's face had been white as a sheet. The moment Maria saw her face, she knew. The form said little, only that Alfie had 'died from wounds (gas)'.

'What happens with gas? Is it bad?' Maria had asked Charlie. 'Or do they just fall asleep? Like ether?'

She liked the idea that he might've simply inhaled this gas and slept. He simply didn't wake up, that was all. His death could well have been painless. That was a comfort of sorts, she told herself.

Charlie couldn't look at his wife when she asked him. He merely muttered some words about her being right, though he knew it was the opposite. She'd stopped reading the papers a year or so ago now, unable to cope with the barrage of negative information. She'd said hearing the news every damned day was driving her mad. So she hadn't read about the use of poison gas and Charlie wasn't going to disabuse her of her ignorance. He knew that the truth was the polar opposite of what she thought, that death by gas was one of the worst, most painful and unpleasant deaths. The horror of that fact could have paralysed him but the thought of protecting Maria from the truth galvanised him more. He just had to make sure that she never read anything about the war ever again.

The next day, after the news came, another letter arrived for Jo, this time from a captain by the name of Shearwater. Such an extravagant name, it seemed out of place.

On behalf of myself, the Officers and men, I extend sincere condolences to you on the passing of your husband, Private Alfred Woodvine. Alf was a good soldier and well liked in the Company. He was especially proficient at digging duties and organised the other men efficiently and with good humour.

Your husband was killed by a gas attack. He fell unconscious immediately and died the next day having suffered no pain.

Charlie knew this was a complete lie. He was glad the man had protected the women. But Charlie had a gnawing hunger to know the details. What followed were some burial details, a makeshift graveyard in France, near an area called Somme. Then, it finished thus:

If you have any questions or I can help you further in any way, please do not hesitate to contact me. I send with this letter my deepest condolences for you and your little boy.

I remain, yours sincerely,
Jolyon H. Shearwater, Capt.

It was a kind letter, Charlie thought, in that it was brief and went into no details. He wondered, maybe he could write to this captain, ask him what really happened, man to man. He went to write down the name and details of the address. But what good would it do him to know? If he were this Shearwater, he wouldn't tell his soldier's father the horrible truth anyway. Instead, Charlie copied down the burial details. One day, after the war had burnt itself out, he knew he would go there and search for his son's grave. It was the least he could do. For there was nothing else to do, nothing at all, except protect the women. That was his job from now on. Maria wasn't speaking. Charlie didn't know what to do. What could he do? What could anyone do? It was the worst news in the world and he himself barely wanted to go on living when he heard it. He couldn't even imagine how hard this must be for Alfie's mother. It was different for women. They carried them inside their bodies. He knew his own pain was unbearable. Equally difficult to bear was Maria's silent pain.

Maria went to her darkroom the day after they'd received the captain's letter. She'd barely slept since the first news of Alfie's death. As dawn was breaking, she slid out of bed as quietly as she could, so as not to wake Charlie. She was most worried that he'd have a breakdown at the news. She knew how strong she could be, she knew she'd cope with this better than him. She worried he'd never recover. She feared he'd take Snap for a walk one day and never come back, letting Snap off his lead in the woods and walking into the Severn and sinking to the depths. Her own parents had drowned in an accident and she could clearly imagine Charlie going the same way, this time by choice. That boy was Charlie's life. Or rather, his heart. His life was busy with school but his heart belonged to Alfie. She crossed the room as quietly as she could, glad Charlie was sleeping. She pulled on a dressing gown and stepped into her slippers and went outside, the grass still dewy. The birds were tweeting and she felt angry with them, for carrying on, when everything in her world was destroyed. How dare they chirp like that! She crossed the garden and went into her darkroom, turned on the red lamp and stayed there, for hours. It was warm in there, getting hotter and hotter as the day went on and the sun grew fierce. She opened the door for a draught, as she hadn't eaten and felt faint. But she did not want to come out. She slept a little, from exhaustion, on the floor. She woke up sobbing, as she'd been crying in her sleep.

She sat up on the floor in the red light, staring at the door. She felt numb. She knew she ought to speak to Charlie. He'd been very patient with her and not tried to force her to talk to him. But she knew he'd be lonely. Somehow it felt as if she'd lost the ability to speak. Her son's death had struck her dumb, like someone in a folk tale. Luckily it was the summer holidays, as she couldn't think of anything worse than being surrounded by children when her boy was lost for ever. She thought of the time when she carried him in her belly and she would've fought off wolves with her bare hands to protect him. In fact, she did beat off a wolf – his blood father, Oskar – and how she thought she'd killed Oskar – she did that while pregnant, to protect herself and her unborn child.

And now, her son had been sent far away across the sea and there was nothing she could've done to protect him. She felt that she'd failed him as a mother, that she should've moved heaven and earth to stop him marching away with the army that day. But she knew deep down it was all nonsense. It was out of her hands. The powers that be had decided to start this war and take those boys – boys they had been and boys they still were – innocent lambs to the slaughter on the fields of France and Flanders. Jo was right, when she used to complain about the suffragettes being shoved aside by this men's war – war was made by men, but what Jo was wrong about was that war doesn't sacrifice men – it sacrifices boys. Her boy. Her only child. Her Alfie.

When Charlie woke up and found his wife gone, he panicked. He rushed downstairs in only his pyjamas and looked around the house. He didn't call her name as he thought she wouldn't answer. He rushed outside, barefoot on the grass, and then saw her open the door of the darkroom from the inside, just a crack, probably to let the air in. It was a warm morning already. He couldn't believe how late he'd slept. Snap was wandering about the garden looking forlorn. He knew that the collie sensed there was something wrong.

As Charlie stood and stared at the darkroom, its door tantalisingly ajar, he wished he could go in, take Maria in his arms and comfort her, as he'd once been able to do about anything they faced. And they had faced troubles before; indeed, their whole relationship had begun in the deepest trouble, when he found her in Shrewsbury, wandering away from the flat she'd shared with von Schoen, her face and body beaten, her hair wild, her eyes glazed over. She thought she'd killed him, the violent father of her child. But they'd found he had survived the blow to the head she'd given him with his own camera. They tussled in the street when he'd come back at them with his gun and Schoen had taken a bullet to the foot. It all seemed ridiculously melodramatic now. This fool, this chemistry student and a pretentious photographer – who had lied about being a professional one, indeed wasn't even an amateur, his attempts were so pathetic – they had left him there in the street. They had run from him and started a new life back in dear old Ironbridge. They had feared they'd be found and made to pay for what they'd done to Oskar's foot. But they weren't. They only received a letter from his sister, offering help with her nephew, which had a proprietorial tone that had enraged Charlie at the time, still did. They'd burnt the letter and put it behind them. Charlie became Alfie's father from the moment he knew of his existence. That was a true father, not the coincidence of blood. Why was he thinking about all this now? It was the loss of him that brought it all back, how he'd fought for him, for his son. For Alfie was his son, in every way a boy could be.

Snap nudged his nose into Charlie's hand and he looked down at the sweet-tempered dog.

'Come on, then,' he said, gently, and went to get dressed, fetching Snap's collar and lead and taking him out onto the path beside the river.

Charlie walked past the remains of the old Bedlam Furnace, disused now for decades. Here and there in the woods sloping up and away from the river were other remnants of a lost industrial age, overgrown with weeds, taken over by natural things. As he walked past the ruins of old industry, he had a sense of history as he went, as if he were walking back in time, seeing the land change, through the industrial revolution, to the agrarian times and beyond, back and back to pre-history, the mysterious past. As he went on, there grew a heavy summer fog about the river that shielded light and space and Charlie began to feel that he really could be anywhere, at any time. He realised as he walked that this was exactly what he wanted, to go back in time, just like in that book by H. G. Wells he'd read extracts from to the children in class just a few weeks ago: *The Time Machine*. What an extraordinary imagination Wells possessed. Charlie wanted to take that time machine and turn back to the moment just before the poison gas entered his son's lungs. He'd swoop in and take him away from that cursed field and bring him home. His son, Alfie, alive again, saved by his father, his true father.

Nobody but Charlie and Maria knew that Alfie was not his blood. It didn't matter anyway. It had never mattered to him.

Except Anny Malone. Ah, yes, Anny had known. He'd told her, when they escaped from Shrewsbury and recovered at her house in the deep woods. Dear Anny, a Woodvine by birth. They were related somehow via a distant cousin. She had looked after Maria until they'd married. She'd known the whole story and never judged them for an instant. She'd worked at Charlie's school for years, teaching the children the skills of ordinary life that the curriculum had not. She was a working-class woman who had come from poverty and then, via her daughter-in-law and adoptive daughter, Hettie, had come into money late. She'd used her privilege to help others. Her father had worked at the Bedlam Furnace, Charlie remembered. He'd died there in an explosion. Not an accident, by all accounts, but due to the carelessness of the rich King family who'd owned it. Anny had seen her fair share of suffering. She was gone now, had died in her sleep five years before, living to a ripe old age. Charlie was glad she hadn't lived to see them lose Alfie, as she doted on the boy as much as she did her own grandchildren and great grandchildren. Her Peter had gone a year before her and Charlie had watched her lose interest in this mortal coil. She was tired of living, but not in a sad way; she was ready. It was a natural way to go, a natural order of things. It was Anny's time.

But this death, his son's death, was different. For your child to die before you was unnatural. Charlie felt an anger rise in him then. He cursed the war. He cursed the German army. He cursed whoever invented that poison gas. Some German chemist somewhere, no doubt. How revolting that connection was, that Alfie's blood father had been a chemistry student. They had heard in that letter from his sister that he worked with a great chemist in Germany. Perhaps it was them that created the poison gases that killed his own son. Charlie wouldn't be surprised. He wanted to burn down the German laboratories where the noxious stuff was made. He wanted to burn down the British Army HQ of the commanding officers who sent his boy on that final walk into the arms of death. He wanted to burn down Parliament for agreeing to this war and calling his boy and countless others to their deaths. He wanted to burn down the modern world.

'It's bloody stupid!' he cried aloud, into the mist. 'Progress, ha! The modern world is stupid.'

Charlie wept then, walking along through the summer fog, nobody about on the river path, only Snap, who whimpered as he listened to his master's sobs.

Chapter 26

Jo

July to August 1916

Jo couldn't take it in. She somehow thought it would never happen to her Alfie. It seemed impossible. Impossible! She couldn't believe it at first. She wouldn't. She told Charlie that they should write and double-check, that it was really him. Charlie said no, it wasn't a mistake, as this captain had written as well and he would know. Jo refused to believe it and said she wouldn't accept it until she saw his body, which then Charlie made her realise that she never would, of course. Alfie's body was buried over there in some battle-torn field in France. They would never see him again.

She dealt with her grief by denying its existence. She harboured the idea that it was some terrible error, that some other Alfred or Alfie or Alf had been killed, not her Alfie. But Martine was the one who helped her most. Martine, in her recuperation, had spent a lot of quiet time with Jo, as she regained her strength in bed. Sometimes Jo would sit beside the bed and weep as Martine held her hand. Martine had had losses of her own and said she recognised Jo's denial. She said she'd done it herself, firstly, when her parents died and later when her husband was killed. Her kind words did aid Jo, but the weight of it felt to Jo as if it would crush her. Jo hated herself for spending so much time arguing with Alfie before he left, even starting to curse the suffrage movement for driving a wedge between them. She didn't know how she'd ever explain it to their son, Harry, who was only three years old and would, in all likelihood, retain no memories of his father, since Alfie left to go to war two years before and, though he came home once, Harry would be too young to remember. This cold fact dropped like a stone in Jo's consciousness. She would watch Harry playing and talking to her. He was happy, she thought. He didn't ask after his father, ever. She'd lied to Alfie about that in the last letter she'd sent him and she was glad she'd told Alfie that white lie. And she found she couldn't talk to her son about his father, because every time she tried, the wave of sorrow would overcome her and she knew she'd sob in front of him and that was unacceptable. Thus, she didn't say a thing about his daddy, which felt terribly wrong. She ought to be talking about Alfie, to keep the boy's memory alive of his father. But how do you tell a three-year-old their daddy has died? It was unthinkable. One day, she told herself, one day she'd start talking about him again, when the boy was older, when he could understand. But the fact remained that, whatever Jo told her son about Alfie, Harry would never know how wonderful his father truly was.

Nothing made sense any more. She felt like a lost soul, wandering in a white mist, detached from her life, from others, even from Harry. She felt as if she were barely a person any more, instead simply a heart beating pointlessly in a body and a mind throbbing with grief.

To stop herself from losing sight of the real world, she knew she had to do something, an activity to get her moving again, moving forwards, and not keep her mired in past miseries.

Just as the suffragette meetings had saved her from her sadness after Harry's birth, she decided to take Dr Hale's advice and volunteer at the new hospital. It had been set up in the grounds and the house of Rowland Hall. Dr Hale had put in a good word for her and arranged for her to go and have a chat with the housekeeper to discuss a possible role there for her. Though she couldn't carry out nursing duties, she could do a range of other things that were desperately needed, the foremost being helping out in the kitchen that prepared meals for the recuperating soldiers. She was happy to do it, two or three days a week. It would get her out of the house and it would take her out of herself. She left Harry with his grandmother one day in early August, a day that didn't feel like summer, instead like a nip of autumn. It was a breezy day, with dark piles of clouds whipping across the sky and, though it wasn't cold, the wind made her shiver, as did the little gusts of fat raindrops that swept by. The bus took her near to the gatehouse of Rowland Hall, the same bus Alfie had taken from time to time, as he usually preferred to walk, so much did he love the outdoors.

She couldn't believe she'd never visited, when her husband had spent more time there than he had with his own family. There was a lane she had to walk up towards the hall, tree-lined with silver birch trees whose spindly pale trunks waved in the wind as she passed. She'd been told to walk around the house to a red side door opposite the fountain. She passed through a courtyard, past the stables with the whiff of horse dung in the air, across a gravel drive that swept round past a sunken garden with a large, rectangular pond. It was all so fancy. Should she really be here? She felt utterly out of place. As she moved on down the gravel drive, the house to her right, a circular lawn flanked by dark trees to her left, she suddenly felt cold. What if seeing soldiers in the beds there or strolling around the grounds would make her feel sadder, missing her Alfie and hating these men who had survived?

She hadn't thought about this at all. It made her shudder. A heron appeared in her eyeline above the house, winging its way, almost motionless, towards the pond she'd just passed. She stopped to watch it fly overhead. Was it Alfie's heron? The wise old one he'd told her about. It could be. She watched it intently. There was such a stillness about it. Alfie was right about herons. This one, at least. It was just what Alfie had said: majestic, mysterious. She saw the great bird slow itself and alight with grace beside the pond. It made her smile to think it might snaffle up the elegant fish that the Lord and Lady kept there, just as Alfie had told her.

She carried on walking, feeling lighter. She saw the fountain, then found the red door. She knocked on it but there was no answer, so she gingerly turned the door handle and went inside. There was a long corridor, quite dark as the only window was long, thin and near the ceiling. She could hear the clattering of pots and pans, so followed the sound and found the kitchen. A little woman with light-grey hair curled about her ears, wearing a mucky apron, looked up from kneading dough with floury hands as Jo stood at the open kitchen door.

'The suffragette wench?'

Jo was taken aback.

'Yes?'

'Good. You're needed. The other lass is off sick and the last one's gone off to France for adventure. Get a pinny on.'

Jo looked about her and saw clean aprons hanging up on hooks on the opposite wall. She put one on and the woman directed her to peel a huge bag of potatoes, which Jo started immediately. As she peeled, the woman continued kneading her pastry dough, then slapped it down on the kitchen side.

The room was large, with two full ovens, scrubbed shiny. The heat in there warmed up the autumnal August day and, before long, Jo was perspiring. She glanced over at the woman who was now rolling out the pastry, then manhandling a huge round of it onto an enormous pie dish.

Then, she let out a huge 'Phew!' and Jo looked up.

'I canna converse when I'm working pastry. It takes up my whole head and heart and hands and I canna say a word. Right, lass. I'm Mrs Simkiss, housekeeper, chief cook and bottle-washer!'

Jo laughed, as Mrs Simkiss had such a jovial mood, it just made you smile.

'I'm Jo Woodvine. Pleasure to meet you.'

'Good, good. I canna tell you how glad I am you're here. Like I said, the other two have jumped ship. And we've got thirty-seven souls on board for lunch, plus the nurses' meals to do after. Are you ready for a day of hard work?'

'Aye, aye, cap'n,' said Jo.

The rest of the morning passed in a whirl. It was only the two of them and they were making three huge leek and potato pies for lunch with peas and carrots from the garden. Jo had never peeled so many vegetables and shelled so many peas in her life. By late morning, her hands were aching from being curled up in a peeling position for so long.

They talked as they worked. Mrs Simkiss asked her a lot of questions and was quite the town gossip.

'Did you get up to mischief in your suffragette days, then? That's what everyone said you did.'

'Nay, not really,' Jo lied. There was no way on earth she was going to reveal what she'd got up to with Barbara Rose that time in Shrewsbury. Ah, Barbara Rose. She'd never replied to the letter that Jo sent, all those years ago. It was another time, aeons ago, it felt like. Another life.

'What's those Belgian types like, the ones staying with you? Everyone says they're quite sweet, for Belgians.'

And Jo told them what golden people they were, Martine and Brigitta (who everyone now called Bridget).

Mrs Simkiss answered, 'Well, when that Dr Hale came here to tell me all about you and why I should take you on, he then spent the rest of the time talking all about the mother, the Belgian one. They say he's sweet on her and is going to propose! That's what they're saying anyway and he certainly couldna curb his tongue about her when he spoke to me. She's a winsome young woman, I mun say. Will she settle down to the life of a doctor's wife, though, with all that fiery red hair? Red hair is never a good sign of constancy, you know.'

Jo kept her mouth shut on that one. She'd seen how attentive Dr Hale had been during Martine and Bridget's recuperation and just assumed that he was a very good doctor. Which he still was, of course . . . yet in recent days, in their house of mourning, no mention had been made of Dr Hale or anyone else while the shadowy pall of gloom hung over their days and nights. However, a few days back, Jo had noticed when out shopping that Martine and Dr Hale had seemingly met by chance by the fountain in the marketplace and were talking animatedly, like old friends . . . or more. Now, with Mrs Simkiss's gossip, it seemed that Jo's inkling was confirmed. When Jo had seen them there in town, chatting away like that, she'd felt a twinge of envy so painful it made her eyes water, not because she had any interest in Dr Hale that way, but simply because she wished she could be standing talking to her Alfie, her own eyes shining with love and not tears. But then, she'd told herself, Martine had lost her husband too, years ago now, and since then her whole family was gone. Of course, Jo wished her well. Of course, Jo wanted the best for her. And Dr

Hale was the best kind of man, the same ilk as Charlie. And as Alfie.

By lunchtime, the kitchen began to fill with nurses, ready to take the food out to the men. They were VAD nurses, Jo knew, as she'd seen them around town here and there with their smart white uniforms on with the red crosses on their chests. She found she envied them, their position in society as angels of goodness, their confidence in their roles, even if a couple were quite arrogant, looking down on Jo as a kitchen maid, while one even called her 'girl'.

But Mrs Simkiss heard this and said, 'That's no "girl". You're the girl round here, missy. That's Mrs Woodvine, the war widow. Show some respect!'

That shut everyone up and Jo felt queasy. She turned away and got on with washing the pots, which she focused on entirely. Then, she felt the tears coming and had to force them back. She'd never heard herself called a widow before. It was such a lonely-sounding word, so final. She hated it. Finally, every meal had been taken by every nurse and the kitchen was thankfully quiet again. And Jo began to weep, as silently as she was able. Mrs Simkiss might've been a bluster of an old woman, but she wasn't tone deaf. Jo felt a hand touch her gently on the shoulder. She didn't want to turn around. She didn't want to betray her tears.

'Why dunna you go to the chicken coop and fetch some eggs for me, dearie, eh? They're by the door to the kitchen garden. And while you're there, pop in and see old Cork and get me a jar of his bees' honey. Then, when you come back, you can sit down and have your lunch. I've put you a plate aside. Off you go.'

'Thank'ee,' murmured Jo, taking the egg basket Mrs Simkiss gestured to on the table, and then she told Jo how to find the chickens and Mr Cork's office. Jo nodded and got out of the kitchen as quickly as she could. The moment she pulled the door to, she broke down, hurrying away from the main house. She followed the path up beside the dark trees, overhanging the walk so that the day turned dark under them. She let herself sob, as everyone was inside having lunch and she was all alone in this grand place. She followed the deep green hedge Mrs Simkiss had described and found the opening through it to the flower garden, resplendent in its summer garb, swathes of nodding flowers in every hue. Alfie would know the name of every one of them. He'd probably planted most of the perennials and tended them year on year, man and boy. This made Jo sob even harder. Shades of Alfie seemed to haunt her here. Perhaps it really was a terrible mistake to come here to Rowland Hall. Then, she heard the flap of a wing and looked up. The heron was there again, sailing low over the walls of the garden, to the woods and water of the estate beyond. She watched it until it vanished in the distance behind the tall tops of faraway trees. And by that point, she had stopped crying and was able to go on.

She found the door in the wall through the vegetable garden and saw immediately, in a scrubby little area to the left, the chicken coop. She went in and closed the little gate behind her, reaching into the straw and pulling out a great number of eggs from the prolific, clucking hens. Once she'd found all she could, she managed to stop crying, focusing on the task in hand. And it was a good job she had, because she had to go and face old Mr Cork now, Alfie's former boss. She was dreading this, dreading his sad face, dreading his sympathy. She knew Mr Cork, of course. She'd not visited Alfie's workplace until today, but they'd see Mr Cork in town from time to time and he'd come and give little Harry a gentle pinch on the cheek with his long, weathered fingers, the texture of oak.

She crossed over the vegetable garden, the beds bursting

with growth and a cornucopia of food. These soldiers were certainly living the high life being sent here to recuperate. Food shortages had no sting when it came to Rowland Hall. She approached the greenhouses and potting sheds, then passed through the brick archway to the gardeners' office. There, underneath the arches, sat two tortoiseshell cats in perfect loaf shapes, their legs and paws tucked in under them neatly. Jo remembered Alfie talking of them, how old Cork had called them Apple and Crumble. This made her smile. She'd not seen a soul in the gardens since she'd arrived, except these two cats. They looked at her curiously, though did not move a muscle. They were clearly very comfortable there, unofficial guardians of the gardeners' office. The office door beyond them was open and she could see a pair of muddy boots sticking out from under a desk, yet she stayed behind the threshold out of respect and reached round to knock on the open door.

There was a scuffling of boots and the head gardener appeared.

'Why, Mrs Woodvine!' he said, and his lined old face broke out into a great beaming smile, one that Jo was not at all expecting.

'Mr Cork,' she said, and nodded, returning the smile. It was good to see him.

'And how is Master Woodvine? Is our Harry hale and hearty?'

Jo nodded. 'He is, Mr Cork. As wriggly as a bag of snakes. Never sits still.'

'That's good to hear. Very good to hear. Such a handsome boy, with that mop of flaxen hair.'

'And Mrs Cork? How is she these days?'

'Bearing up, bearing up. She gets the odd twinge but remarkably healthy for a woman her age. She's much older than me, you know. All of eight month.'

Mr Cork had a twinkle in his eye and caught Jo's glance. And then a moment passed between them, of utter pathos, where the knowledge of what connected them – and who had been lost – was brought home to them.

Both looked away. Jo moved on with her task in hand, to calm the groundswell of feelings she sought to quell.

'I'm working at the kitchen now as a volunteer, helping out with the soldiers' meals. I've come to fetch some honey back for Mrs Simkiss.'

She said the whole thing staring at her shoes. They were dusty already, simply from walking through the gardens, clean and dry as they were in high summer. The sun was coming out now, the dark clouds blown away from Rowland Hall. To think what a fuss she'd made for all that time about Alfie's muddy boots coming in the house and now she'd give a hundred pounds to see his boots walk over that doorstep again, a thousand pounds or more.

'I'll get you two jars, if you'll follow me, Mrs Woodvine.'

She crossed over into the gardeners' office and he bid her put her basket of eggs down on a sturdy wooden table. She looked up to see the pigeon holes where she knew Alfie used to keep his lunch tin that she had prepared for him, day in and day out. Only two pigeon holes out of the four rows of them had possessions in. All the others were vacant. Behind them were shelves with some hand tools and gloves here and there, yet again the majority were empty.

As Mr Cork reached up to take a jar of honey from a row of them neatly stashed on a high shelf, Jo asked him, 'How many staff do you manage these days, Mr Cork?'

'Only me and my brother-in-law now. He came out of retirement to help when all the lads went off. Which reminds me. I have summat to show you, Mrs Woodvine. Follow me again, will you?'

Jo nodded, as he slipped the jar of honey into his jacket pocket. He showed her behind the shelves to a further area in the outbuilding, a place where two pairs of neatish shoes were neatly lined up against the wall, where against the far wall, two lonely-looking coats and hats were hanging on pegs. Jo guessed they belonged to Cork and his brother-in-law, the only two gardeners left here at the hall.

'This is the gardeners' cloakroom,' he said. 'Once upon a time, this used to be filled with coats and hats and shoes every day of the week, every day of the year. There was always work to be done and plenty of young men and old, keen to do it. Plum job this is, at Rowland Hall. Any man'd be lucky to get it. And look here.'

He took Jo over to the hooks on the far wall and lifted his great hand to show her. At the end of the row, there was written on the wall in thick dark pencil a list of names, all higgledy-piggledy, in varying types of spidery handwriting.

'Before they went off to the war, every man and boy who worked here signed his name on this wall,' said old Cork. 'I dunna know why they did it. Maybe for luck. Maybe to make their mark. To be remembered. To say they'd be back. Who knows? But they did. And here's your Alfie's, Jo. Here it is.'

He pointed a tremulous finger at the name scrawled out in large, generous script: *Alfred Woodvine 1914*.

Seeing Alfie's signature hit her like a punch in the stomach and she bent over as if winded, letting out a sob and a cry the like of which she'd never made in her life. All of her pent-up grief for Alfie – that she'd held in so as not to upset anyone, not her son, nor Charlie nor Maria, nor Martine nor Bridget – it all came out in a flood. She howled like an animal, her body heaving with it like a sickness. The old man offered his hand and she grasped on to it like a lifeline, as he put his arms about her and she sobbed into his chest, his worn waistcoat soft against her cheek. Cork never said a word. He simply waited silently for her to finish.

When the sobs ended and she had no more sounds within her, she pulled herself away from him and wiped her eyes with a hankie from her pocket.

'So sorry,' she croaked. 'I dunna know what came over me.'

'Dunna be daft,' Cork said with a blessed gentleness. 'My great-nephew's name is on the wall there too – see? – John. Little Jonny Cork. He was a navy boy and drowned in the Battle of Jutland in the summer just gone. Every single name on that list is gone now. Every one of them. And the last one to be lost was Alfie. He lasted longer than any of these gardeners of Rowland Hall. He outlasted them all. I thought you might like to know that. And now they're all gone, I'm fixing to paint some varnish over this wall to make sure their names stay there for ever. Would you like that, Jo?'

She couldn't think of a more poignant epitaph for Alfie, and all the others lost like him, than the flourishes made by the hands of excited young men before they trooped off gladly to war, never to return.

Chapter 27

Jo

August 1916

The following days passed, filled with work and endeavour. Jo had felt so welcomed by Mrs Simkiss that she decided she wanted to go and help more often and agreed to do three or four days a week at the kitchen, with Harry going to Maria or Charlie, or staying with Martine. Jo wanted to spend time with her son – of course she did – yet she also missed the kitchen when she wasn't there. An older woman – the well-to-do wife of a dentist from Broseley – came on the other days that Jo wasn't there, but she knew Mrs Simkiss preferred her, as the housekeeper was such a gossip that she told Jo so quite clearly.

'She's too lah-di-dah,' Mrs Simkiss said. 'Not like you, easy to be with, Jo.'

The two of them were a grand team, making a variety of dishes for the patients with few resources, largely due to voluntary rationing and food shortages. Would this damn war never end? This was the question heard in the kitchen, the wards, the streets, the pubs and the parlours at home. The war that was to be over by Christmas had stretched into its third year and now food shortages were a significant headache to cope with every day for families, as well as the hospital. The private money that came from Lord and Lady Rowland to help was all very well. However, bacon now being double its pre-war price was usually a no-no, yet with the extra income, sometimes Mrs Simkiss was able to order it and the soldiers loved it – Jo and Mrs Simkiss did too. Jo hadn't had bacon for years, though she only had a taste, as she wrapped up the rest of her rasher to take home and divide up between Harry, Bridget and Martine, who all had a taste too, to a chorus of 'mmm's. Everyone missed the salty goodness of bacon.

In the hospital kitchen, Jo and Mrs Simkiss worked hard together to plan a weekly menu based on whatever ingredients they'd been able to have delivered. The Red Cross's representatives regularly came by to supervise the nursing team and liaise with soldiers about contacting their families, as well as helping out from time to time with the kitchen planning. Mrs Simkiss had been given a Red Cross cookery manual that had lots of obvious stuff in, yet also the odd good idea, including a page on nine different ways to cook a potato. There were the regular items that they often cooked, such as the perennial porridge for breakfast, but sometimes cold ham or fishcakes instead. Often they cooked tripe or mutton for dinner. Puddings were the most popular thing and they were able to offer bread-and-butter pudding, which always went down a treat, as did jam roly-poly or rhubarb and custard. Then there were the special diets for soldiers with facial injuries, such as whisked egg whites. One thing that went down well with such men was a dish called 'egg flip', where raw eggs were mixed with sugar and either brandy or sherry, whatever was available. These were for men who, according to Mrs Simkiss, 'couldna chubble', meaning they were unable to chew.

Jo was responsible for these specialist concoctions, which she handed over to the nurses with a sense of somewhat morbid curiosity about the poor men with damage to their jaws or mouths whose fate it was to eat such strange food while they healed. She heard the chatter of the nurses as they came and went, talking about the men and dividing them into types – the 'flirty' ones, the 'nice' ones, the 'hopeless' ones. This latter category sounded a little bit of a harsh name for such men, the ones with wounds that would never heal, for some had been shot with these awful things called 'dum dum' bullets, which would expand inside and many men never recovered, which sickened Jo. Who could invent such a thing as a 'dum dum' bullet? What kind of monsters? The same as those who created poison gas, whichever devils had done that.

Jo grew particularly upset when she heard the nurses talk about the gas cases. She didn't want to hear a word about it. But she couldn't plug up her ears and heard two nurses talking about the 'panting gas boys' who would never get better and were slowly suffocating to death. Maria and Charlie had told Jo that Alfie would have passed out from the gas instantly and never felt a thing. Why, then, were these men still alive and shipped all the way to England to pant and gasp in a bed at Rowland Hall until they died in pain? She heard one nurse say some of the gas boys begged to be put out of their misery. Had she been lied to about Alfie's death? Mrs Simkiss told her that she could ask the Red Cross to look into it for her. They could liaise with service personnel and be told details about deaths. She considered it, then decided against it. What on earth good would it do to know how terribly her beloved had suffered at the end? Jo decided it was better to remember him as the man – a good husband and father – who wrote his name on the garden wall and went off to war. She didn't want to think about it any more than that and, to be honest, she was very glad she was in the kitchen at Rowland Hall and didn't need to visit the injured soldiers beyond, as she knew it would set her off about Alfie.

One day, in the midst of kitchen duties, Jo's keen ear for the nurse's gossip caught something of great interest to her. One of the nurses said they had a woman in, which was highly unusual. And not only that, she was once a suffragette. Jo rarely tittle-tattled with the nurses. She found them to be a bit high and mighty, and more, she found most of their gossip unkind, though she imagined that perhaps they did it to blow off steam after the no doubt difficult long hours they spent with the men, so Jo couldn't blame them too much. But this was something she wanted to know about. And she wasn't the only one.

'Did you hear that, Jo?' called Mrs Simkiss. 'We've a suffragette in!'

Jo looked up from her work and said, 'That's a turn-up. You've a woman in, then?' she asked one of the older nurses. They were generally less silly than the younger ones and easier to have a sensible conversation with.

'An ambulance driver, fresh from France,' replied the nurse, looking shattered, wiping her eyes with the back of her hand, trying to rub some wakefulness into her eye sockets by the looks of it. 'She was up on the front lines and lost an arm.'

'Well, to goodness!' cried Mrs Simkiss. 'Women losing arms? Whatever next?'

'What a brave woman,' said Jo, in awe. She'd done her bit of war work, helping with the refugees and now this, but that felt like nothing beside driving an ambulance at the Western Front.

The nurse added, 'She's having to learn to write again with her other hand. She's in good spirits but fed up. She needs someone to write to her family. I dunna have the time, though. I've a million things to do.'

'I'll do it,' said Jo, without thinking. 'Can I?' she asked Mrs Simkiss. She'd done the pots for the day and all the food for dinner was prepared and was now being kept warm or finishing off baking. It would need serving up but perhaps Mrs Simkiss could manage.

'After dish-up,' said her boss, then added, 'Want to see an old suffragette butty, eh? You might know her from before.'

'I might do, but I didna know that many. I kept myself to myself in meetings. But I'd like to talk to her, help her write some letters, if that's all right?'

'Fine by me,' said the nurse, holding her hand in front of her mouth as she yawned, then told Jo in which room of the mansion the woman could be found.

Jo rushed through the serving, eager to go. She hadn't been this excited about something in ages. To see a fellow suffragette would be a great boost to her morale. She'd been thinking recently about when this damn war would end and she could get back to it. The work she was doing was important, she knew that, not only in the kitchen here but also as Harry's mother. Somebody had to hold the home and family together. It was a sacred duty, as far as Jo was concerned. But here now was a whiff of her former life, before the shadow of war was even an inkling, before everything went into darkness.

The second Jo had finished, she threw off her apron and grabbed a pencil and pad off the side where they wrote down notes on menus, recipes and special orders. She hot-footed it out of the kitchen and down the long corridor to the main house. She'd not walked around it before, yet the nurse's directions were clear. She had to walk past the main staircase, a grand affair that opened out onto a chequered entrance hall. Once there, she saw her first close-up view of soldiers at Rowland Hall. She'd seen them go past the kitchen window some days, but only from afar. These two were led by nurses to go outside for a walk. One of them looked at her, his ear gone, healing up well from the looks of it. He walked with a pronounced limp. Jo smiled at him and he smiled back. She thought of Alfie. She moved on. She knew it would be hard to see the soldiers. She'd see them around town all the time – healthy, fit ones, home on leave; and the sick ones, recuperating; and the men who never went because they were exempt for whatever reason, mostly valid, surely. She hated them all equally. They had done nothing to her. They had done nothing wrong. Many of them were scarred terribly, in their minds or their bodies or both. She knew she should pity them and had no right to hate them. But she hated them nonetheless because they had lived. They were alive while Alfie was not. And she could not forgive them for that.

She hurried away in the direction of the library, where sat several more. One was with a nurse at a table, a book splayed in front of them. He was completely still. The nurse was trying to interest him in a book but he was just staring vacantly into space, his eyes wide yet dull. He wasn't even there. Jo hurried onwards. She had to go through the library and after that, apparently, there was a small reading room that had been put aside for this female patient, since it was, of course, unacceptable that she would be put in with the men.

Jo reached the door she thought it might be and knocked quietly on it. No response. She tried again and still no response. She thought to turn back but she'd come this far, so she thought she'd go on. She gently opened the door a crack. Nobody shouted at her. She popped her head around the door, to see a figure sleeping in the bed, lying on her side, the uppermost right arm off at the elbow, wrapped tightly in bandages, the head of dark wavy hair turned away towards the window, the face unseen. Jo tiptoed in, past the wall-to-wall shelves of books, taking a chair from the corner and bringing it over nearer to the bed. Then she sat down on it to wait for the woman to wake up. She felt rather odd, waiting for this woman who was sleeping, who she probably didn't know at all. But just hearing that there was a suffragette was a clarion call to Jo. She hadn't spoken of such things deeply in so long, and to think, here in Rowland Hall, was another person – another woman – who fully understood what the suffrage movement had meant to Jo and many other women like her before the war interrupted it all . . . well, it was too good to miss. She could wait. Maybe she'd choose a book to read. She got up and perused the shelves. Jo didn't read much but she was willing to try. There were books in Latin that would be hopeless, some old encyclopaedias. A bit of poetry that she took down and looked at briefly. At least the pages were mostly blank. Still, Jo was not a big reader and felt intimidated by books like these, fancy, old ones with gold lettering on the covers.

'Jo Woodvine, as I live and breathe,' said a voice.

Jo whipped round, clutching the book. Was it a nurse, telling her off for being there? But no, it was the woman in the bed, who had woken up, turned over and was now staring at Jo and smiling. She knew that face. She knew it very well.

'Barbara Rose! I'd no idea it was you!'

Jo shoved the book back on the shelf in the wrong position and came quickly over to the bedside.

'You're saying this is a coincidence?' said Barbara, her eyebrows raised quizzically.

'Nay. I mean . . . well, it is and it inna. I heard there was a suffragette here. So I came for a chat about old times, with whoever it was. I didna know it'd be you. It's so good to see you, Barbara!'

Jo couldn't help but smile. Her old heroine, the woman

she admired for a time more than any other, here again, in the strangest of circumstances. But, then it hit her, Barbara Rose had lost an arm in the war. What a terrible turn of events. Her face went from beaming to sympathy.

'You're thinking about my arm.' Barbara's face was resigned, rueful.

'I'm sorry. I didna mean to look.'

Barbara's voice was calm, gentle. 'It's fine. Look on, Jo. I'm proud of it.'

'How did it happen? If you . . . if it inna rude . . . to ask.'

'Sit down, Jo,' she replied, nodding at the chair, which Jo pulled over. 'We can have a nice little chat.'

'I'd like that,' said Jo, taking Barbara's change of subject as confirmation that she didn't want to talk about it.

But she was wrong, as Barbara went on, 'I was driving ambulances around the Somme area. Terrible battle round there.'

Jo knew the name. It was where Alfie had died.

Barbara went on, 'My ambulance was hit by a shell. Blew it on its side. My arm was crushed. They couldn't save all of it. But I've still got the top bit.'

Jo said, 'I'm so sorry that happened to you.'

Barbara replied, 'Well, I can still throw bricks through windows with the other hand, eh?'

It was a serious subject, losing an arm, wartime, all of that. But Jo burst out laughing and so did Barbara, surprising themselves.

'I wrote to you, you know,' said Jo, her cheeks growing warmer as she recalled the growing disappointment when she'd never heard back.

'Did you? I never got it!'

Barbara shifted awkwardly in bed and grimaced at the pain.

'Oh, I'm an idiot,' said Jo, appalled at her own selfishness.

'Here I am banging on about a letter and there you are . . . armless.'

They laughed again. Jo felt like they were old warriors, easy with each other, because of what they'd been through.

'Dunna be sorry. I'm annoyed I never received this letter. I'd have written back, no question! I'd have loved to have you as a correspondent, Jo. I went to ground for a while, hid out from the authorities. I knew they were putting suffragettes back in jail on any flimsy excuse around 1913 and '14. Then when war broke out I joined up with the FANY straight away and went to France. I've been there since the early days. We could've been writing, all this time! How infuriating!'

Jo asked, 'What was it like? France?'

Barbara was quiet for a moment, staring into middle distance. Jo could see that images were playing out across her mind.

'You dunna have to say. I'm sorry, again. I keep saying the wrong thing.'

Barbara smiled at her. 'You dunna have to fret. You inna saying the wrong things at all. It's just hard to explain. It's this bizarre mixture of . . . of the greatest fun you've ever had . . . and the worst horrors you've ever imagined. I dunna think I'll ever get over it. I dunna think I'll ever stop being angry about my arm, my lovely arm, my lovely hand, that wrote for me and fed me and brushed my hair and was kissed by charming men. I dunna think I'll ever forgive the war for that. But working on the ambulances, the people I've met, the things I've seen: it was all somehow a great adventure too. That sounds a dreadful thing to say. But it's honest. Do you have anyone over there, Jo?'

Jo looked down at her hands, that were wringing in her lap without her realising. She had two hands, one more than Barbara. She had to remember that.

'My husband, Alfie. He was killed last month. Gas.'

Barbara's face turned, her eyes full of earnest sympathy.

'Oh, dear, dear Jo,' she said, a tear rolling down her cheek. Her emotions tipped Jo over and she felt the tears coming too. 'I dunna have a right hand to hold yours. But will my left do?'

Barbara reached over awkwardly and Jo grasped it, their fingers interlaced, their understanding of each other's pain deeply comforting.

Chapter 28

Martine

September 1916 to December 1917

Autumn in Ironbridge really was a sight to see. The trees flanking the river were a riot of red, yellow, orange and brown. Mists hung in the air mysteriously, softened the solidity of the iron bridge. The town had its beauty, and it had grown on Martine in the last few weeks, during her recuperation. She had taken short walks for her constitution along the riverside, breathing the cooling air into her healing lungs. This new-found appreciation for the town was significantly assisted by her companion, Dr Malcolm Hale. He knew so much about the world, not only medicine, yet other interesting subjects too, like art, music, architecture and history. He told her about the building of the iron bridge, about how the town had grown up around it, a community born from the industrial revolution. He told her stories of the men and women who built the industry from the ground up – those who dug out the ironstone, the coal, the clay. Those who stoked the fires and lost their lives in explosions, falls down mineshafts, house fires and even murders.

'This little town has had its fair share of history,' said Malcolm to her one day, as they strolled from Jo's house on a new route away from the bridge. Martine followed happily, allowing Malcolm's sure yet leisurely pace to guide her. He did not walk too quickly as he could not manage it, due to his limp. He managed perfectly well, though, and he had his pride, a quiet, stoic pride, not showy or arrogant. Everything felt luminous to her that day. She had almost lost her daughter, but she had survived. She had almost died herself, but she had lived. All thanks to Jo, to this man and to God. The town seemed to glow with the joy she felt at walking again, at seeing the world again, at being with this kind and handsome man at this moment, as his eyes crinkled up, smiling at her. He had deep, dark brown eyes and when she was talking and worrying about her accent, he was gazing at her drinking in every word she said. He did not view her difference as a problem, instead seeming to find it captivating.

'Tell me more of Leuven,' he said.

'Surely you have heard enough from me on that subject,' said Martine, recalling her acute feelings of loss only a few months before.

'Never,' he said emphatically. 'When you were delirious and I sat at your bedside, you'd say its name several times: Leuven, Leuven. Mostly you'd say Brigitta, Brigitta. Sometimes you would call for Emiel.'

'That was my husband,' she said. 'I'm surprised to hear that I called for him. He's been gone these past years. I don't think about him as much as I used to.'

They proceeded along the street, Ironbridge citizens tipping their caps or nodding their hellos to the town doctor, eyeing his companion with some interest.

Malcolm was quiet for a moment, then replied, 'I am very sorry for the loss of your husband.'

'Thank'ee,' said Martine, taking on a few of the Shropshire dialect words these days, mostly subconsciously, surrounded by it as she was. She sensed that Malcolm wanted to know more, so she gave him a morsel of it. 'He was a good man, a good husband and father. His death . . . was unfortunate. Pointless. Yes, that's the English word for it. A pointless death.'

'Indeed. I am rather too familiar with death in my profession. Some are expected and even sought for. One tired boatman recently was lying down on his settee when I called. He seemed quite bright. I had hopes for his recovery. He sat up, quite suddenly, and said very clearly: "I'm off upstairs to see the old ones." I told him he was going no such place but he was determined and staggered across the room, climbing the stairs slowly. By the time he reached the top step, he knelt on the landing, stretched out upon the floorboards, closed his eyes and he was gone, just like that.'

'He was ready,' Martine said.

'He was. Did you know, Martine . . . how very nearly we lost you?'

Martine looked at him. The trauma of being near death had not been spoken of by anyone, as life moved on, but Martine found she was haunted by it, the terrible thought of leaving Brigitta alone in this new country. But it hadn't happened. She had to keep reminding herself of that. Malcolm was the first to say anything about it.

'I think so,' she said. He understood, about her sickness, about her fear. 'But I was going to stay. I was determined.'

'And so was your daughter. The two of you fought your way back to us. And I'm gladder of that than I think I have been about anything in my life.'

She was about to speak, to thank him, to tell him that his care for her had meant something to her too. But he stopped in the street and pointed.

They had arrived at the railway station.

'What is this about?' she asked him.

'We're going on a little trip, not far, to Shrewsbury, our county town. I know you've been missing your home city. So, I thought it might help to see another beautiful city, full of fascinating architecture and replete with history.'

'Oh, Malcolm!' she cried, and could've kissed him. But she held back and followed him into the ticket office. What an adventure! She had been nowhere else in her time in Ironbridge and this short trip felt as thrilling as a balloon ride to her hemmed-in soul.

On the train, they chattered away happily and at one point, in a rare, serious moment, Malcolm said to her, 'When all of this war madness is over, I would like to see Belgium. Perhaps even with you as my guide, if I may.'

She smiled sweetly at him and answered, 'I shall buy you a *kramiek,* warm from the baker's oven.' He had no idea what that was and she told him it was a little brioche with raisins and he said he had no idea what brioche was either, but that he had 'infinite faith in her judgement'. She liked the way he talked, very much.

Once they'd arrived, he led the way, strolling at his customary gentle pace through the streets, pointing out a fifteenth-century inn here, a thousand-year-old church there. Martine ran her fingers across the stone, as if by touch she could absorb the centuries it had seen. Shrewsbury was stunning and it lifted her spirits in just the same way her favourite Belgian pastry used to. She thought of the ruins of her old home and looked about her at the sturdy buildings and ancient streets and she made a decision then, about old homes and new places, about families you've lost and families you've found, or who found you.

They went to a small park and found a bench, as Malcolm's

leg was aching and her breathing felt a little short, though she had recovered well. They sat and looked at the trees, bushes and lawns, some summer flowers dotted here and there on their last gasp, a flash of pink among the autumnal robes nature wore. Martine felt utterly content, something she had not felt since the early summer of 1914, only two years since and yet it felt like aeons ago. It was a different world then and she was a different person.

'Martine?' asked Malcolm.

'Yes, Malcolm.'

She looked into those deep brown eyes of his and saw how nervous he was. She saw him fumbling in the pocket of his inside jacket pocket with his right hand.

'Kiss me first,' she said. She wanted the feel of his moustache against her skin and his arms about her. She wanted him to relax, to know he was wanted, to feel her lips on his and for herself to breathe in the scent of him. She wanted to know him that way before she said yes.

Jo

The autumn of 1916 came quickly and furled itself up against the winds of winter, spent by Jo in two worlds: those of work and home. Her life at home was filled with her son, who would be turning four next year, and next autumn would be starting at school. It seemed unfeasible that little Harry could be old enough to start school. Surely only yesterday Jo was weaning him. Martine and Malcolm Hale were newly engaged and quite adorable together. Bridget was thriving at school, chattering away in English with the best of them. Martine still spoke Flemish with her at home, when the two of them were pottering about together. It was lovely to see that Martine kept up the old traditions of their homeland. She was even teaching Malcolm how to speak a few words of Flemish, which was charming to see.

At work, Jo was now taken on as an official employee of Rowland Hall alongside Mrs Simkiss, with an actual wage, which made life much easier all round. Jo continued to visit Barbara every day she was in. Her recovery was going well and Barbara was released in January of the new year 1917, yet she and Jo had become such close friends that Barbara would regularly come back and visit Jo at intervals, usually at work, so they could walk around the grounds of Rowland Hall together and talk. Barbara had had to wait months for a prosthetic arm, as being a woman, there was no provision for such things, as she was seen as an anomaly. She fought it tooth and nail and finally got her arm in May and came to show it to Jo.

'Let's go for a walk in the spring weather round the grounds and show off my arm!'

'The next time I have a sherry, I shall raise a glass to your arm,' said Jo, as they went outside after Jo's kitchen duties had finished.

'By the way,' said Barbara, 'I have news. News of old times.'

Walking down the sweeping path past the dark trees, both in pastel-coloured spring coats and hats, they went to sit by the large pond where the fancy fish were to be found, those that hadn't been eaten by the resident heron.

Barbara asked Jo, 'Have you been reading about the progress of the new suffrage bill?'

'I never read, you know that,' said Jo. 'No time with a little boy and a part-time job. I've not heard a thing about suffrage in years.'

'Well, it's back in the news. The bill was introduced this month and it'll be going through the House for the next few months, I reckon. There's a lot to be ironed out but the word on the street is that it has huge support in the House. It looks like there really might be an Act of Parliament perhaps next year, Jo. Votes for women!'

'What? Really? Actual votes for actual women? Women like me?'

Jo could barely believe it. Could it possibly be true, that after all these years, the stick-in-the-mud men of Parliament had finally seen the light?

'Well . . .' said Barbara and made a face.

'What?'

'From what I hear, it's likely to be men over twenty-one of any or no property. But the same rules are unlikely to apply to the women. They're saying that it'll probably be only women over thirty and only women with property over a certain amount of money. It wonna be you, Jo.'

'But . . . but that inna fair!' Jo cried. This enraged her. How could it be right that only some women would get it, only older ones and richer ones? 'After all that was fought for? This is wrong!'

'It's a first step. I feel as angry as you do. It inna fair, you're right. But we must see this bill gets through first. And when it does, how would you like to go to London with me and the old gang and protest it? What do you think? We need to let them know that it's a first step, but it inna enough. Women must be on equal terms with men with the vote, that is, over the age of twenty-one and with no property clause.'

'Absolutely, I will!'

They made a pledge that when the act was finally passed, they'd meet in London in Parliament Square and protest its passing. Jo couldn't wait. Just like old times, as Barbara had said. The months passed by and Jo started to read the newspapers, to follow its progress, but it was slow going. During the year of 1917, her work carried on as busy as ever, and in September Harry started school. She already knew he was bright as a button, brilliant at all things to do with numbers, just like his dad. He was the spitting image of Alfie, so much so it was painful for Jo to see at times. She knew Maria and Charlie saw it too, especially on his first day, dressed up in his school uniform. Jo could see it in their eyes that they were reliving Alfie's first day too, the sadness and loss in their eyes matched by their pride and joy in the little boy they all adored.

Throughout that year, Jo had spent more time with the soldiers than she'd ever thought she would when she first arrived at Rowland Hall, raw with grief. She would sit with them and read to them, write letters for them, listen to their stories if they wanted to talk. They all lacked something, a limb, an organ, or less neatly, great chunks of them, bitten out of their bodies by war. Alfie had said to her, that last night they were together, that war was butchery. How right he was. When she sat with them, she saw Alfie in some of them, which pained her. Yet in truth they were all so different from one another, a ragtag collection of individuals who just happened to be thrown together by war. In fact, war was the only thing they had in common. She'd begun the war railing against it, as a suffragette, as a colossal waste of time by men, to distract from the raised voices of women. But as time dragged on through the long years of war, she had recently begun to feel quite differently about it. It was not just made by men for men. She realised instead that it was made by those in power and yet it was always those without power – the ordinary men like Alfie – who paid the ultimate price. War was all about class, it occurred to her, not about men or women. People with power started the war and people without power fought it. And they were so often the ones ruined by it.

Tending to those brave men by cooking them good hearty meals and sitting with them, Jo realised that her feelings about most men being, by dint of their sex alone, agents of the male-dominated system that kept women in their place, the old idea that had fuelled her from her suffragette days . . . well, she just felt it wasn't true any more, if it ever had been. Yes, she knew that there were certainly many men like that, and it was also even in the best of men, as they had been brought up to see women in those roles. But they needed educating, to learn that tradition had been smashed to pieces by the war – women had proven themselves in the workplaces and on the home front to be able to do any job a man could do, or at least most of them. Just look at Barbara driving her ambulances and sacrificing a limb for the war effort, not to mention all the kind folk who took in refugees, and the refugees themselves who worked hard in jobs also supporting the war effort, whatever some of the naysayers said. For Jo, spending time with the broken men in the hospital, helping them to mend in the ways she knew how, not as a nurse, but nourishing them, and listening to them, it made her feel closer to Alfie, and also made her feel quite differently about men. The male-dominated system had done nothing good for these men, had it? The powers that be had made sure of that. What was the answer, then?

One weekend near Christmas time, at the senior Woodvines' house, Snap the dog curled up by the fire, Maria and Harry coloured with crayons together at the table, while Jo and Charlie sat in the chairs beside the fireplace and debated. Jo had shared her new ideas with Charlie.

'If men inna the problem, what is it, then? Is it just rich men?'

Charlie replied, 'I think it's even more complex than that, Jo. Think about Lord and Lady Rowland, the way they've taken in all those folk and been so kind. They're good people. But they're rich too. Alfie always said they were good bosses to him. And there are others like them. They exist in the system but they dunna always profit by it. Did you know the Rowlands' grandson was killed in the first months of the war?'

'I didna know that, nay. That is sad.'

'War touched us all, in different ways, rich and poor.'

Jo was thinking. Her ideas were starting to coalesce.

'Do you think . . . do you think, Charlie, that this war . . . maybe it'll change things. It'll make us all the same, somehow. That's what I think when I'm tending the men. They're all individuals, each one of them is unique. But they all share the same enemy – not the Germans or other foes, but the war itself. Death is . . . it makes us all the same.'

'War is a great leveller. And so is death,' said Charlie, nodding slowly, staring into the fire.

'This is all a bit morbid,' said Maria from the table, looking over her shoulder and glancing sideways at Harry.

Jo and Charlie got the message and stopped talking about all that serious stuff and instead came to the table and sat down to do some colouring too. Harry was doing his best to draw a robin, or at least, a jagged circle with a scribble of red in the middle. Maria drew a Christmas tree with brightly coloured baubles.

'Germans invented Christmas trees, you know,' said Charlie with a disapproving sniff.

'Stop complaining and draw a snowman,' said Maria.

Charlie quickly sketched one out.

'How many buttons should this fellow have?' he asked Harry.

Jo watched her son muse on this problem. 'Sixteen,' he replied.

'Six-TEEN?' cried Charlie, which made Harry giggle. 'Always good with numbers, this boy. Just like your dad.'

The four of them were all quiet then; only the sound of the wax crayons could be heard, filling their pictures with colour, along with the crackling of the fire and the low whine of Snap snoring.

'There's nothing to colour in on this snowman,' muttered Charlie, 'except his nose. Bad choice, Woodvine.'

Harry said, 'What are you drawing, Mummy?'

Jo outlined the bird as accurately as she could, determined to get its shape just right. The long neck, the almost box-like body, the elegant wide wings keeping it aloft.

'It's a heron.'

'What's a heron?'

'Your daddy's favourite bird.'

She ruffled her son's beautiful yellow hair, then turned back to her drawing.

Beneath the lone heron, Jo sketched in tall trees, coloured in with forest green. The bird flew high above them, heading away, into the free and far distance.

Epilogue

February 1918

'The buildings!' Harry cried, his hand tugging on his mother's so she'd look up. 'They're the biggest in the world!'

'Maybe not the world,' said Jo, squeezing her son's hand, as they walked down the vastly wide street, flanked on both sides by a row of tall trees, the buildings behind towering over them. 'But bigger than most in Shropshire, that's for sure.'

'Look at the men in bowler hats. I shall be one of them one day. I shall work in London one day, just like them.'

'I dunna doubt it,' replied his mother, smiling, proud. He'd been at school only a few months and already he was outstripping all the children around him. He had his father's gifts with numbers and his grandfather's gifts with letters, that was certain. His sense of wonder, Jo liked to think, he got from her perhaps. But where this proficiency with all things scientific came from, she couldn't fathom. He was just a one-off, their Harry. She knew he'd outgrow his grandfather's school and even his town, and soon. She didn't know what she'd do about that yet, but she'd work it out. She had big plans for her son, to make his life extraordinary and give him everything she'd never had. She was bursting with delight as she led him along the London pavements, hurrying towards their destination, not because they were late, but because Jo was so eager to get there and show him what they'd come all this way to see.

'Jo Woodvine, as I live and breathe!' came a voice, shouting across the road.

Jo stopped abruptly and Harry nearly fell over.

'Let go, Mother! I wanna walk on my own like the men in bowler hats.'

Jo scanned the crowd and then saw the figure running across the road to them, dodging horse-drawn carriages, wagons and omnibuses as well as man-powered bicycles and motor cars galore across two carriageways to reach them.

'Barbara!'

The friends ran towards each other along Parliament Street, laughing.

'You made it!' said Barbara, in a sumptuous purple coat with fur at the collar and cuffs. Even Jo had a new outfit on, bought with her earnings from her job at Rowland Hall. Hers was not as fancy but she was still proud of the green skirt and white blouse, with the customary man's tie at her neck, and a new winter coat on that kept her warm, and a matching green hat with little white flowers in a spray at one side. Maria and Charlie had said she looked like a model from the magazines in it and had offered to have Harry while she went for her day out to London. But she told them she'd be taking him with her, for an important reason. He looked smart too in his new suit of a belted and buttoned-up jacket, wide white collar, breeches tucked into long socks, shiny new boots and straw boater, quite the little man.

Barbara put her left arm about Jo's shoulders and they hugged briefly, as Jo fought to keep hold of Harry's hand.

'I can walk alone,' he was whining. 'I'm at school now. I'm a schoolboy.'

Jo and Barbara laughed, then moved over to the side of the pavement, beside the stone balustrade that ran alongside one of the enormous buildings.

'You brought your young lad, then?' said Barbara, adding quietly, out of the side of her mouth, 'You didna want a break from mothering for a day?'

'Nay, not today,' Jo replied, emphatically. 'Harry needs to see this. It's historic. I want him to say, when he's older, I was there when women got the vote.'

Barbara nodded approvingly. 'Good point. Men need to see this too. And see us protest. Got your sash?'

Jo told Harry to hold onto the railing beside him, as she pulled her old suffragette sash from her coat pocket and wrestled it on over her shoulder, Barbara doing likewise. Then they hurried on, keen to get there. As they reached the end of the street, they turned the corner and Harry nearly exploded with the thrill of seeing the grand old clock tower that held Big Ben. Jo had never been to London either, just like her son, and had nearly got them lost several times on the way from the railway station. But they were here now. As they crossed over the road to arrive in Parliament Square, they saw some other women across the other side who were marked out by their green, white and purple sashes too. Barbara waved like mad and one of the women called out to them, 'Votes for Women!'

'Votes for Women!' Barbara shouted back.

A man in a top hat walking past heard that and stopped in front of them, his face twisted with disgust.

'Suffragettes? While there's still a war on?'

Barbara and Jo just laughed in his face, so happy were they to join their friends across the way.

But the man wouldn't stop, blocking their path.

'You should be ashamed of yourselves, you hussies!'

'Dunna speak to my mother like that!' cried Harry.

Jo was furious. She didn't want her son hearing that. But also, she didn't want to escalate things. She remembered the Shrewsbury march only too well.

'We dunna want any trouble with you, sir,' Jo told him. 'We are here to protest the vote, as is the right of everyone in our country, to make our voices heard.'

The man wouldn't give up. 'But the bill's being passed this week for women's suffrage!'

'Not for all women,' said Barbara, attempting to sidestep the man and gesturing to the others to follow.

But he was determined to have his parting shot. 'Are you never satisfied, you women?

'Never!' cried Barbara.

'Not until we have equality for all,' added Jo. 'And we're not there yet!'

'Go and jump in the river!' cried Harry, causing his mother and her friend to burst out laughing.

With that, she squeezed Harry's hand and they broke out into a run together, to escape the man.

As soon as they were free of him, Jo stopped and crouched down at Harry's level, straightening his collar, which had come awry in all the kerfuffle.

'I'm so proud of you,' she said.

He beamed at her.

'I'm proud of you too,' he replied, breathlessly, a little unnerved by what had happened.

Jo looked Harry square in the eye and said, 'I want you to remember this day, Harry. I am raising you in a household that knows about the world, that debates and discusses, that never stops learning. And we shall always stand up for what is right, just like your daddy did when he saved me in the school queue, and just like he did against the Germans and gave his life for. We'll always stand up to bullies, eh, Harry?'

Harry nodded. 'Can we go and see Big Ben now?'

'In a bit,' said his mother. 'We've got women's business first.'

Glossary of Shropshire Terms

Argufication – debate
Bezzler – a heavy drinker
Butty – mate/friend
Cakehole – mouth
Canna – can't
Chapper – little boy
Chinwagging – gossiping
Chubble – chew
Clemmed – hungry
Cwtch – a cuddle or squishing up beside someone while sitting
Didna – didn't
Dunna – don't
'ee – thee, i.e. you (e.g. thank'ee)
Fiddle-faddle – nonsense
Fussock – big, dirty, greasy, old woman
Gonna – going to
Inna – isn't
Jockey – term for a male friend/mate
Mon – man

Mun – must
Nay – no
Shouldna – shouldn't
Snap – packed lunch
Summat – something
Tara-a-bit – goodbye for now
Wanna – want to
Wench – a charming old Shropshire term for a young woman, with no disrespect intended or taken.

Author's Note

Dear Reader,

It's Mollie here. I just wanted to add in a little detail about the writing of this book, particularly for Walton fans who may well have read the other books before this one was published. I've added in to this story what is termed in the trade as 'Easter eggs'. If you're not familiar with the term, it basically means adding in mentions or moments or characters who hark back to other books in the same series, like going on an Easter egg hunt, I suppose. Thus, if you've read the Raven Hall saga, here are some of the Easter eggs present in this book that you might remember from those books.

You may have noticed that Brigitta in this book eventually comes to be known by all as Bridget. When she's a grown-up woman with a husband of her own, she will travel to Yorkshire one day and visit Rosina Calvert-Lazenby with some very bad news, introducing herself as Harry Woodvine's cousin. You may remember the scene . . . but I won't give away the spoiler here, for those readers who haven't read the Raven Hall books. She calls herself Harry's cousin as, even though they aren't related by blood, their time living together during the Great War led to the two mothers feeling that they were honorary sisters and their offspring cousins.

The other main Easter eggs appear in Alfie's life in the trenches. Firstly, there are two sets of characters related to Raven Hall. Alfie's friend Precious is in fact Helena Bairstow's secret lover, mentioned in *A Mother's War* – Bairstow is Rosina's housekeeper and tells her about how she lost the love of her life during the Great War, a married man who went off to war and never came back. The others related to Raven Hall are the Lazenby brothers, Basil and Douglas, Rosina's brothers, whom she also mentions in the series as having died during the Great War. Lastly, is a more personal inclusion and that is the character of Alfie's friend Chadwick. This is a little tribute to my grandfather, Arthur Leslie Chadwick, who fought in World War One and survived. He was as nice as the character in this novel, also as wise and with the same dry wit. He died when I was a teenager and I still miss him today, forty years or so later.

I hope you enjoyed these little cameos. They're so fun to do and make the series of books feel like a real history with recurring characters who continue to live their lives even when they're off-stage. That's how they feel to me, anyway. I've always said about my characters that I don't invent them, I just find them, already perfectly formed. And when I'm not bothering them, they're busy doing their own thing and certainly don't need me snooping into their business.

Thanks, as ever, for reading my books.

Very best regards,
Mollie Walton

Acknowledgements

A huge thank you to:

Shroppiemon, AKA Stuart Geoffrey Davies, for all of his help on dialect and WW1 Shropshire, my research buddy and my Shroppie expert par excellence.

David Giddins, for expert help on rail routes from London to Ironbridge in 1914.

Russell Beeson, for his expertise on chalk soil, clay soil, plants and entrenching tools in WW1 France.

Everyone in the Facebook group Memories of Shropshire (run by the legend that is Shroppiemon) who responded to my posts on WW1 Ironbridge in May and June 2025, including: Norman Beech, Annette Burgoyne, Flissy Tipton Burke, Stuart Geoffrey Davies, Neil Evans, Pauline Jones, Tony Mugridge, Wendy Haynes Palin and Rhiannon Urquhart. A special extra mention for Pauline Jones, as she always goes above and beyond with research help, as well as for her constant support for my other work.

Jenni Edgecombe, my previous and wonderful editor who started this project with me before she moved on from Headline, and Jessie Goetzinger-Hall, my new editor, who took up the reins so brilliantly and just 'gets' me and my writing. I could not do this work without editors like these of such high calibre. An extra thanks to the whole team at Headline, who get Mollie's stories out into the world so well.

My agent, Laura Macdougall and her assistant, Eleanor Horn, for their tireless support and help throughout the writing of this book plus all my trials and tribulations, as ever.

My fabulous audiobook narrator, Lu Corfield, for breathing life into my dear characters, as always.

My early readers – Lucy Adams and Pauline Lancaster – who always read my early drafts with such speed and thoughtfulness.

And, as ever, my family, friends (virtual and IRL), my daughter Poppy and my partner Clem, for keeping me sane, happy and writing. Love to you all, my darlings.

DISCOVER THE RAVEN HALL SAGA

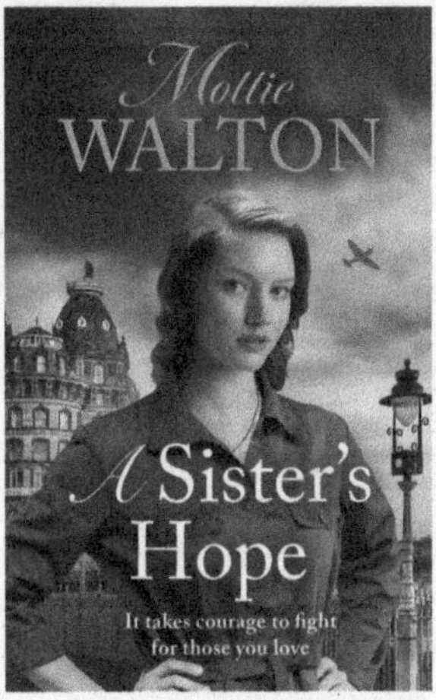

About the Author

© Claire Newman-Williams

Mollie Walton is the saga pen-name for historical novelist Rebecca Mascull. She has always been fascinated by history and has worked in education, has a Masters in Writing and lives by the sea in the east of England. Under Mollie Walton, Rebecca is also the author of The Raven Hall Saga.

RAISING READERS
Books Build Bright Futures

Dear Reader,

We'd love your attention for one more page to tell you about the crisis in children's reading, and what we can all do.

Studies have shown that reading for fun is the **single biggest predictor of a child's future life chances** – more than family circumstance, parents' educational background or income. It improves academic results, mental health, wealth, communication skills, ambition and happiness.[1]

The number of children reading for fun is in rapid decline. Young people have a lot of competition for their time. In 2024, 1 in 10 children and young people in the UK aged 5 to 18 did not own a single book at home.[2]

Hachette works extensively with schools, libraries and literacy charities, but here are some ways we can all raise more readers:

- Reading to children for just 10 minutes a day makes a difference
- Don't give up if children aren't regular readers – there will be books for them!
- Visit bookshops and libraries to get recommendations
- Encourage them to listen to audiobooks
- Support school libraries
- Give books as gifts

There's a lot more information about how to encourage children to read on our website: **www.RaisingReaders.co.uk**

Thank you for reading.

hachette UK

---

[1] OECD, '21st-Century Readers: Developing Literacy Skills in a Digital World', 2021, https://www.oecd.org/en/publications/21st-century-readers_a83d84cb-en.html

[2] National Literacy Trust, 'Book Ownership in 2024', November 2024, https://literacytrust.org.uk/research-services/research-reports/book-ownership-in-2024